"Don't you go up there again."

Trish turned so they faced each other only inches apart. "Listen. This is my house, and I plan to check out any and all repairs. How else can I know everything is done correctly?"

Craig held up his iPhone. "Pictures." They were close enough that he felt her warm breath against his face, caught the scent of perfume. That was something new. She never wore perfume back when they were kids. "I guarantee my work." He paused, diminishing the space between them so they were nearly nose to nose. "Don't go up on the roof unless someone's here. Namely me. You understand?"

"All right, already." She stepped onto the ground. "When did you get so bossy?"

Trish's cheeks were bright pink in the cold. Why hadn't he kissed her when he'd had the chance? Every part of his being had wanted to. Still did. But...

They weren't kids anymore. She was spoken for, committed to someone else. So was he. There would never be any Trish and Craig together.

Dear Reader,

It's a sad time for Trish when she returns to Riverbend, New Jersey, after a ten-year absence. She just lost a grandmother who was so special, and now she's back to collect the house her grandmother left her. She loved this place while growing up, as well as all her childhood friends. And of course Craig, the friend who'd wanted to marry her from the time he was nine.

I raised my family in northern New Jersey in a town similar to Riverbend and spent countless hours completing projects on our hundred-year-old farmhouse. Many of the windows had been painted shut decades before we bought it. Although our home wasn't as spacious or as attractive as Trish's inheritance, it did provide me with numerous projects, some of which I could include in her story. I became skilled at plastering, painting and repairing, and I can appreciate why someone wouldn't want an old house.

I love hearing from readers and can be reached through my website, marionekholm.com, or heartwarmingauthors.blogspot.com.

Marion

HEARTWARMING

Forget Me Not

———

Marion Ekholm

HARLEQUIN® HEARTWARMING™

Recycling programs
for this product may
not exist in your area.

ISBN-13: 978-0-373-36802-0

Forget Me Not

Copyright © 2016 by Marion Ekholm

HARLEQUIN®
www.Harlequin.com

Printed in U.S.A.

Marion Ekholm was writing stories and reading them to her friends back in fifth grade, in Plainville, Connecticut. She always wanted to be either a writer or an artist. Neither one seemed like a possibility in her day, when most women became either teachers or secretaries. But she had determination on her side and a mother willing to help with her dreams. She earned her BFA at Rhode Island School of Design and became a lace designer in New York City, met her husband and moved to New Jersey. Years later, she took stock of her life. She had a career, two children, a beautiful home and opportunities to travel extensively—but she'd never written anything other than letters. She began writing for real and eventually became an editor of a newspaper and sold numerous short stories and magazine articles. Thanks to Harlequin Heartwarming, she's now a novelist. Her third novel, *Forget Me Not*, follows *Just Like Em* and *An Act of Love*. She's found signing her books and talking to people who've read them an absolute delight.

Books by Marion Ekholm

Harlequin Heartwarming

An Act of Love
Just Like Em

Visit the Author Profile page
at Harlequin.com for more titles.

This book is dedicated to Shelley Mosley, my critique partner, mentor and friend. Her encouragement over the years has been a driving force in my career. Thank you.

Acknowledgments

My thanks to the many people who helped me gather all the information for this book.

To my friend Fran Deming, who interviewed volunteer firemen at the Company No. 1 Fire Department in Mahwah, New Jersey. Although both of our husbands had belonged to that organization, I couldn't remember all of the details. She managed to get answers to all my questions. Even so, my book is fiction, and a few artistic liberties may have been taken.

To my nephew Matt Suess, a fabulous photographer who told me what kind of camera Craig would use.

To Glenda Chagolla for her technical knowledge. I've enjoyed working with her at Glendale Community College, where she teaches CAD (computer-aided design) programs.

I learned about scissor lifts and knuckle booms from my son, David, a skilled electrician and handyman who answered any questions relating to DIY work.

Additional thanks go to Harlequin's Dana Grimaldi, my personal editor, who provided directions for the story.

CHAPTER ONE

"ARE YOU GOING to marry me now that I'm all grown up?"

Trish placed her hand on the door frame and leaned closer to the storm window for a better view of the man on the front porch. Marry him? What on earth was he talking about?

"Do I know you?" There was something familiar about the grin that spread so quickly across his face. His deep blue eyes held an unmistakable twinkle.

"How've you been, Trish?" He chuckled. When she still couldn't make a connection, he added, "You were the best babysitter I ever had."

Trish sucked in her breath. "Butch?" she yelled. "Butchy Cadman? Look at you! Last time I saw you…"

"I was a good foot shorter."

Trish pushed open the door, came onto the porch and stood next to him. She looked up and laughed. "Not quite that, but you sure have grown." He had to be four or five inches taller than her five foot eight. She took a few steps back to get the full view of him while he watched her with equal interest.

"I always told you I'd catch up with you one day," he said. "Don't I get a hug for old times?" She held out her arms, and he enfolded her in a bear hug.

She reached up and ruffled his dark wavy hair. "I didn't recognize you. Little Butchy Cadman." With a sigh, she stepped out of his embrace, then caught his smirk.

"You blushing?" he asked.

Trish pushed away and tried to look undisturbed, but warmth radiated from her cheeks. "Still planning on marrying me, huh?" She grinned. "You should be over that by now. What's it been? Ten years?"

"Me? Forget my first love? Never." He sobered. "I'm really sorry you had to come back under these circumstances. I know how close you were to your grandmother."

She swallowed and nodded thanks for his sympathy. Gram had left her this house in her will with the hope Trish would move back, keep it in the family and reestablish her roots. That wasn't likely.

Trish rubbed her arms to fight off the November chill. With only two and a half weeks before Thanksgiving, they couldn't expect the Indian summer to last much longer. "Okay if we go inside?"

"Sure."

Trish and her parents used to live here in Riverbend, New Jersey, near Gram. Moving away had been difficult—Trish left a grandmother she adored as well as all her friends while starting her junior year in high school. Her father's promotion had taken them to Virginia, where he could commute to his new job in Washington, DC. When her grandmother became ill a year ago, Trish moved to New York City so she could be close by. If only she'd relocated earlier. Their time together had been so short.

"So, Butch," she said once they were in the large vestibule, "are you here on your father's behalf, or will he stop by later to give me an estimate?"

"Dad died nearly two years ago."

"Oh." She placed a hand over her mouth. "I'm sorry. I didn't know."

He nodded. "I took over the business, so I do all the estimating and most of the renovation work. And there's another thing. I don't go by Butch anymore. It's Craig. Now that my dad's gone, there's no more confusion."

"Okay. Craig it is." She hesitated. The senior Cadman had had a sterling reputation not only for his integrity but also for his superior craftsmanship. Her grandmother had trusted him to do all the repairs on the house, from the plumbing to the electricity. But Craig, being so young...

"Do you need references?"

Trish shook her head. "Of course not. I just remember you tagging along with your dad..."

Craig took in a deep breath. "My father taught me everything he could, and before he died, I earned my contractor's license. Besides that, I work with an experienced crew who also worked with my father. My mother can supply you with names of people I've worked for." He chucked her chin with his knuckles and smiled. "Always ask, Trish. There are too many people out there who will do a rotten job and take you to the cleaners."

Her faith restored, Trish waved toward the arched entrance to the living room. "Shall we look at the house?" They stopped at the large staircase. "No one's lived here since

Gram went to a nursing home. Neighbors kept an eye on it, and I've been up a few times to check. But I'm afraid there's damage from the roof leaking when the last hurricane came barreling through."

"Right. We've taken care of a lot of damage from storms this past summer." Craig removed his heavy blue windbreaker and placed it over the staircase's carved newel cap.

"I'll need the roof repaired or replaced. I'd like an estimate on both. While I'm here, I'll start on the central staircase, sanding it down and refinishing it. I'm hoping to get it back to its beautiful oak finish once that carpet's removed."

They walked into the living room, which was still loaded with heavy, outdated furniture. "No damages here. Just some ratty-looking wallpaper I'll need to remove."

Craig made notes on his iPad, scrutinizing the fieldstone fireplace as well as taking a quick picture. "When was the last time this was used?"

Trish shrugged. "I remember one Christmas…" She sighed. "But that was a long time ago."

"I'll check it out. Don't want any unwanted fires messing up the repairs."

When he looked in the direction of the old-fashioned furniture, Trish asked, "Do you know where I can donate all of this?" She swung her hand around, indicating several items in overstuffed maroon velvet. "I have no use for it, and I'd really prefer having the room cleared before I remove the wallpaper and paint."

"Sure. Several churches in the area have banded together to help people affected by the hurricane. I'll contact them and have it moved out."

Trish clasped her hands together in delight. "That will be wonderful."

"Except..." Craig walked over to the tall mahogany secretary before turning back to her. "Remember this?" His face lit up again with that grin. "We searched all those hidden compartments in here, expecting to find treasures." When she didn't reply, he added, "Right before you moved." Craig's expression sobered.

Trish glanced at the polished wood and remembered all too well. It was a memory she'd prefer to forget. Her parents had informed her that day they'd be moving, taking her away from all her friends and Butch. Checking Gram's secretary for its secrets had been the last time they were together.

"Have you gone through any of the secret drawers since you came back?"

"I never did," she said.

As Trish came to his side, he caressed the dark wood. She grasped the large panel that served as a writing surface, pulled it down and exposed all the various compartments. "You suppose there are any treasures we could have missed?" When she reached for one of the carved containers that fit seamlessly into the background, Craig placed his hand over hers.

"Your grandmother had some wonderful antiques, things you should keep."

The warmth of his hand brought back more memories, ones she'd thought were long gone. She pulled her hand free and traced the carved surface with an index finger. "Is this valuable? Do you think I could get a good price for it?"

He looked at her as though she'd spit on his shoe. "Sure. Henry's Antiques is always in the market for family treasures."

She grabbed his forearm and felt his muscles tense. "Keeping family treasures isn't a luxury I can afford. As it is, I'll be using what Gram left me plus everything I have just to get this place ready for sale."

Craig shook off her hand and turned toward the vestibule. "Let's see the rest of the place." He carried a yardstick that he swatted against his hand and occasionally used it to point to different areas.

They took the stairs to the second floor. Several rooms had ugly water stains on the ceilings. Trish opened one of the doors and scrunched her nose in distaste. "I think the bathrooms on this floor need a major renovation." She had avoided the bathrooms yesterday when she'd arrived, using the smaller powder room on the first floor instead.

Craig stepped onto the linoleum and made a cursory examination. "If you want to get a good price, you'll need some major modernization here. Bathrooms and kitchens can sell a house."

"With some major expense," Trish added as they backed into the hall.

Finally Trish stopped at the door to the attic staircase. "This was my favorite place to play. Remember all the times we stayed here on rainy days and dressed up in old clothes?" Her grandmother had made hot chocolate and provided cookies for Trish and all her friends in the neighborhood. She'd felt wanted and cared for, none of the indifference she found with her own parents. Trish had often wondered why her parents even bothered to have her. Whenever those thoughts invaded her mind, she'd run to her grandmother for all the love and hugs anyone could provide.

"Right. Your grandfather's top hat and fedora. You still have them?"

"I'm not sure. Most of the things stored here were moved to drier areas, and I haven't had a chance to check. Oh," she said once they reached the top stair, "you can see the roof damage." She pointed to the cracks in the roof where light came in.

Craig walked around, examining different beams, poking with a yardstick in places that looked particularly bad and snapping pictures. "This problem could get worse, especially if we get more rain. We should cover it with a tarp until it can be repaired."

After checking the two attic windows for any leaks or damage, they went downstairs to the basement. "You're lucky there's no water damage down there," Craig said after a quick tour. "That hurricane ruined more than roofs. Lots of homes were flooded. Fortunately, this place sits on a little rise."

When they came back upstairs, Craig grabbed his jacket before they headed for the kitchen.

"You mentioned kitchens can sell a house, and most of these appliances are dated." The country-style kitchen featured a pastel fridge, windowed cabinets, wallpaper with sunflower borders and colorful flower pictures. Canisters in a sunflower motif sat on the counter. She'd bought them for her grandmother. How many times had they taken flour and sugar from them to make cookies? She lifted the coffeepot, an old electric percolator. "Would you like some?"

Craig nodded and settled with his things at the kitchen table.

Trish poured coffee into large mugs and brought them to the table, where Craig continued to make notes. After putting some of her cleaning supplies back under the sink, she joined him. Once he stopped writing, she took a deep breath. "What do you think? Is this going to cost me a fortune?"

"Probably." He glanced around a moment before taking a sip of his coffee. "This kitchen is pre–World War II. It definitely needs modernization, and you'll find it well worth any expense. You'll have a lovely old house to leave your own grandchildren one day."

"I thought I made myself clear. I want to sell the place." The words came out softly, forced past the lump in her throat. "I plan to spend my vacation fixing it up so I can get a better price. Should I bother or just let it go as a handyman's special?"

A disapproving scowl crept across his face. Then his expression went blank, and he looked away.

Trish bit back a sigh. Hadn't she already suffered enough guilt over her decision to sell? She stood and leaned against the sink, waiting for his verdict.

"It's a sound structure. If you don't mind my helping on some of the interior areas, I can have my crew do all the tough stuff." He sat back and watched her with an intensity she found disturbing. "I was hoping you'd decided to come back and stay."

"Why?" She laughed and propped her hands in the back pockets of her jeans. When she shook her head, her hair swished along the top of her shoulders. "You may have gotten taller, but you're still three years my junior, and I have no intention of marrying you. You'll just have to find another girl."

"I have."

All her playfulness vanished, and she stared at him, unable to think of anything more to say.

"You didn't give me much hope," Craig added.

"Anyone I know?" Trish asked, regaining her composure.

He sat up and folded his hands on the table, looking at her with way too much satisfaction. "Cyndi Parker."

"Cyndi Parker! From down the street?"

"Always liked older women."

"And shorter ones? Unless she's grown, she has to be…" Trish held her hand out to where she pictured Cyndi might come to.

Craig swatted himself at a halfway point on his chest. "She comes up to about here in her heels." That grin again. "What about you? You have any romance in your life?"

An image of Harrison came to mind. He was six years older than her twenty-six years, nine years older than Craig. "As a matter of fact, I'm engaged." Trish pulled out the ring she'd slipped into her pocket for safekeeping while she cleaned and placed it on her left hand. Harrison had given her the diamond only a few days after her grandmother's funeral, a little after the reading of Gram's will. Both the inheritance and engagement had come as happy surprises. "My fiancé, Harrison Morris, and I are going to use the money from the sale of the house for a down payment on a new condo."

Craig acknowledged her remark with a raised eyebrow but didn't offer a comment. She looked away, remembering her disagreements with Harrison over the house. Even though he'd never seen it, he'd already said he wouldn't consider moving into an old house in suburban New Jersey. If only Harrison liked traditional architecture instead of the stark lines of steel and glass that he'd shown her in and around New York.

"I'll get started on this," Craig said, standing and grasping the iPad, "and get back to you in a day or two." He pulled on his jacket, bringing their meeting to a close.

With a nod, Trish followed him to the back door that led onto the porch. She grabbed her grandmother's old camel-colored coat off the hook by the door and slipped into it. "When will you contact someone about the furniture?" They walked the large deck that

made a half circle around the house until
they reached the front.

"I'll wait till you call Henry's about the
antiques. He'll come by and give you an ap-
praisal. That way you won't give away anything of value."

"You don't approve, do you?" Trish asked
as they walked to his large white van. Handyman Specialist, LLC, was emblazoned in red
on the side along with his phone number and
website address. Another website address in
blue and a different font, cadsbycadman.com,
sat under his name.

"We all have to do what we have to do."
Craig turned to survey the Victorian-style
home. "I've always liked this house." His
hand on his chin, Craig stood there for several seconds before hitting the side of his van
with an open palm. "I'll get back to you with
the estimate. Great seeing you again, Trish."

Trish walked back to the house, remembering when she'd babysat for the Cadmans. Craig
was nine and she was twelve. She loved children and always wished she had brothers and
sisters. Starting as a mother's helper, Trish took
over the full duties of a babysitter eventually
when both parents had to work. When he no
longer needed a sitter, they spent a great deal

of time together as friends. Extremely precocious, Craig had skipped a grade. He adored her and insisted she wait till he grew up so they could marry.

He skipped another grade. By the time she was a junior, Craig entered his sophomore year and seemed determined to catch up with her. Although he was shorter than his entire class, he stayed ahead of everyone scholastically. When she had trouble in algebra, he offered to help and their roles switched.

The memory made her smile. Craig turned out to be far beyond his years in more than academics. The day tutoring led to a kiss, her mother walked in and put a stop to any further education. Her father was transferred soon after, and they had to move.

The three-year age difference seemed less important now than it did then. Thinking back to some of the men she'd dated, Trish couldn't recall their kisses. But Craig stood out.

CHAPTER TWO

CRAIG TRIED TO concentrate on his driving, but thoughts of his meeting with Trish continued to play havoc with his mind. He was over her, wasn't he? Of course he was. Hadn't he been dating Cyndi for months? Then why did seeing Trish drag up all those memories and send his hormones into overdrive?

She hadn't checked those secret drawers in the secretary. If she had… He had to find some way to get back there and remove his note. He'd been so upset when he learned she was moving. No way would he want that note surfacing now.

Craig drove to the back of Moody's Lumber Company and stopped at the small office. His father had first rented the place from Moody when Craig was an infant, and it had served them well over the years. The Cadmans' business had grown thanks to his father's well-known integrity, and Craig was determined to fill his father's shoes. Not much chance of that with everyone still referring to him as Butchy, Craig Cadman's kid. Bringing Trish's house back to its original splendor might be exactly what he had to do to prove he was as good as his father.

When Craig stepped inside the office, his mother was looking over some papers with Maxwell Moody, the owner of the lumber company. Craig's little brother, Noah, was sitting in her lap.

"How did it go, Butch?" she asked. "Trish give you the job?" Besides being a wife and mother, Rachel Cadman had served as secretary and journeyman to his father over the years. In many ways she'd provided the stability that kept the business from faltering when her husband became ill and died. Rachel also worked for Maxwell, who provided the crew that assisted Craig in his repairs. He looked up as Craig advanced. They acknowledged each other with a nod.

"Butchy," Noah shouted. A moment later, he came around the desk and propelled himself into Craig's arms.

Craig attempted to balance himself while the boy squirmed. "Noah. What are you doing here? Aren't you supposed to be in school?" The boy placed a stranglehold around Craig's neck.

"Teachers' meetings." Rachel came around the desk and took a reluctant Noah from Craig's arms.

"I want to show him the hat I made for Thanksgiving," Noah said, still reaching out to Craig.

"It's at home. He'll have to wait and see it when we celebrate with the big turkey dinner." Noah pursed his lips and gave her his grumpy face. "How about you build a house? Your brother and I need to talk." She placed the boy on the floor and watched him run to the box of wood pieces.

"I told her to call me Craig." His mother raised an eyebrow and pursed her lips but didn't add anything. "I want her to think of me as a grown-up, not the little kid she babysat."

Rachel pushed several strands of light brown hair behind her ear. Sometime during the past six months, she'd started dyeing away the gray. "I know." Rachel sighed. "It's just…"

"I understand it's hard, Mom, but if she calls…"

"*When* she calls. Trish hired you, didn't she?"

Craig gave his mother a peck on her cheek. "I think we're in once I finish some estimates. I'm sure the roof needs to be repaired. And the bathrooms are way out of date." He took out his iPad and showed her the pictures he'd taken. Maxwell strained his neck so he could see, as well.

Noah came over with several pieces of two-by-four and tried to look at the pictures. Rachel held the iPad so he could see, too, and flipped slowly through the album. She stopped. "What's this?"

Craig leaned over. "Oh, that's her old secretary. She's getting rid of everything and I thought… I'm going to offer her something, maybe deduct it from the cost of the repairs."

He took the iPad from her then. He'd forgotten he'd snapped Trish's picture and didn't want his mother asking questions about it.

With a shrug, Rachel went back to her desk. "What we really need is money," she said, rubbing the tips of her fingers and thumb together. "Antiques may be nice, but you can't eat them."

Craig nodded. "It's just…"

"I know. You want something for the

house you'll build for you and Cyndi," Maxwell said, assuming Craig's relationship had gotten that far. Craig didn't bother to correct him. There was no chance of that, but he knew most people seeing him and Cyndi together would come to the same conclusion.

Cyndi was an enigma. He never knew what to expect. One minute she'd throw herself at him, kissing him to distraction, and the next she'd be flirting with someone else.

They'd grown up just a few houses from each other and often played together with Trish and other kids in the neighborhood, usually at Trish's grandmother's. He thought of Cyndi as a butterfly that flitted here and there and didn't offer any kind of permanence. He still enjoyed her company, but he wasn't interested in marriage to Cyndi or anyone else.

She had come up to him at Moody's, having returned to live with her parents after a divorce. They'd talked a bit and caught up, and then she asked him out. The most popular girl in high school, head cheerleader, prom queen, and she asked *him*. Back in his nerdy days, she'd forgotten he existed.

Maxwell stood and picked up his empty coffee cup. "Don't go overboard with an offer on that antique. The woman probably inherited a good deal from her grandmother, and you don't have to be overly generous."

Craig nodded but didn't comment. Price wasn't the issue in this instance. "I'll cover her roof with a tarp tomorrow and decide if we'll need to replace it."

"Good. The crew finished their last job early. It will be nice to get them working on something other than inventory and sweeping floors." Once he went through the connecting door to his own office, Maxwell turned and raised his cup toward Craig. "Sorry, kid, but you'll always be Butch to me, just like Craig will always be your father." He sighed and shook his head. "But…your father would probably approve if you took his name, so I'll give it a try."

Noah came over with his selection of wood. "Wanna help me build something?"

Craig bent down to his level and brushed his brother's hair with his fingers, something he remembered their father doing. Unfortunately, Noah probably didn't even remember their father. An unplanned child so late in life had come with joy, but also unexpected problems when his father died. Craig stood and took the piece of wood, examining it closely. "Any other pieces this size? We'll need several."

Noah did an about-face and ran back to the large crate containing all the scraps. He looked over his shoulder, a smile lighting his face. "Yep, we got enough to build a house."

And so it began. Every day he spent time with Noah, teaching his brother the way his father had taught him—how to hold the hammer, center the nail and hit it without destroying his fingers. But Craig couldn't help feeling that their father should be doing this. And maybe his dad's time wouldn't have been cut short if he hadn't had to deal with all the ramifications of a new child.

"HI, MOM," TRISH said when she finally reached her mother. "How are you enjoying your trip?" Her parents had bought an RV and were traveling the Southwest after her father's early retirement.

"Unbelievable. We just left the Grand Canyon, and we're heading south to some warmer weather. Actually had a little snow. How's it back East?"

"Indian summer. Everything's settled with Gram's house, so I moved in to start fixing it. You sure you don't want anything? Furniture? Antiques?"

"Absolutely not. We were delighted that she left everything to you, and we don't want anything to tie us down. Right, Tom?" A deeper voice made an acknowledgment before her mother continued. "Your father and I plan to see the world before old age robs us of our faculties."

Trish chuckled. "My goodness, Mom, you haven't even cashed your first Social Security check yet."

After a long pause, her mother asked, "So, what's new with Harrison? Has he seen Gram's house?" Harrison was one of the few men she had dated who managed to impress them.

"No. I've decided to sell it."

Her mother took a quick, deep breath. "Really? But I thought…"

"We're going to use the money for something closer to our work in the city."

"And can he come up with an amount equal to what you'll be contributing?"

Trish resented her mother's tone. "Of course. He owns a condo that he plans to sell, and it more than equals what Gram left me."

"I only meant that your grandmother gave

everything to you because she thought you would appreciate it and want to live there."

With a sigh, Trish said, "I do appreciate it. And like you and Dad, I need to live my life the way I see fit. I never gave you any flak over you selling everything and getting that trailer."

"It's an RV, dear, a recreational vehicle, and you'd better not give us any flak, or we won't drive up to your wedding. When is it, anyway?"

Since she and Harrison hadn't settled on a specific date, Trish hesitated. "Sometime after the house is sold."

"Well, make sure your plans are for the spring. Your father and I don't like to travel in the snow."

Trish chuckled. "I'll be sure to take that into consideration."

For a moment, her mother didn't respond. "I suppose you connected with Butch again."

She sounded almost reluctant to mention him. At one point, Trish's parents and Craig's had been friends, but for reasons Trish had never understood, they weren't speaking to each other by the time her family moved to Virginia. "He goes by Craig now. His father passed away a few years ago, and he's taken over the business. I asked him for some estimates on the repairs that need to be done here."

"And that's it? He's not still madly in love with you?"

"He has a girlfriend, Mom." For a moment, Trish wondered why that thought filled her with an unexpected sadness. She shook off her reaction. Silly. They'd both moved past childish crushes and had new directions in their lives.

SETTLING ON ONE of the kitchen chairs, Trish reached for a cup of coffee. She'd risen to the ringing of her cell phone before seven. The birds hadn't even been up.

She pulled her blue bathrobe tighter. Maybe she should have Craig check the heating system. The temperatures outside were close to freezing despite the sunny skies, and the inside didn't seem much warmer.

"This is your inheritance?" Harrison had asked, referring to the picture Trish had sent on her iPhone.

"Yes!" She hoped the joy in her voice made an impression over the phone. "I can't wait till you get here to see it. So many memories. I've started cleaning and hope to have it livable while I'm here."

"You still planning to take off from work for a whole month? Won't that jeopardize your job?" Had Harrison started the day on a sour note? He sounded critical. This was not exactly the bright, sunny good cheer she wanted in the morning.

Trish hadn't taken a vacation in over three years. She deserved one, and it would give her a little rest before returning to her new promotion. Right now she and Harrison worked in the same department; however, once she received her promotion they'd be working down the hall from each other. And once they married, and lived in the same house, they'd be able to commute together. Unfortunately, it wouldn't be from her grandmother's house.

Now, with matrimony on the horizon, she was considering other career moves. Harrison made enough to support them both, so eventually she could be a stay-at-home mom and take care of the many children they'd talked about having. Just thinking about it made her smile.

"I needed this chance to get away." Not about to slog through her decision again,

Trish asked, "When can you come see the place?"

Trish had wanted moral support as well as some physical labor from Harrison to get her grandmother's house spruced up. They'd even talked about spending their vacations together to get as much completed as possible before the eventual sale.

"I'm so rushed, flying in and out to different locations in California. I can come on Sunday." He provided a date and Trish looked it up on a calendar.

"You'll be gone the week of Thanksgiving?"

"Right. The company wants all this training completed before Christmas. You know how people go crazy with credit-card problems before and after the holidays." Her plan to surprise him with a turkey and all the trimmings slowly slipped away.

But no one should skip a proper Thanksgiving, and if it meant taking time away from work on her grandmother's house, so be it. "How about we celebrate on that Sunday when you're here? I make a mean turkey."

"Don't." He hesitated. "I thought you wanted to get painting done…finish some projects on the house. I'm not doing them all by myself while you're busy cooking."

Trish considered this a moment and tried to control her voice, something she had plenty of practice at in her customer-service job. Keep your voice pleasant. Don't antagonize the patrons even more. They were already stressed-out calling about problems with their credit cards.

She took a calming breath. "So you'll be here only that one day?"

"Right." He waited a moment longer before adding, "Sweetheart, I wasn't going to mention it, hoped to keep it a surprise, but… I can't stay any longer because I put in for a promotion. I've got reservations in Los Angeles and San Francisco for interviews. How would you like to settle in California? It's a possibility if the interviews go well."

Trish hesitated. California. She'd always lived on the East Coast, never even seen the West Coast state. But that certainly had exciting possibilities. For him. Why hadn't he mentioned it before? "Let's talk about it when you arrive."

CHAPTER THREE

AFTER THE CALL, Trish forced herself to concentrate on anything other than her disappointment. She'd hoped to spend some time working on the house with Harrison. With so much to do on her own, she decided to tackle the furniture problem. Which items would interest an antiques salesman? She began by taking pictures to show Henry of each piece that might have value.

The large secretary drew her attention. Where had they found those secret hiding places? Had the carvings moved to create openings? Trish had made several unsuccessful attempts to push and pull the sculptured leaves and flowers when the doorbell rang.

Abandoning the secretary and its secrets, she glanced down at her attire. Still dressed in pj's and a robe, she pulled the robe's belt tighter before heading to the front door.

She saw Butch through the large oval window etched in a lovely art-nouveau design of flowers and ribbons.

Trish opened the door and said, "Oh, hello, Butch…" She placed a hand over her mouth. "…I mean Craig."

"Listen," he said, "you can call me Butch if you want. Lots of people still do." He sounded frustrated.

"But you'd prefer Craig?"

Wearing a green ski sweater with white deer marching across his chest, he leaned against one of the posts that supported the porch roof. In his youth he'd lacked height and hadn't participated in sports. Since his interests gravitated to books, he'd remained a thin teenager, labeled by most people as too intellectual. At some point, he'd definitely matured, having a well-developed body and… Trish gave herself a shake and forced herself to concentrate on the paint peeling on the post, and not the man resting against it.

"I'm here to check out the roof." He pointed to an extension ladder lying parallel to the sidewalk. "Also, do you have your grand-mother's flag?" He reached up to the flag holder attached to the post before glancing back at her. "I remember her putting it out on Veterans Day, and just about everyone's flying one. Lets people know someone's occupying the house."

"Of course. I'll get it. Can you put it up while I get dressed?" Trish hurried to the closet. After retrieving the flag, she headed to the small room off the kitchen that contained a single bed. It had served so many purposes: a sewing room, a library and even an office when her grandfather was alive. When her grandmother became ill, it served as her bedroom so she wouldn't have to climb the stairs.

Trish dressed warmly in several layers so she could go outside. In her worn jeans, red turtleneck and sweater, she headed out the front door to check on Craig. She found him on the ladder, pulling leaves out of the eaves trough.

"You're planning to put that on your bill, aren't you? Cleaning gutters?"

"Absolutely." He grinned and tossed a handful of multicolored maple leaves at her, which she swatted away. "You need a free flow of water during the next rain so it doesn't puddle on the roof. I'm coming down."

When Craig reached the ground, he pointed to the flag. "Looks very patriotic for Veterans Day. Your gram would be proud."

"Come in. I've got coffee ready. Have you finished the estimates?"

"Started but not finished, and no, thanks. I don't need more caffeine. I told a few people about your furniture and…" He turned and extended his hand toward the truck pulling into the driveway. "They're quite anxious to get started." Several older men and a teenager exited the truck and came onto the porch. "This is Reverend Meyer from the Methodist church, his son and his grandson, and they'll be happy to take anything you want to get rid of."

Reverend Meyer grasped her hand in a firm shake. "I knew your grandmother. A wonderful woman and a pillar of the community." With that said, he walked past her, obviously anxious to get started. And she hadn't even determined what she wanted to give away.

Deciding certain eyesores had to go, Trish pulled the door open so they could enter. "You'll be able to fill your truck."

"So kind of you. We have several families who were devastated by the floods, and we can use anything you want to give us. All tax deductible, of course." He followed her into the living room. "Just point out what we can take."

"Everything in this room—couch, chairs, tables and lamps. Leave the secretary." She turned to Craig. "What do you think? Anything else in here that Henry's Antiques might have an interest in?"

Reverend Meyer stopped moving one of the chairs. "I'm sorry. I didn't realize you hadn't consulted the antiques dealer yet." He swept a hand around the room. "Just about everything here looks like something Henry might want."

Trish hesitated, weighing the financial benefits against helping people who'd been devastated by a flood. "You take what's in the living room. That should pretty much fill your truck, and I'll get back to you about the rest after I've spoken to the antiques dealer. You can have anything else he won't consider for his store."

After several nods in her direction, Reverend Meyer motioned his helpers over to the sofa. "Let's start with this." While they worked on removing the furniture, Craig directed her to the secretary.

"I'd like to buy this once you find out the value from Henry." When she didn't immediately reply, he added, "You were going to sell it, weren't you?"

Trish's ambivalence had her wondering, not for the first time, if her decision to sell everything might be a mistake. With her fingers barely touching the wood, Trish felt a connection to her past. "It has memories. So many." After pressing her lips together to keep from getting too sentimental, she turned to Craig. "You're first on the list."

He reached over and drew his finger under her eyelash, sweeping away the tear that had slipped onto her cheek. "Maybe you shouldn't rush into anything."

She forced a laugh and backed away. The touch was too sweet, too intimate. "I don't know why I'm getting so emotional. I'd have no place for this desk. It's too large." And she doubted if Harrison would ever want anything this archaic.

Reverend Meyer came back into the room. "Okay if we take the matching chairs?"

"Of course."

The reverend hesitated. "I don't mean to be unappreciative, but what we could really use is a few beds. Do you have any of those? Something basic. So many people haven't a decent place to sleep."

"Of course. Come upstairs and I'll show you the beds that can go." Trish went up the large curved staircase and motioned for the men to follow.

"I'm heading for the roof," Craig said and disappeared out the front door.

Once they reached one of the guest bedrooms, Trish pointed to the double bed. "There are linens for this. I'll get them for you." While the men removed the bed, she gathered sheets, pillows and several blankets from the hall closet.

When they returned, she pointed to two of the other bedrooms and had the men remove the beds. "The mattresses have seen better days, I'm sorry to say." She followed through with the linens needed for those.

"Anything we can get is a blessing."

They left the nightstands and dressers, saying she should find out their potential value. Her grandmother's room she left intact for now. It contained several antique pieces, including an elegant armoire. She'd have to take a picture of that to show Henry.

She found several large plastic bags and stuffed them with usable items from the closet while the men worked. It made her feel as though she'd finally managed to make a dent in all that she had to do, and she was grateful to Craig for finding people who needed all these unwanted items. Once she was ready to leave the house, she could give up the cot in the downstairs bedroom, as well.

"That's it for now," the reverend said. "The truck's full." He handed her a list of the items he'd packed away. "You can add the values for tax purposes. The church's logo is at the top with our phone number. Call us whenever you want another pickup."

"Will do." Trish shook his hand and grinned. With the beds gone, along with most of the living room furniture, she had more space to move around and see the condition of the rooms.

Craig came in just then. "You won't need a whole new roof after all. Just a section. I can give you the estimate on that now." He handed her a printed paper with a detailed description of all the items needed practically down to the last nail, including a meticulous drawing of the roof section in three dimensions.

Trish glanced at it before looking back at him. "How'd you do this?" Had he prepared the information before coming over here and actually looking at the problem? She hadn't heard him drive away to go print out a report. And how did she know if it was accurate?

"I inspected the roof."

"When?"

"A few minutes ago. While you were working with Reverend Meyer."

"How did you do all of this?" Trish waved the sheet in front of him.

Craig's eyebrow went up, giving him a quizzical expression. "On my computer." He nodded toward his van. "I have everything I need in there." He grabbed the paper from her hand. "Come on. I'll show you."

Trish followed him and waited while he slid the side door of the van open. "My office." He stepped in and offered her a hand to pull her up onto the metal floor. "I took a picture, put that and all my figures in a program I've developed, and out comes what I'll need to complete the project."

"Craig Cadman, you invented this?"

He grinned. "Well, yeah, pretty much. I've taken courses in CAD…" When her eyebrows went up, he explained, "…computer-aided drafting/design, and created something that combines several programs. It's patented, and a few other people have shown an interest. I sell

it through my website, cadsbycadman.com."
He paused while she continued to stare.

"Show me what the roof looks like now."
She jumped out onto the driveway and waited
for him. He hesitated before following her.

"Trish, I don't think you should go up
there."

"I've been on that roof so many times.
I used to help my grandfather hang all the
Christmas decorations."

"Yeah, when you were a kid."

Ignoring him, she headed for the ladder
at the front of the house and placed one foot
on the bottom rung. Craig came up behind
her and lifted her off.

His voice came out in a warm breath against
her ear. "I'll go up first, and you stay on the
ladder. Don't you dare go on the roof." After
releasing her, he nudged past and hurried up
the rungs. Once he was on the roof, he waited
until she came near the top rung. "Now you
stay put." He held out his hands, palms facing her. Craig turned and scrambled across
the tiles toward the damaged area. When he
looked back, she was right behind him. "I told
you—"

"Oh, stop having a hissy fit. I'm not afraid
of heights."

Craig sat on his haunches and chuckled. "I should have remembered you always have to do everything your own way." He reached out and took her hand to pull her closer before turning to indicate the section that needed repair. "It's not too bad, and I can get it done today if you approve."

"How did this happen?" Trish poked at several shredded shingles.

"I found bits of branches embedded. The hurricane must have torn some limbs from one of the trees and shot them against the roof."

"Definitely start on this as soon as possible." After taking a seat next to him, she focused on the maple trees that lined the street. All the leaves had dropped, been raked into the street and carted away. She stretched out her legs and leaned back on her elbows, duplicating Craig's stance. "I can see all the houses from here, and you're right. Just about everyone's put out their flags. It reminds me of Fourth of July. Remember marching in the parades?"

"Yep. Happy times."

Trish pointed to an empty area on one of the corners. "Didn't Mr. Flurry have a house there?"

"It was damaged during a fire. I was hired to demolish it."

"Anyone hurt?"

"No. Luckily Mr. Flurry and his wife were on vacation at the time."

She remembered Mr. Flurry, not exactly the nicest man around. "The people who bought my parents' old house did some major additions, totally destroyed the cookie-cutter image of all those Cape Cod houses built after World War II. Have you made any changes to your place?"

"No. We don't own it anymore. Not since my father died."

Trish turned to him, wondering if she should pry. Why not? They'd always been able to talk to each other. "What happened?"

He cleared his throat. "Long story."

"If you'd rather not…"

"No. It's okay. Just don't know where to begin." He ran a hand over his jaw. "My father had problems, getting tired and unable to work a full shift. Mom forced him to go to the doctor. He needed a bypass." Craig took in a deep breath and let it out slowly. "He didn't make it, and his hospital bills were staggering."

"Where do you and your mother live now?"

Craig sat back and relaxed next to her. "She and Noah moved in with her sister, that blue cookie-cutter house over there next to Mr. Flurry's vacant lot." He pointed to a house not too far from where Trish had lived. "My aunt Jenny didn't have enough room for all of us, so I took an apartment near the lumberyard."

Trish remembered his aunt, a pleasant woman who always had a full cookie jar. But the other name... "Who's Noah?"

"My brother."

Trish sat up with a start and stared, leaning toward him. "Your brother?"

Craig grasped her arm. "Watch it. We're a good forty feet above the ground, and I don't want to scrape you off the sidewalk."

She slid over until they were hip to hip. "How did you get a brother?"

With a chuckle, Craig placed his arm around her shoulders and held on to her. "How do you think? Do I have to explain about the birds and the bees?"

Trish rolled her eyes and leaned against him. "I've got a good idea. However, wasn't your mother a little old to be adding to your family?"

"Forty-three. And it wasn't planned."

"Obviously a welcomed surprise." The two shared another laugh.

"So, Trish, where do you live?" he asked, not releasing her. His arm around her felt comfortable and something else...safe.

"In Queens, just a short subway trip to my job in Manhattan."

"You planning to stay in Queens once you're married?" Craig was staring out across the street.

"No. I have a lovely studio apartment, but it's too small. Harrison has an older condo on the Palisades in New Jersey, overlooking the Hudson. Once he sells it, we're hoping to combine our funds and get something closer to the city." Trish concentrated on the toes of her sneakers and wiggled them a little before looking past them to the landscape spread before them.

"And this house wouldn't do? You know we're called the bedroom of New York for a reason. The train runs right through the town." Craig pulled his arm away, leaned forward and pointed. "See? There it goes now. You just sit in a comfortable seat, take a nap or read a book, and you're in Manhattan in no time."

"My point exactly. I've tried talking to Harrison about it, but so far no luck." She turned toward him, adding a smile. "Maybe you could convince him when he comes here."

"Then you want to keep the house? Live here? Raise a family?"

With a sigh, Trish watched the train disappearing in the distance. "I want something we'll both enjoy. If this place isn't going to work for both of us, we'll find something that does."

Trish pulled her knees up, wrapped her arms around them and leaned forward. Craig sat up, as well, duplicating her position.

"Why did you stop writing to me?" he asked.

HE HAD TO KNOW. Before she left for Virginia, they had been best friends, talked to each other every day. They had shared everything. Their thoughts, their hopes, their dreams for the future. Why had their email correspondence suddenly stopped?

"I was new to the school… I'm sorry. I… We were so far away from each other." She paused. Would she continue? He didn't want to spook her, certainly not on the roof, but he remembered those months after she left as an agonizing time.

"I wanted to come back, live with my grandparents. But Gramp got sick, and Mom said I couldn't." Her gray-blue eyes, with flecks of gold, revealed a sadness that equaled his own. "My mother got on my case, said I had to adjust to my new life, meet new people."

Trish turned away and pressed her face into her knees. "I did. Had a boyfriend, and he… well, he had a fit when he saw I was emailing you." Her expression hardened. "It was ten years ago, Craig. Life goes on. Yours certainly did."

She moved away and started for the edge of the roof when Craig grabbed her arm.

"Wait. I'll go first," he said and maneuvered around her.

"You plan to catch me if I fall?"

"No. Figure I'd have a better chance to get down if I'm not hampered by all your blood and guts covering the ladder." He reached the first rung, swung his leg around and started down. "Be careful, now." When she didn't respond, he stopped, his head even with the edge of the roof. "I mean it, Trish."

"Okay. I'll be careful. You plan to move so I can come down?" He nodded and started his descent. A few moments later, when Trish reached the bottom rung, Craig trapped her against the ladder.

"Don't you go up there again."

Trish turned so they faced each other only inches apart. "Listen, mister. This is my house, and I plan to check out any and all repairs. How else can I know everything is done correctly?"

Craig held up his iPhone. "Pictures." They were close enough that he felt her warm breath against his face, caught the scent of perfume. That was something new. She never wore perfume back when they were kids. "I guarantee my work." He paused, diminishing the space between them so they were nearly nose to nose. "Don't go up unless someone's here. Namely me. You understand?"

"All right, already." She stepped onto the ground. "When did you get so bossy?"

Trish's cheeks were bright pink in the cold. Why didn't he kiss her while he had the chance? Every part of his being wanted to. But…the moment passed and sanity returned. They weren't kids anymore. She was spoken for, committed to someone else. So was he. There would never be any Trish and Craig together.

CHAPTER FOUR

AN HOUR LATER Trish came out of her house to discover Craig on the roof again, this time with a crew of two men she didn't recognize. He came down the ladder and walked over to her. "There are one or two more places that need repair, but I checked with Max. Moody's Lumber replaced the roof about ten years ago. You should get at least ten more, providing you're not hit by another wicked storm. We'll do that one side so you won't be able to see any difference with the older shingles."

"Thank you," Trish said. "Anyone with fewer scruples could have insisted I needed the whole roof replaced. Can I get you anything? Lunches for you and your men?"

"That's a nice thought, but we've already made plans with some other guys from the lumber company. We meet at Drexel's Deli whenever we're working. You're welcome to join us."

A voice from on high said, "Yeah, join us. We could really use someone with a little more class."

Craig glanced up before turning back to her with a chuckle. "Ignore Ray. He's the only low-class jerk in the group."

"I heard that," the man shouted, "and he's right!"

"Thanks for the invite, but I bought some groceries yesterday. Another time," she said to the men on the roof. Smiling, she turned to Craig. "If I'm not needed here, I'll head into town."

Craig started for his van, which was blocking her Toyota. "I'll get this out of your way."

"No, that's okay. I'm going to walk. I'd like to check out several places, and I don't need my car."

"Okay. We should have all the roof repairs completed this afternoon, and I'll finish the prospectus tomorrow morning for the other projects we discussed."

"Sounds like a plan."

Trish started down the street at a brisk walk, listening to the rat-tat-tat of hammers ringing their song throughout the neighborhood. Once she and Craig went over the repairs, she could prioritize, budget her money and get the most for her dollar. In the meantime, Trish planned to check out Henry's Antiques and show him the pictures she'd taken.

The temperature had become a little nippy, and she double-wrapped her green scarf around her neck. The sound of leaves crunching under her sneakers gave her the true feeling of fall. Some chestnuts had fallen, and she picked them up along with a perfect red maple leaf that had escaped the street sweepers. She twirled the stem and stopped in front of the house once owned by Craig's family.

Several people were outside raking the leaves. They turned to wave to her. "Hello," she called out. "Beautiful day, isn't it?"

"Yes. Before you know it we'll have snow."

How sad for Craig to lose his father and then his home. Yet the joy that lit Craig's features when he mentioned Noah warmed her heart. What would it be like to have a sibling that young? Craig and Trish had often regretted being the only children in their families. Now Craig had one up on her. The thought brought a smile, and she continued to Henry's.

Center Street, in the older part of town, had turned into a mixture of commercial and residential buildings with several businesses in some of the older homes. One magnificent brick estate, built more than a hundred years ago, posted a doctor's sign in front. Across the street, Gram's lawyer had taken residence. Trish had spent the day there when all her grandmother's possessions were transferred.

The fire department sat on a corner with Moody's Lumber Company farther down the block. A portion of the grammar school Trish and Craig had walked to could be glimpsed behind the pharmacy, where one could still sit at the counter and order a sundae.

She stopped in front of Henry's Antiques. At one time a five-and-dime, the shop had remained unoccupied until Henry moved in and removed the sign. Thanks to the dark green trimming, the dusky red building had a Christmas look. Trish glanced at some of the items displayed in the crowded windows before stepping into the store. An armoire in pale blue with a floral design painted on the large doors looked elegant and expensive. Very similar to her grandmother's. Would Henry want her grandmother's things in this shop? Determined to find out, Trish headed for the counter.

"Hello," a man called. Although out of

sight, he continued to talk. "Look around. I'll be with you in a moment."

Trish waited by a tall golden dresser, something with a Chinese influence and definitely pricey. The other items arranged around the room had a classiness beyond her grandmother's dusty collection. She turned when a thin man with gray hair and a matching goatee approached. "How may I help you?" Definitely a different voice from the one that had invited her in.

"Henry?"

"One of them. I'm Stanley Henry." He turned and motioned to the younger man with similar features coming from the back. "This is my nephew Dave. And you are…?"

"Trish Lowery." She expected some recognition of her last name. After all, her family had lived in the town for nearly one hundred years. Nothing.

"Were you looking for something specific?" Stanley asked.

"No. I'm interested in selling some of my grandmother's antiques. I have pictures, if you'd like to see them."

Dave Henry, who had a pleasant smile and blond hair, came over. "Lowery, you say. As in Helen Lowery?"

Stanley looked at his nephew with a quizzical expression. "Of course, Helen Lowery, from one of the founding families, the lady who recently died?" He turned back to Trish and approached, his hand extended. "Our condolences. And you have something to show us?"

With his demeanor becoming more gracious, Stanley gripped her hand. Trish suddenly felt like a field mouse trapped by a marauding hawk. She pulled free. "Um, I have a question. Do you purchase antiques outright to sell in your store?"

Stanley sighed. "Unfortunately, we can't. Not enough space." He smiled, helping to displace the hawk image. "Most of the items here," he said, waving his hand around the shop, "are on consignment. I run another store in Manhattan, and we also advertise on the internet. I'm sure we can give your grandmother's items a proper showplace and get you the best possible price."

Trish held out her cell phone, displaying the picture of her grandmother's bedroom furniture. Stanley took her phone as Dave came over to join his uncle. "We really need to see your treasures in person. May we make an appointment?"

Trish pulled her phone back. "Of course."

"Okay if I handle this?" Dave asked. He nodded toward his uncle before turning back to Trish. "When are you available?"

Trish appreciated Dave taking over the conversation. "Anytime today. The sooner the better. I have a limited time here, and I need this resolved before I leave."

"Would this afternoon be appropriate? At two? I know the address." He turned to his uncle. "If you wouldn't mind watching the store for me?"

With a nod, Trish thanked them and headed for the door, followed closely by Dave. After opening the door for her, he said, "I'm sure your grandmother has lovely items, and we'll be able to work out some satisfactory plans for them." He offered his hand. "Very nice meeting you, Ms. Lowery."

Just as she exited, a noisy blast echoed through the town—one, two, three times—and Trish stumbled. Dave grabbed her arm and steadied her.

"That darn fire horn." He glanced down the street. "Better watch it. Any moment, we'll have volunteers speeding toward the firehouse." He pointed to the brick building across the street and pulled her away from the sidewalk's edge. "Here they come now."

Trish stood there watching as one vehicle after another came down the road with lights flashing and pulled into the firehouse's parking lot. Was that Moody's truck? The front was filled with several men...men who'd been on her roof. How could they appear so quickly? The horn had just sounded.

"I've got to go," she said, slipping away from Dave's grasp. She headed down the street at a near run.

When she reached her house, she saw Craig taking down the ladder. "What happened?" How would anything get finished if they took off anytime the fire horn blew?

"Most of my crew are volunteers." He placed the ladder on the ground and headed for his van. "Including me." Trish followed him to the driver's side. Was he about to take off, too? She grabbed the sleeve of the OSHA green shirt he had pulled over his sweater.

"When will you be back?"

Craig got into the cab, holding on to the door. He leaned over toward her. "When the fire's out." She stepped away as he slammed the door and backed out of the driveway, his headlights flashing.

"You okay?"

Trish turned to see Dave Henry standing there on the sidewalk. "Did you think your house was on fire?" he asked as he approached. "You took off looking very upset."

"I saw Moody's truck with all the men who had been on my roof. They didn't finish."

"They'll be back." He glanced at the house and rubbed his arms. "I didn't take a jacket. Didn't realize how cold it had gotten."

Small towns. She had forgotten how familiar people were with each other, how concerned they were for each other's welfare. She needed to remember that. "Would you care to come in, Mr. Henry? I can offer you some coffee."

"That sounds wonderful, and please call me Dave. Whenever anyone calls me Mr. Henry, I'm expecting to see my uncle behind me." He followed her into the house, pausing several times to look around the vestibule before they reached the kitchen.

"Sorry, the heat isn't up to par. I plan to have Craig look into it when he gets back." She handed him a cup of coffee from the electric percolator she had left on. She pushed over the cream and sugar. "This should help to warm you."

Dave stopped rubbing his hands together and reached for the mug without adding any condiments. He held it several moments before taking a sip. "Oh, this hits the spot. So, are you planning to live here? It's a beautiful house."

"No. My fiancé and I want to sell it. In the meantime, Craig is fixing whatever needs repairs."

"Craig Cadman, the handyman who drove off to the fire?" Dave waved a hand in the direction Craig had taken. "I know him. Does fantastic work, and his mother has refinished several antique dressers for us. You're not the girl he's been dating, are you? I'd heard he was dating, but I didn't hear that he'd gotten engaged."

Trish couldn't help but chuckle. "No. We're old friends, but he's dating someone else." She held the mug to her lips and looked over the rim at Dave. His blond hair was a little mussed, probably windblown from following her. Otherwise he was as neat as his uncle, although not as intimidating.

"Would you care to look at the antiques

while you're here?" She put her mug down. It would be wonderful to get this chore taken care of so she'd know what other items could be donated to the church.

Dave nodded. "That would be great." He walked to her counter. "I've been checking out these dishes." After picking one up and looking at the back, he turned to her with an expectant smile. "Any chance you want to get rid of these?"

Trish joined him. "It's a complete set, with several of the larger pieces in the china cabinet." Her finger traced the delicate cream-and-gold edge with its tiny pink and yellow roses and some miniature blue flower that looked like a forget-me-not. It had always been her favorite. When she and Harrison had looked at china, though, they'd gone for a more modern geometric pattern. No sense in having two full sets of dishes. "Sure. I'm interested in selling it."

"Okay if I run back and get a few things? I'll need to take my own pictures, and frankly, this place isn't much warmer than the outside. The only thing you're missing is the arctic breeze." He gave her a heartfelt smile while he continued to rub his hands.

"Why don't I drive you?" Since all the

work vehicles had gone, she could easily get to her car.

"That would be great."

They headed out the front door just as Craig pulled in beside her car. When he got out of his van, Trish asked, "You put the fire out already?"

"Nope. I got there too late. The truck had already left." He stared a moment before extending his hand. "Nice to see you again, Dave. Hope you can give Trish some great deals."

"Take care of her heat, will you? I've got to get back to my place to warm up."

Craig's eyebrow went up, and he looked at Trish. "Heat?"

"I forgot to mention, I couldn't get the furnace to work. The key's under the mat, and we'll be back in a little while."

Once she had the car started, Dave got in on the passenger side. "You have heat in this?" he asked, blowing into his hands as he rubbed them together.

"Yes. You'll be toasty by the time we reach your shop."

CRAIG RETRIEVED THE old-fashioned three-inch key and headed for the basement to check the furnace, an oil burner probably installed a good fifty years ago. No wonder it wasn't providing any heat. No fuel. When was the last time they had a shipment? He went upstairs, sat on one of the kitchen chairs and dialed the local oil company most people used in the area.

"Hey, Marty," Craig said. They had been classmates, and Craig graduated a year before Marty did. "When was the last time you delivered to Mrs. Lowery?"

"You mean before she died?"

Craig took a deep breath. "Yes, before she died."

"Sometime last winter, I guess."

"Okay, she needs another fill-up."

"Why, is she alive again?" He cackled, a sure sign he wasn't taking Craig seriously.

"Since when did you turn into the town's comedian? Her granddaughter is staying here, and there's no more fuel. She's freezing. When can you make a delivery?"

"Who's paying for it? I already closed Mrs. Lowery's account."

"You'll get your money from the granddaughter."

"Okay, I'll make it my last delivery today.

Say, isn't she the Lowery gal you were sweet on?"

"The pipes are freezing, Marty."

"She's back in town and you've got another girlfriend?"

"Take care of it, Marty."

"Cyndi Parker, isn't it? I remember her doing all those splits and backflips as the head cheerleader."

"Just deliver the oil." Craig disconnected the call. Living all your life in a small town had definite disadvantages. Who else had been tracking his love life?

About to return the key to its not-so-secret hiding place, Craig stopped. Perfect time to check out that secretary and find that note. He went to the living room and lowered the large desktop just as a car pulled into the drive. Great. Trish was back.

Craig returned the large panel and headed for the front door. He opened it as Trish walked up the stairs with Dave Henry following her. This might be a good chance to get the price for the secretary.

"Found out why there's no heat. You ran out of fuel. I ordered a fill-up from Marty Cassidy's Homefuel. It should arrive later today."

Trish paused by the open door, rolling her eyes. "Oh, for heaven's sake. I never even thought about that. Thank you." She walked past him, motioning Dave to follow. "I'm making lunch—warm soup so Dave and I can defrost. Have the men come back from the fire?" When Craig shook his head, she added, "Would you like some soup or are you going back on the roof?"

His crew would probably stop for food after returning from the fire, and he didn't want to miss out on lunch. "Warm soup sounds fine." Once in the kitchen, Craig leaned against the counter, his arms folded across his chest, while Trish pulled out packages from the refrigerator. All the ingredients looked like his favorites, and he wondered if she had bought them for him. "You making grilled cheese?"

She grinned. "Of course. Can't have tomato soup without grilled cheese sandwiches."

"With ham?" He moved closer and opened one of the wrapped packages from Drexel's Deli. "You remembered?" That had always been their preferred treat. "The grill still in the same old place?" When she nodded, he headed for the pantry.

Sure enough, the grill was right where he remembered. A little dusty. Probably hadn't been used in years. He placed it on the counter and opened a drawer filled with dish towels. After a wipe-down, he plugged it in.

"You're sure familiar with everything," Dave said, coming over to stand by the counter. His gray winter parka was zipped to his neck even though the room had to be close to sixty degrees, despite no additional heat.

When the doorbell rang, Trish glanced at Craig. "You think that could be the oil delivery?"

"Doubt it. Marty said he'd do it on his last run. Why don't you answer the door, and I'll get started on the soup." He headed back to the pantry, where he'd seen several cans. After checking the dates, he realized all the cans were new. He smiled and started to whistle, right up until he heard her gasp of delight.

CHAPTER FIVE

"HARRISON! WHAT ARE you doing here? Come in and relax." She pulled at his red tie so it wasn't so tight around his neck, something he'd never allow on the job. "Here in my house, the casual look fits perfectly. You fit perfectly." She couldn't stop smiling. He was handsome in his dark gray suit. "I'm so glad you could make it."

"I missed you." He grabbed her hands then looked down at them. "Your hands are freezing." He pulled her into a loving embrace and kissed her with a fervor she appreciated and rarely experienced from him.

Since they worked together and their company frowned on any fraternization between employees, they always maintained a proper working relationship. Even when they had total privacy, he never showed the same tendency to hug and give affection the way Trish did. Maybe their short separation had ignited some romantic flames.

"Even your lips are cold. You been working outside?"

"No. It's just that we don't have heat."

When he gave her his "I told you so" look, she slipped outside, still holding his hand. "Come on." She hopped down the porch stairs and looked at the house. "What do you think?"

"So this is the relic?" Harrison stood, hands on hips, and looked at the house her great-grandfather had designed and built around the turn of the twentieth century. His son, her grandfather, had added his own imprint, making it a showpiece. "Wow. Is that what they call gingerbread?"

"I suppose some of it is. My grandfather liked to work with wood and—"

"It's coming off, right? No one needs all that fancy trim nowadays, and a lot of it is just hanging there."

"No, it's not coming off." Sure, some of the pieces had broken away, but Craig had assured her he could replace them.

Harrison raised his eyebrows. "You mean you won't change any of this…" He swished his hand in an arc toward the house. "…this…"

Trish ground her teeth a moment before

deciding to add her own comment. "Don't say it. I mean it, Harrison. I love this place, and it's important for me, so keep any negative opinions to yourself."

Clamping his lips together, he nodded and placed an arm around her shoulders, pointing to the flag flipping around in the breeze. "Is that for something special?"

"Check out the neighborhood, Harrison." Trish swung her arm around to take in all the houses on the street. "Everyone's flying them because it's Veterans Day."

He shrugged but didn't offer any other comment.

When she escorted him back inside, past the wide circular staircase and into the living room, she hoped to spark some enthusiasm for the old place. He remained unimpressed, but at least he didn't offer more criticism. She warmed only slightly to another of his embraces. "What?" he asked. "I'm in the doghouse now for not jumping on your bandwagon?"

Trish sighed. How could she expect him to love this Victorian house when he had none of her memories? She cuddled against him and smiled when he pulled her back into his arms.

"You're planning to spend a month here? I don't see how it's possible to fix all that needs to be done in that time."

"I've hired a handyman. He'll do most of the work."

"How do you know he's any good?" Harrison nuzzled her cheek. "I don't want you to end up with more of a mess and possibly get cheated."

Trish appreciated his concern. "It's okay. I grew up with him, and he's the best."

"Good," Harrison said, moving slightly away and brushing his hand through her hair. "Then you won't have to stay here. My main concern has been you being so far away from—"

"Anyone hungry?"

Harrison and Trish jumped apart. Harrison was the first to recover. He strode toward the intruder, his fist clenched as though he planned to strike. "Who are you?"

"Right now I'm the cook. Lunch is served in the kitchen." Craig made a quick pivot and disappeared into the hallway.

Trish grasped Harrison's arm and felt the

tension there. "That's my handyman, Craig Cadman."

"And he cooks?"

Trish patted his arm, hoping to relieve the unexpected hostility. "Not usually. Let's go eat."

So this is the fiancé, Craig thought as he returned to the kitchen.

Dave looked up from stirring the soup on the stove. "What was that? Is she okay?"

"Yeah." He stopped speaking when Harrison and Trish walked in.

"I'd like you both to meet my fiancé, Harrison Morris."

Craig offered his hand. "I'm Craig, the handyman."

Dave came around, also extending his hand. "And I'm Dave, the antiques man." He gave Craig a wink and went back to stirring the soup. "Do we have bowls for this?"

Trish picked up four of the china bowls she'd washed. "Do we have to use those?" Dave asked. "I thought I was buying them."

Trish laughed and brought the bowls to the table. "They've gone through hundreds of meals over the past seventy-five years. I'll wash them when we're through, and as long as no one starts to juggle them, they should make it without any problem." After opening several drawers, she placed napkins and spoons by the bowls.

Dave sighed, then went back for the pot of soup.

"What's this?" Harrison thrust his hand in a dismissive gesture. "I planned on taking you out for lunch. And instead we're settling for soup in a freezing kitchen." He managed a convincing shiver and paused before adding, "With the help." A moment later Harrison started laughing. "Oh, this is getting ridiculous. I'm sorry, guys. I just never expected…" He offered Trish a chair before taking one himself. "Let's just do it. I took an extended lunch hour, and I need to get back to the city."

Craig brought the grilled sandwiches to the table while Dave dished out the soup. At any moment Craig expected his crew to return. And he didn't want an interruption, not when he had an opportunity to observe Harrison. Maybe an inch or two shorter than Craig, Harrison had trimmed dark hair that hadn't started to thin, even though he was older than everyone else at the table. He looked as though he worked out, probably in some office gym.

What did Trish see in him? Was he the right one for her?

Craig reached for his sandwich and let old memories wash over him. "Remember when we sat in this kitchen, eating our favorite meal with your grandmother's cookies baking in the oven?"

Trish grinned and pointed to her mouthful. She swallowed before adding, "Yes. Dozens of times." She glanced at Harrison before concentrating on her sandwich again. He looked miffed.

Craig decided continuing down memory lane might not be the best idea. But Trish did remember. Was she experiencing the same nostalgia? Was the same knot tying up her insides?

He put down the sandwich, not able to deal with what was lost and could never be.

"So, WHAT DO you think this secretary is worth?" Trish asked Dave.

He started to reply, but Harrison came over and wrapped her in his arms, pulling her away from Dave. "When I come here in the future, I'll expect one of your home-cooked specialties." He gave Craig a look that could only mean the meal he'd just consumed wasn't up to par. "Really sorry I'll be missing out on Thanksgiving."

Did Trish know how to cook? She used to help her grandmother, but back then they were always happy with nothing fancier than a plate of cookies. Craig turned his attention back to the secretary. What would he do if Dave discovered the note? What would Harrison do? Laugh himself inside out?

"I'm sorry you'll miss it, too." She and Harrison embraced only a few feet away from him. Did Harrison really have to act so touchy-feely in front of everyone? And did Trish have to enjoy it so much?

"You'll only have one day to help me paint?" Trish looked away, and Craig saw the hurt in her eyes. *The rat.*

"Right. I'm taking all of that Sunday off. We can get most of it done then."

Sure. One day of painting and they'd be lucky to complete one room out of the half dozen that needed work. Didn't the guy know anything about how long it took to mix the paint, put up tape, cover the walls, trim the woodwork and clean up afterward?

Harrison kissed her again on the cheek,

and Craig considered bashing him in the head with one of the antique ornate brass lamps. As much as he wanted to know more about the secretary, Craig felt like leaving.

"Don't your parents live in Chicago?" Trish asked. "Will you be joining them for Thanksgiving?"

"I may stop by, but it wouldn't have much meaning if I can't bring my fiancée." Another embrace. At least her response was less than enthusiastic this time around. Was it the subject matter? Why wasn't he taking her there to meet his family?

Trish managed to slip from under Harrison's possessive arm and walked closer to Dave to re-ask her question. "So, what do you think, Dave? What kind of price can I get for the secretary?"

"Could one of you help me move it away from the wall? I'd like to see if there's any signature or an indication of who might have made this. Do you have the history on this, Trish? Where it came from?" Craig moved over to the opposite side and helped swivel the large piece around to expose the back. Trish joined him.

"It's always been here. I think Gram mentioned once her grandfather bought it for his wife as an anniversary gift. In fact, most of the items in the house were purchased by her father's parents or grandparents. Gram didn't see the point in replacing anything with a newer model unless the old one no longer served the purpose." Trish chuckled. "She did upgrade to a flat-screen TV, though."

"Oh, my!" Dave traced his finger on a faded mark while everyone else came over to see what had intrigued him. "This WW is from Willard Williams, a cabinetmaker back in the early eighteenth century. What a find! I'll have to do a little more research, but we're talking thousands. Especially since it's in pristine condition."

Thousands! Craig caught his breath and wondered how he'd ever come up with that much money for something that served no practical purpose.

Harrison again embraced Trish. *Dollar signs must be floating in his head. Can't she see where his interest lies?*

Dave came around to the front and pulled down the writing section. "Yes, this is definitely Willard's. See all the carved leaves and flowers on the drawers? And if I remember… Yes, the one with an animal opens…" Dave reached for the tiny carved squirrel and tried twisting and turning the decoration. Nothing happened.

To Craig's total relief. Sweat trickled down his back. Had the heat kicked in? He searched for any excuse to leave. "I think the crew has returned. I'd better get back to work."

"Thanks for lunch," Trish said.

"You provided the ingredients. Dave and I merely threw them together."

She reached for his arm. "I'll walk you out." When she disentangled herself from Harrison, he gave Craig a fish-eyed glare but didn't join them.

"The meal brought back great memories, Trish. Thank you."

"And it tasted just as good as when Gram served it." Trish chuckled. "I don't think Harrison appreciated it much."

"How could he? It's only special to us." Craig reached in his pocket and pulled out her key. "I didn't get a chance to put it back."

She took it from him, gripping his hand. "I'll take care of it." Her fingers felt cold in his.

"You might not want to keep it in such an obvious place. Especially if what Dave said is true. Your antiques have some great value." He held on to the old-fashioned metal a moment longer while he thought about it.

"Yeah, what a surprise." Trish removed the key from his hand. "I'll find a better hiding place."

"You know, you really need these locks upgraded to dead bolts."

"But this works well." She reached up and kissed him on the cheek. "Thanks for everything."

Surprised that she'd be affectionate in front of Harrison, Craig turned toward her just as Harrison came over and placed an arm around her shoulders. As he pulled her out of Craig's reach, he said, "He's right. Dead bolts are a must."

"I'll look into it."

"You do that. Nice meeting you," Harrison said, but his expression didn't reflect any pleasure.

"Same here." Craig gave the lie back, not adding any warmth in his reply.

DAVE WENT THROUGH each room, scribbling notes in a small loose-leaf notebook. Occasionally he took pictures, and he appeared extremely pleased at each new encounter. Although the upstairs bathrooms held no treasures, Dave said that claw-foot tubs were a real find. In one bathroom, he kicked at the linoleum that had begun to curl against the wall before he dropped to one knee and held on to the tub's rim.

"These tubs are magnificent." He examined it thoroughly both inside and out. "I rarely see so many beautiful details in an old house like this that haven't fallen into decay."

"Can I get a good price for the tubs?"

Dave straightened. "Is it true you plan to sell the house?"

Trish glanced at Harrison. "Well, yes."

"Then I suggest you leave the tubs. You'll fetch a much higher price."

Harrison chortled. "Really?" He leaned over and pulled on the linoleum, managing to rip off a good chunk of it. "How much will this add to the value?" After showing the curling piece to Dave, he tossed it into the tub. "Who buys this kind of stuff?"

"I would." Dave stood straighter. "In fact, I've been giving it more thought. Craig said he's keeping the building's integrity intact. I particularly like that he's not removing the gingerbread. Yes, I'm definitely considering it." He turned to Trish. "Do you have any other buyers in mind?"

Before Trish could say no, Harrison took over the conversation. "We're looking into all possible avenues. And we'll certainly consider any offers." He wrapped an arm around Trish's shoulders and drew her close. "Right, honey?"

Dave beamed. "Good. I'll talk to my uncle and see what he thinks."

By the time Harrison was ready to leave in his gold Lexus, the nail drivers had started again on the roof. "How can you stand the noise?" Harrison held her hands and pressed his lips against them. "I'll be back early Sunday in my jeans and some old sneakers so we can get going on the painting. I hope the heat will be back on so we can work in some form of comfort."

"It will be. Craig will…"

"I don't know about this Craig. Is he really competent?" Harrison glanced at the roof. "He seems awfully young."

"He is, but I'd trust him with any project. He was trained by the best."

Harrison's expression hardened. "I'd prefer you didn't stay here. It's not safe. Especially with those locks."

"Don't be ridiculous. I grew up here and know almost everyone in town. Besides, the police department and fire department are just down the block. This is a hundred times safer than either of our apartments back in the city." She waited a moment before adding, "So, you're really looking forward to transferring to California?"

Harrison placed his fingers against her mouth. "Let's not talk about it before I go. I don't want to jeopardize my chances."

Harrison wrapped his arms around her, pulling her close and nearly squeezing all the air out of her lungs. She pushed away to be able to breathe. "I wish you didn't have to go."

"Training sessions. They'll take about ten days. Sorry I'll miss Thanksgiving, but I'll get a turkey sandwich and wish I was with you." He kissed her, one of those passionate kisses that promised so much more. He started to laugh as he pulled away. "Hey, you could be doing training sessions now that you're taking that new position. I told you the job had its perks."

Trish watched Harrison leave, waving until

he disappeared down the street. How nice of him to take time away from his busy schedule just to see her. She thought about the possibilities of her new job. An office of her own. A pay increase. Travel. For some reason she couldn't muster any enthusiasm. Nor did she want to think of the ramifications of moving to California.

Now that she had returned to Riverbend, she realized this house, this neighborhood and the people she knew intimately were still important to her. Her heart felt ready to burst with affection.

She turned as Marty Cassidy drove his truck into her driveway. "Marty," she called as she walked to the driver's side. His door opened and he dropped to the ground, his flaming hair still as untamed as she remembered from high school. She transferred the passion she'd just felt for her hometown onto him with a warm hug and ran her hand through his unruly locks. "You look exactly the same." She pulled away. "Except for a few extra pounds."

"What can I say? My wife's a great cook."

Someone nudged Trish's back, and she turned to see Craig reach past her. "Glad you could make it today."

The two men shook hands. "Yeah, I know the pipes are about to explode."

"So who did you marry, Marty? Anyone I know?"

"Mary Ellen Sinclair." He grinned and Trish nodded, remembering Mary Ellen from their high school classes. "And we have three girls. Triplets."

Trish grinned. Wouldn't it be wonderful to be blessed with three girls? "You planning on any more?"

"No, just the triplets for now. Mary Ellen said we wait till these three are out of diapers." Marty turned to Craig. "So how many kids are you and Cyndi planning to have?"

Craig exhaled in a puff. "Zero."

Trish waited for an explanation while Marty dived right in with a question. "What do you mean? No children or no Cyndi?" Marty began unloading the hose from the truck.

"You know, Marty, I always knew there was something about you I didn't like. Maybe it's the hair." Craig made an abrupt turn. "While you pump the oil, I'll go check on the furnace and make sure it's ready to function."

"Whew. What's got his dander up?" They

both watched Craig's determined stride into the house.

"I haven't a clue," she said barely above a whisper.

"So, Trish, you planning on staying here, living in your grandmother's old house?"

They continued to talk while Marty filled the oil tank. "You've got to come by and see Mary Ellen and the girls."

"I'd love to."

"And what's up with Craig? Hostile. I only asked about Cyndi because everyone knows they're dating."

"I'll ask him."

When he was through, Trish went into the house to find Craig. She followed the banging noises coming from the basement. "This should work. It's primed." He stood, brushing off his hands. "Why don't you stop by and see my mother? She was asking about you. The furnace will take an hour or two before it warms the whole house. I noticed before your hands were freezing."

He reached over and grasped her hands again. His felt decidedly warm and comforting. "What did you mean before?" she asked.

"Before what?" They started up the stairs.

"About zero kids. Does Cyndi feel the same way?"

When they reached the hall, Craig stopped to feel the register. "This won't warm up until the water flowing through it is heated."

Trish pulled on his arm to get his attention. "Why wouldn't you want kids? When you talked about your brother…"

"In case you haven't noticed, Trish, my brother doesn't have a father. Dad didn't even reach fifty, and heart conditions run in my family. I'm not bringing children into this world if I might not see my own son through college or dance at my daughter's wedding."

"What about Cyndi? How does she feel about this?"

"The subject hasn't come up."

"Well, it should if you're planning to get married."

"Who said we're getting married?"

"Didn't you say…?"

"We've dated. Nothing more than that. And I can't help it if some of our nosy classmates come up with their own interpretation." He maneuvered past her. "I'd better get back on the roof and see how things are going up there."

Trish watched him, feeling a terrible ache.

What if her parents had decided not to have children? She had often felt unwanted, as though she interfered with their lifestyle. They rarely took vacations as a family. Her parents liked adult entertainment—a trip to Las Vegas, a cruise to the Caribbean. Most of the time she was dropped off with her grandmother whenever her parents went on a trip. The few times they did go as a family, it often included Craig's parents.

Not that Trish had any regrets. She camped, hiked and played with Craig and his parents, so she knew firsthand what a family should be like.

She and Harrison planned to have many children, something they'd talked about at great length when he proposed. She'd raise them differently from how she'd grown up.

No sending her children off for someone else to care for. She'd play with her kids, get involved in their lives and help them with their homework, something her parents never did. Homework was done at Gram's, usually with Craig's help. Her father didn't get involved in any physical recreation, but Craig's dad often participated in softball or went for bike rides. All the things she couldn't get her own parents to join in. Now they roamed the country "playing" in their RV.

Maybe Craig had a point: don't have kids if you really don't want them. Trish planned to be a stay-at-home mom, and Harrison had agreed. Thank goodness they were both on the same page.

CHAPTER SIX

TRISH WALKED OVER to Franklin Avenue and headed to Craig's aunt's home. She paused in front of the two-story Cape Cod structure built at the end of World War II. It was similar to the one Trish had lived in down the street. The homes had serviced returning GIs, one of them Craig's grandfather. When he died, the house went to his oldest daughter, Jenny.

A flag fluttered by the door, snapping close to her head, and she pushed it aside. Before Trish could ring the bell, the door opened.

"I thought it was you." Rachel came out and swept Trish into an embrace. "Come in, come in. I want you to meet Noah."

A young boy, a replica of Craig, avoided looking directly at her. He glanced up at his mother as Trish went down to one knee and held out her arms.

"This is Butchy's friend Trish. Say hello, Noah. Don't be bashful."

"Hi, there." Noah came over shyly and allowed Trish to hug him. "I met your brother when he was about your age. We're old friends."

Noah backed out of the embrace. "You want to see my room?"

Trish stood and looked at Rachel for permission. "Sure. You go ahead. I'll make us some hot chocolate. Craig said you've been freezing over at your place." She disappeared into a kitchen.

Noah grasped Trish's hand and pulled her to a dining area. He scooted under a large brown sheet that lay across the tabletop and invited her in. "This is all mine."

Trish succeeded in ducking under without banging her head and took a seat hunched among a multitude of stuffed animals. "Which one is your favorite?" Noah reached past her and grabbed a dog that might have been a golden retriever at one point before it lost some stuffing. It had suffered further from dirt and grass stains. "Nice. What do you call it?"

"He's Butchy, for my best friend, my big brother." Noah reached for another animal, what appeared to be a bear, looking equally well loved.

"This one is Max. I named him after Mr. Moody."

"I haven't met Mr. Moody yet. Does he look like this?" Trish picked up the rangy bear and twisted it back and forth.

Noah started to giggle and reached for the animal. "No."

Rachel's toes were visible at the edge of the tent. "You want to come out and have the hot chocolate? I'm afraid I'd spill it if I came under there."

"Let's go," Trish said to her new friend. "I could really use a warm drink." She crawled out and headed for the tray table set up in the living room. Settling on the couch, Trish patted the seat next to her so Noah could join her. "I really like your room. Did you make it all by yourself?"

"Butchy helped."

"Some of us still call him Butchy. A hard habit to break." Rachel set a plate of oatmeal cookies next to the steaming hot-chocolate mugs. "He told me you call him Craig. He likes that."

Trish took a sip of hot chocolate and re-laxed against the couch. "Craig said you might be able to help me at the house. The two of you are partners?"

"Yes. What do you need done?"

"I plan to remove the carpet on the staircase, but the tacks made holes. I need to sand it down and patch it so the holes won't show. Also, the living room wallpaper is faded and nasty-looking. Could you show me how to remove it?"

They continued to talk shop until Noah lost interest, finished his snack and went back to his tent.

"He's a darling boy," Trish said, leaning closer to Rachel.

"Thank you. Craig said you're engaged?"

"Yes, and I hope to have a half dozen like little Noah."

Rachel's smile faded. "I wish Craig felt that way." She stood and began retrieving the dishes. "He had a hard time accepting I was pregnant. Maybe it embarrassed him, what with him graduating from high school at the time. He wasn't pleased when I had Noah." Trish grabbed the other items on the tray table and followed Rachel to the kitchen.

That didn't make sense. "When Craig told me about Noah, he said it was a happy accident. He adores the boy."

"Oh, it was an accident, all right. I never thought at my age…" Rachel placed the dishes in the sink before turning back to Trish and leaning against the counter. "The doctor said when I had Butchy, I'd never be able to have more children. You can imagine my surprise when it happened."

Rachel took a deep breath and whispered, "He thinks that's what killed his father, all those added pressures." Rachel turned back to the sink and began running water over the dishes. Several times she brushed at her eyes with the back of her hand. "At the time, we had no idea Craig…" She paused. "I mean Craig Senior…had a heart problem." She sniffled. "We both wanted that child. Even if my husband had known about his condition, he'd have wanted that boy. But it did give him anxieties in the end. How I'd care for everything with him gone. The debt, losing the house." She sighed. "I really wish my oldest son would get over it, though. Life goes on and you adjust."

Trish wrapped her arm around Rachel's shoulders and squeezed. It made no sense. How could a child have anything to do with his father's death? What could she say to offer comfort? After giving the woman a kiss on her damp cheek, Trish decided it was time to leave. "Give me a call when you can help with the stairs."

"How about tomorrow morning after I leave Noah at the nursery school?" Rachel asked.

"Sounds like a plan." As she went through the dining area and passed the tent, Trish leaned down and said, "Nice to have met you, Noah. I'll see you around."

He peeked under the sheet and gave her an endearing smile. How could anyone be upset about this lovely accident?

FROM UNDER THE welcome mat to under a clay pot holding artificial flowers didn't seem like much improvement, Craig thought as he collected the key. Harrison would have a fit. The guy had no idea he was broadcasting his concerns right below the roof, and Craig and his crew had heard every word, including that business about Craig's competency and youth. *The jerk.*

Now that Trish had gone to his mother's and the roof was complete, he should have enough time to go through the secretary's hidden drawers. Craig pulled down the writing surface and examined the different carvings.

Besides the squirrel, there were numerous leaves, flowers and one acorn. What did squirrels eat? He grasped the acorn and squirrel at the same time and pulled. Like magic the two drawers opened and unlocked all the others. He went through each one and found nothing more than a paper clip and a pearl button. No note. *What could have happened to it?*

He could never afford to buy the secretary, so that was one less thing to worry about, he thought as he returned all the drawers to their proper places. Someone had removed the note. If it wasn't Trish, then who?

Well, at least he could show Trish the secret to opening the drawers. He replaced the writing surface and headed for the upstairs bathrooms. He was glad that Dave had liked the claw-foot tubs. Craig's crew could never have gotten them out without destroying them, and Dave's endorsement might have been exactly what Trish needed to keep the relics in place.

He took out his iPhone, went on the internet and pulled several vanities and other items into a folder to show Trish. Several of the pieces he could get from Moody's and save her quite a bit.

In the meantime, Craig had to do something about that curling linoleum. With the heat working its way back to normal, he started with his large scraper and began wedging it under the linoleum.

By the time he finished, sweat covered his forehead and his sweater lay tossed in the hallway. The hissing radiators indicated the heat had returned.

So had Trish.

"ANYONE HERE?" TRISH CALLED. Rachel's remarks about Craig still gnawed at her. Should she mention it to him, find out if he knew how much his mother suffered from his accusations? Or should she just stay out of it? Trish decided to not get involved unless an opportunity presented itself.

Craig came to the head of the stairs. "You might want to be more careful. Your newest hiding place for the key isn't much safer than the last. I could be a raving maniac up here waiting to pounce on you."

"I saw your truck, Mr. Maniac."

"Well, my next project is finding dead bolts for your doors with enough keys so you don't have to hide one where any burglar could find it." He paused before continuing. "And don't give me that bit about your grandmother never replacing anything if it wasn't broke. This is a necessity."

"Okay, but they have to blend in. I don't want the look of that beautiful front door ruined by modern hardware."

Trish started up the stairs, removing her scarf and undoing her sweater. "Good. The heat's back on. So, what are you working on now?"

"Come look." Trish followed him into the bathroom and stepped over a pile of shredded linoleum. "All this had to come out. I'm thinking vinyl tiles, maybe in black and white."

"Linoleum again? Why not ceramic tiles? They're so much more attractive."

"True. But they're triple the cost and triple the weight. Ceramic tile plus the heavy tub filled with water will put added strain on the floor."

"Is there something the matter with the floor?"

"It flooded when the pipes burst a few years back. No reason to believe it isn't sound, even though it is over one hundred years old, but why take the chance?"

Trish nodded agreement. "Your mom's helping me with the stairs tomorrow. I'm going to remove the rug and sand the wood." Trish started to grin. "I met the most darling little man today. Someone who looked a lot like you."

"Yeah, I'm a cutie, all right." When she attempted to swat him on the arm, he grabbed her wrist. "What? You don't agree I'm cute?"

"Cute?" Trish shook her head and pulled her arm free. Should she tell him just how attractive he'd become? Why not embarrass the heck out of him? "I'd say your movie-star good looks no longer put you in the category of cute."

But instead of backing away with cheeks turning crimson, Craig grinned. "I wondered if you'd noticed."

Trish chuckled. "Aren't you the reigning king of modesty?"

With his smile growing, Craig moved closer. "If you've got it, why not flaunt it, I always say."

"Oh, cut it out. You never said that in your life." She walked over to the top of the staircase. "Want to help me get this old rug off?" It was a beautiful Persian design but terribly worn.

"Sure. I've got something that will slip under the rug and help get it up with the least

amount of effort." He came out of the bathroom carrying a long wooden handle with
what looked like a flattened hoe on the end.
"Let's start at the bottom and work up. And
be sure to collect the tacks."

"Why? Do they have value? What about
the rug? Can I sell that?"

When they reached the bottom stair, Craig
turned to her and leaned on the wooden handle. "We collect the tacks so they don't end
up in our shoes. As for the rug, I doubt it's
worth anything, but check with Dave."

"Where's your imagination? What if it's a
magic carpet?" Craig ignored her and slipped
the metal tip under the rug. "We can sit on it
and fly around the world."

He stopped and stared at her. "You're paying me by the hour. Do you really want to
have flights of fancy attached to the bill?"

Trish sighed. "I can remember when that
cute kid I knew was a lot more fun."

"Yeah, well, that's before he turned into a
movie-star-handsome working dude."

CHAPTER SEVEN

TRISH DIDN'T SLEEP well that night. She kept thinking about Harrison. Why had he dropped in without calling first? And why all those hugs and kisses? He often referred to her as the "hugger," an instinct that didn't come naturally to him. For a man who didn't display emotion in front of people, his actions today seemed out of character. Was he worried or jealous about her working with two very attractive men? Certainly she had no interest in Dave, someone she'd just met. And Craig...

She laughed quietly about Craig's reaction to her comment about his looks. That wavy dark hair over his ears. Those blue eyes that seared through your skin when he stared at you. And when she caught him looking...

Trish flipped over and attempted to block out the image of Craig gazing at her, something she'd noticed a few times. Just a look, and it made her all fuzzy inside. Ridiculous.

Why pile all these fantasies onto Craig? She was engaged. She had to focus on that.

Another flip and she tried concentrating on Harrison. What was his eye color? Gray or hazel? She couldn't be sure. She'd have to check that when he came over to paint on Sunday. But her thoughts wouldn't stay with him. She kept thinking about Craig and his mother. Did he know how much his placing blame hurt? As much as Trish wanted to put that out of her mind, she couldn't.

She forced her thoughts back to Harrison. They had met when she worked for Metro-Mintro Credit Cards in their branch just outside Washington, DC. Harrison had visited the global company for training sessions. No sparks flew then. But when she got the opportunity to transfer to the New York office, where he worked, she decided to take it so she could be closer to her grandmother. While there, Harrison had become her mentor, encouraging her progress in the company.

Eventually she came to love Harrison's quick humor, intelligent conversations and thorough knowledge of Manhattan. He'd impressed her parents, something no other suitor had been able to do. And he had accompanied her when her grandmother moved to a nearby nursing home, comforting her when she died.

Come to think about it, not once did he kiss her in front of her parents, her grandmother or anyone else. All this pent-up passion didn't occur until he came to her grandmother's house and met Craig and Dave. Was he staking a claim?

Another flip and she yawned, finally feeling sleep's relaxing harmony. Maybe Harrison had decided he liked being romantic, kissing without restraint. Truth be told, she enjoyed the change.

THE NEXT MORNING, Trish noticed the flag still flying. Wasn't she supposed to take it in before nightfall? She removed it and placed it back in the closet just as Craig arrived. He went right up the staircase. "Already had my breakfast," he said when she offered him coffee.

"Your mother's coming over to work on the stairs with me."

"I'll keep out of your way."

He placed a stepladder under one of the water spots on the second-floor ceiling. "What are you working on now?"

"I'm putting sealant on to make sure the discoloration doesn't bleed through, and then I'll paint all the ceilings later."

"Okay." Trish took that opportunity to go to the kitchen for a cup of coffee. So much to do. How would she ever empty the house of all her grandmother's things? She looked out the window and shuddered. The barn! She'd forgotten all about that. She grabbed her grandmother's coat and keys and went to check it out.

Originally the structure had housed horses for the horse-drawn carriage that her great-grandfather kept. Trish had seen photos of the horse and buggy along with the different vehicles housed in the barn. Once Ford made cars fashionable, the carriage was exchanged for a Model T, followed by one car after another. The final one, a black Packard with thirty thousand miles on it, was sold when her father made a trip to help his mother downsize. The thought that Gram once had even more stuff gave Trish an unwanted chill. She pulled open the barn door and saw, to her pleasure, that it was nearly empty.

A few bed frames, some sawhorses and a tireless bicycle sat propped against the wall next to several boxes. Maybe Reverend Meyer could find something of value. The church sponsored a small store where they sold used items. She'd give him a call.

When she headed back to the house, Trish saw one of Moody's trucks stop next to Craig's van. Rachel got out along with a man close to her own age. He took out several large plastic buckets and dropped them by Trish's front door, waved to her and then took off.

"Hi. What's this?" Trish asked as she helped Rachel bring in the buckets.

"Lots of different things. Figured you wouldn't have the supplies we'd need, so I charged these to your account at Moody's. Anything we don't use, we can bring back." Rachel walked to the stairs and waved to Craig. "We'll probably work up a dust storm here. Will that give you problems?"

"Nah, I'll go into another room." Craig packed up his equipment and moved into one of the bedrooms that had a stained ceiling.

"Here." Rachel handed Trish a mask. "Put this on. We'll be taking off varnish and who knows what else. The masks will protect our lungs." She removed different grades of sandpaper along with an electric sander. "This can work on the smooth surfaces, but we'll need to squeeze sandpaper around the carved balusters with our hands. Take a pair of these gloves. I figured you'd be a medium."

"Leather?"

"Yes. That's the only kind that will last doing this work." She handed her a pair of knee pads. "You'll want these, too."

Trish placed the knee pads with their Velcro strips over her jeans, slipped on the gloves and flexed her fingers inside. "Where should we start?"

Rachel stood with her hand cupping her chin while she took in the length of the stairs. Her hair was a lighter brown than Trish remembered.

"How about I start with the sander at the bottom," Rachel said. "There's a vacuum attached that should take care of most of the dust. You start at the top on the balusters. Once your hands get tired, we can switch."

Trish headed up the stairs with a bucket containing the sandpaper and sanding sponges. Within minutes she realized she'd taken on a daunting task. But her determination kicked in. This staircase had once been beautiful, and she intended to return it to its original state.

"Have you done something to your hair?"

Trish asked as she twisted the sandpaper around the curved baluster. "It looks really nice, but I remember it being closer to Craig's dark brown."

"Yes. When I got sick of going gray, I decided to do something about it. I like it this lighter color."

"So do I. My mother's went totally white. I think she'd look much better with some color in it." Trish waited for some comment and wondered why Rachel hadn't asked about her family. They used to be so close. After a moment, Trish continued, "Did I tell you my parents took an early retirement?" Still no response. *Odd.*

Maybe Rachel didn't like to talk while she worked. But Trish couldn't see spending the next few hours in silence, especially when they had always talked freely before. Then the electric sander started, and talking above the noise was impossible.

Later, with her shoulders aching and her hands about to fall off, Trish turned to Rachel. "There has to be an easier way to do this."

Rachel came up to stand by her. "We could use chemicals to strip it, but those require excellent ventilation. It's too cold outside to work with the windows open." She patted Trish on the shoulder. "You know, we don't have to do the whole staircase in one day. Give yourself a rest. I have to go and pick up Noah now."

"Are you bringing him over here later?"

"No. He'll have his lunch and nap time. Nursery school manages to tire him out." She paused halfway down the stairs. "He'll stay with my sister. We'd never get anything done with him here, and it's even worse with Butchy. The two are inseparable."

Trish followed her down the stairs, noting how lovely the light grain in the oak treads looked. "Will there be a problem with those tack holes?"

"No, I have a filler for that. It's coming along. We should be able to put a finishing coat on it by the end of the week."

Rachel turned when she reached the bottom, her hands on her hips. "You know, I've always wanted to have a bed-and-breakfast. And this place would be absolutely perfect. It's on the main street next to everything." She sighed and turned toward the door. "Oh, well. I'd better be getting back to Noah."

Trish wanted so much to bring up the subjects that had kept her awake. How could she help Craig and his mother heal the chasm between them? Did they even know it existed?

"I'll take my break now, too." Trish remembered Craig still working upstairs. Maybe he'd like some lunch. Once Rachel was out the door, Trish retraced her steps and went looking for him. She found him sitting against the wall, checking his cell phone. He looked up and got to his feet when he saw her.

"You finished with the stairs?"

"No, but we're making progress."

Craig pointed to the ceiling. "That has to dry." She looked up and saw sheets of brown paper tacked by some blue tape along the ceiling's edge. "I'm getting it ready so I can paint later this afternoon."

"Your mother went to pick up Noah, and I'm taking a break."

"Want to check out flooring for the bathroom?" he asked, ignoring her mention of his brother and mother. "That's my next project after the ceilings."

"Sure. I'll get my coat."

They took Craig's van to Moody's Lumber. "Don't you ever shop anywhere else?" Trish asked. "Your mother came in with buckets of their stuff, and you work with Moody's crew."

"I get a discount, but if you don't see anything you like, we can go to some other stores. Lowe's and Home Depot aren't too far away." Craig parked and leaned toward her. "I need to get a cherry picker for putting up that gingerbread on the front. Max has several different ones I can rent. And as I said, I get a discount that I'll pass on to you with a better deal."

Once out of the van, Craig walked over to a man about his father's age. She recognized him as the man who had dropped Rachel at the house. They began talking about several pieces of machinery located on the outside of the building while Trish stuffed her hands in her pockets. She needed some warm woolen gloves.

Craig introduced Max to her, then asked, "What do you suggest, the scissor lift or the knuckleboom? I'm working on the front of her house, and I need a cage that will hold a lot of supplies so I don't have to go up and down a lot."

"Personally, I'd go with the scissor, but it has to be placed on a level surface."

Craig turned to Trish. "It's level in front of

your house, right? And the ground's pretty much frozen over the past week." Trish shrugged. "We'll take a scissor that can go about thirty feet. I'll pick it up sometime before Thanksgiving."

As they headed inside, Max asked, "You coming to your mom's place for Thanksgiving? She invited me, and she won't tell me what I can bring."

"Mom prefers to make all the food herself."

"Why not bring something specifically for her?" Trish suggested. Max looked as confused as she had been with the scissor and knuckle thingamabobs. "How about flowers?"

Max turned to a display of colorful chrysanthemums by the front door. "Like this?" Craig took off inside the building while Trish frowned at the potted mums.

He looked so perplexed, Trish felt sorry for him. "Get her something she doesn't see every day when she comes to work. What about Grey's Florist? They have some lovely fall bouquets that would look perfect in her living room." Trish had seen them in a window display whenever she drove down the street and had nearly stopped there to buy one for herself.

Max's eyes lit with wonder. "Yes, I'll do that. Will you be joining us?"

Trish scratched her forehead and searched for a proper excuse. No one had invited her, and she didn't think the invitation should come from Max. "No. I have other plans." She had no idea what they might be, but at least she could get out of this situation without hurting the man's feelings.

Trish walked into the lumber company, wondering where Craig had disappeared to. She heard a piercing whistle and looked to see him waving. She followed him into a display of different tiles. "You see anything you like?" He pointed to a vinyl square that looked as though it was made of one-inch black and white ceramic tiles. "This is pretty retro if you want something that goes with those tubs."

Trish examined it for a while, then looked at other samples. After a good half hour of trying to make up her mind, she went back to the first one he'd shown her. "I'm going with the retro."

Craig had spent most of the time with arms crossed over his chest, propped against one of the displays, watching her. He stood and walked over to the boxes of the tiles she wanted and placed several on a movable platform. "Good choice."

"I appreciate your patience."

"Has nothing to do with patience," Craig said, giving her a sideways glance. "The longer you take, the more money I make. Remember, I get paid by the hour."

"Wha…?" She stopped and stared at him. "You mean you're charging me for sitting there…?" Trish gestured to the boxes he'd been sitting on. She couldn't believe it.

"But," he continued, "I'll forget that amount if you treat me to lunch."

Trish whacked his arm. "Bribery, really?" She took a deep breath before asking, "Where do you want to go?"

"How about Drexel's Deli? I can introduce you to the crew if they're still there."

Craig's crew had left before they reached the deli, which meant they could sit anywhere in the small shop. After ordering, they took a seat by the window. Craig showed her the vanities on his iPad that might go in her bathroom, and they discussed the choices until their sandwiches were ready. "So, what did Max decide to bring to my mother?"

"A bouquet of flowers from Grey's, not anything available where she works."

"I would have suggested perfume."

"That's way too personal." Trish took a bite of her ham sandwich, chewed and swallowed before adding, "Unless there's something going on with your mother and Max."

"I'm not sure. In the last few months I've seen a lot of changes. She's dyed her hair, lost weight. Anytime I go into our office, Max is usually there." They finished their sandwiches, and Craig pushed an opened bag of potato chips to her side of the table. "What perfume are you wearing?"

Trish sat back and stared at him.

When she didn't answer, he raised his eyebrows. "Am I being too personal?"

"No. I'm surprised you noticed. It's Chanel No. 5. Harrison gave it to me."

Craig nodded. "He has excellent taste."

"It's my taste. I told him I liked it."

"Then you have excellent taste. I like it, too." He picked up a chip and examined it before putting it back in the bag. "It seems familiar, but I know I haven't noticed you wearing it before you came back to Riverbend. Last odor I remember on you came from a skunk's spray."

Trish chuckled. "All that tomato juice nearly dyed my hair red, and it didn't help one bit. Never understood how the skunk managed to get me and not you." They had been on a camping trip with his family. Unfortunately, the black kitty they tried to bring into the camp lowered its tail over its head and squirted her.

"Luck, I guess." Craig leaned toward her. "So, who wore the Chanel before? It's in my memory bank, but I can't place it."

Trish propped her elbows on the table and rested her chin on her entwined fingers. "Gram."

Craig sat back. "Boy, you really are into retro."

"Does that bother you, that my grandmother wore it?"

"Not at all. The fragrance fits you. I won't connect it to anyone else."

"Okay, but don't mention it to Harrison. He'd have a fit. Chanel No. 5's been around for almost a century, and he has this idea that only new things have any value."

Her phone started to ring. She pulled it out of her pocket and looked at the screen. "Speak of the devil." She turned it on and considered mentioning she and Craig had just talked about Harrison. She decided not to. "Hi, honey. How was your trip to California?"

Craig got up and walked over to the man at the counter, far enough so that she felt able to talk freely. Although Harrison sounded stressed, they talked for several minutes, discussing his trip. He couldn't give her any feedback on his interviews, only that he finished the one in Los Angeles. He still had to head for San Francisco before he could get back to check on her progress with the house.

"So long for now. See you soon." Trish was about to disconnect when Harrison added, "And, oh, yes, I miss you."

"Love you," Trish said before ending the call. She sat staring off into space, still holding the phone.

AS IF I'D TALK to Harrison about his fiancée's wonderful perfume. Craig waited until Trish finished before coming over to her. She didn't look particularly happy about the call from lover boy, and Craig wasn't about to ask for details. "Shall we go? If my mom's coming back to work, she'll need to get into the house."

"I told her I hid the key under the potted plant."

"What? You know that particular spot is probably the most obvious—"

"Then tell me where else I should put it until you get that dead bolt."

"Why are you snapping at me?"

Her scowl turned apologetic. How could he get them both back to their easy talk? He opened the van door and she got in. After Craig was in his seat he asked, "Could we talk about something else?"

"Sure." She thought for a moment before asking, "Did something happen between our parents?"

"Like what?" As far as he knew, there hadn't been any connection between them since Trish moved away.

"I don't know. I mentioned my parents' early retirement and how they're traveling in an RV…"

"Your parents are camping?"

"Yes. Why that shocked expression, Craig? We all went camping a few times together." She sighed. "I know they never really took to it. I can't understand the appeal now, but that's not the issue."

"What is?"

"Your mother didn't ask one question or show one bit of interest. I remember when our parents were best friends. What happened to break them apart?" They arrived at the house to see Rachel entering the front door. "I'm going to ask her." Trish released her seat belt and looked as if she was about to make a quick exit.

Craig grabbed her sleeve. "Don't. I'll tell you."

Trish turned to face him. "What?"

"Remember when you and I were working on your algebra?" She nodded. "And your mother walked in and we weren't…you know, studying algebra."

"We were kissing, Craig. I remember."

Did she remember it the way he did, the best moment of his life up to that point? "And your mother got upset. Sent me home."

"My mother had a fit. We were kids, for heaven's sake." She started to chuckle. "I was going out on my first date and was nervous about kissing him. When I mentioned it…"

"…I said try it on me." And to his unexpected delight, she had.

"It was nothing, and you were only thirteen."

"Well, your mother called mine and read

her the riot act. She was so happy they were moving to get their precious daughter away from my parents' adolescent pervert." He paused and took her hand. "She figured we were on the road to hell. It got my parents very upset, and they pretty much cut your family out of their lives."

Trish squeezed his hand and sat back. "That explains a lot. Mom didn't want me to have anything to do with you, made it so I couldn't send you emails. She might even have erased some of them. You did write a lot." Trish dropped his hand, leaned over and buried her face in her hands. "What am I going to do? What should I say?"

Craig released his seat belt and shifted closer. "You'll say nothing. She's not going to bring it up. It was ten years ago."

"But it wasn't even your fault. I was the one who initiated it."

When Trish moved to face him, they were inches apart. If only he could kiss her now. "Adolescent pervert? That's what my mom called you?" She started giggling. "What did your mother call me?"

"The female equivalent, and according to my mother, she knew it was all your fault."

They both started to laugh as she fell against

him. He held her close so he could breathe in her Chanel. She pulled away slightly, just enough that he recognized her hesitation. *Those parted lips. Oh, so tempting.* Trish managed to tear herself from his grasp without succumbing to a repeat of their first kiss.

But he remembered.

CHAPTER EIGHT

ONCE TRISH AND Rachel returned to working on the stairs, she took Craig's advice and didn't mention her parents again. "I met Max today. A very pleasant man."

Rachel stopped sanding one of the posts. "Yes, he is. I don't know what Noah and I would have done without him. He has the most generous heart."

What could she say after that? Trish continued working, not able to come up with any other topic. How could she, when her thoughts kept wandering back to Craig? What she really wanted to discuss had happened ten years ago. That overblown kissing incident. Well, if she couldn't talk about it with Rachel, Trish could certainly discuss it with her mother the next time they spoke.

Craig was still working upstairs on one of the ceilings when Rachel left.

Trish went into the kitchen and called her mother, letting her phone ring several times.

When no one answered, she disconnected. She wanted to talk to her, not leave a voice mail.

Next she called Reverend Meyer. "I have more things in the barn you can look at, either for the people who were devastated by the floods or for your store."

"Have you shown them to Dave Henry? There could be some valuable antiques."

Trish doubted that, but she appreciated his candor. "No. I'll give him a call, as well, and… I haven't really looked at what's in the basement. If I could get you and Dave to come over and check that out, whatever neither of you wants will get tossed in the garbage." And if too much more had to be thrown out, she might need to rent a Dumpster.

She called Dave with the same message, and he promised to come over later in the day. The moment she hung up, her phone rang.

"You called?" her mother asked.

"Yes."

"Sorry, I couldn't get to the phone fast enough. What did you want?"

Trish took a deep breath. "You remember when you walked in on me and Craig?"

"I knew it," her mother shouted, not even

bothering to ask for more information. "You need to find someone else to work on your house. That Butchy...Craig, whatever you call him, has always been a bad influence. He's going to ruin you and force you to break your engagement to Harrison."

"Really, Mother? Craig has done nothing to interfere with my engagement. He's been a total gentleman and that incident—which happened a good ten years ago—was blown way out of proportion. We were kissing, that's all."

And today when he could have kissed me, he didn't, because we both knew kissing can't happen again with both of us committed to other people.

"Right. It starts with a few kisses and then, before you know it, you're pregnant and quitting school to have a baby, and I end up taking care of my grandchild for the rest of my life." Her voice ended in what sounded like a panicked gulp.

Where was this coming from? Why hadn't her mother ever mentioned it before? But of course any additional children her mother had to care for would have inconvenienced her to the extreme. Her mother hadn't even allowed Trish to have friends over to play.

To relieve the tension she often felt when talking to her mother about personal issues, Trish took the phone to the counter. She'd keep busy and wash dishes. If only her grandmother were here to intervene. She turned on the water and put the phone on speaker.

"Why did you think it would go that far? I was sixteen and Craig was thirteen, and the kissing happened only that one time." Her voice rose in frustration, and she attempted to get herself under control.

"Right. Because I walked in on the two of you. I shudder to think what might have happened if I hadn't." Her mother sighed. "The best thing your father and I ever did was take you away from that environment. You were so young, so naive, and the two of you were always together."

"Working on my algebra, Mom!"

"Thirteen-year-old boys can't be trusted, and…what do you call him now? It's Craig, not Butchy? For heaven's sake, Trish, he constantly asked you to marry him."

When Craig walked into the kitchen, Trish picked up the phone and turned off the speaker. "Mom, I've got to go. I'll talk to you later." She turned to face Craig. "You hear any of that?"

"Just the last part. I came down to get more tape for the ceilings." He walked over and placed a hand on her shoulder. "You all right?"

"I'm fine. What about you?" She tried putting an arm around his shoulders, and he scooted away from her reach.

"You're a very touchy-feely person, Trish, and so am I. Maybe we'd better cool it."

"You're right." She attempted a chuckle to help relieve the tension from the phone call. A hug would have gone a long way right now. Trish turned back to the dishes. "Harrison refers to me as the hugger."

She needed to stay focused on her goals—the family she planned to have with Harrison—and get Craig out of her mind. "I'll get back to work on those stairs as soon as I finish up here."

CRAIG WATCHED HER for several seconds before whatever was raging in him finally died down. It bothered him to think her parents as well as his own didn't trust him back then. It bothered him even more that he didn't trust himself. Even now he felt a magnetism drawing him toward Trish. He knew she was off-limits, and he had no right to think this way, but still…

Trish had been the only girl who ever kept his interest. And now, as a beautiful woman, she constantly took his breath away. Over the past ten years, he'd dated often, but nothing serious. And Cyndi… Cyndi was a bafflement. She could be fun one minute, but then her mood would turn into some kind of crisis. He had to find some way to break off their relationship without hurting her feelings.

He gave himself a shake and went back to finish the ceiling repairs.

DAVE AND REVEREND MEYER both pulled into her driveway later that afternoon. "So, what have you got to show us?" Dave asked. She threw on her grandmother's coat and directed them to the back.

Craig joined them. "I need to check out the barn. Okay if I tag along?"

"Of course." She slipped her arm through his. Friends did that, and the two of them certainly were friends. "Let me know if you see anything you'd like."

When they finished poking through the items in the large, open space, Dave said,

"Nothing here for me, but..." He looked around. "This place is perfect for storage. The cement floor's level, and the walls look sound. I could store all the items here from the house that we think would sell. Would that work for you?" he asked, turning back to Trish. "I'd pay a rental. I'd have to do that no matter where they're stored, and it wouldn't require transporting them far."

"Sure," Trish said.

"I can take these," Reverend Meyer said, pointing to the items against the wall. "We have people who like to fix things, and I'm sure someone could get that bike on the road."

From there they headed for the basement. After pulling down cobwebs and moving items around in the dust, Dave and the reverend decided on a plan to empty the place. On Saturday they'd get people from the church and workers from Dave's business to set up three stacks in the barn: one for Dave, one for the church and one for trash.

"You can pick through it and see what you'd like to keep," Dave said as they came up the basement stairs.

"I'm just grateful you both found something you can use. I have no place for any of this. In fact, I barely remember seeing any of it before.

"You tell me how much I owe you, and I can have the money ready when you come on Saturday."

"You don't owe us anything," Reverend Meyer said.

Dave merely smiled and shook his head. "I'm getting my money from the percentage I get on the consignments."

After they'd headed out, Trish asked Craig, "How much should I pay them?"

"Nothing. The church will benefit from all your 'junk.'" He placed air quotes around the word. "And Dave will save a fortune not having to cart all your stuff to another storage area."

"I don't feel right."

"Then donate some money to the church, and don't charge Dave a storage fee."

Trish turned to him, grinning. "Thank you. That's what I'll do." She started to give him her usual hug, and he backed away.

"What part of 'cool it' did you not understand? I didn't say anything when you grabbed my arm on the way to the barn. Didn't want to embarrass you, but…"

Trish pressed her lips together and nodded.

"You're right. I need to show a little more re-straint." But as she turned away she thought, *I'm a hugger, Craig Cadman. I couldn't hug relative strangers, like the reverend and Dave, but you and I know each other. And we're friends!*

After the ordeal with her mother and the joy she felt from so many people helping her, Trish needed to hug. She pulled her gram's coat tightly around herself and gave a virtual hug to her grandmother.

CHAPTER NINE

"DON'T STEP ON IT," Craig said two days later, when she opened the door to one of the upstairs bathrooms.

"Just checking. Looks good." A pattern of small black and white tiles covered the floor. A new vanity and sink completed the project.

They had accomplished a lot, with Craig going down their to-do list at celestial speeds. While Craig finished the upstairs ceilings, Rachel and Trish prepared the stairs and removed the living room wallpaper. With the posts and banisters on the staircase already painted with a clear coat, Trish and Craig planned to seal the stairs. Once they finished that, no one could use them till they dried thoroughly.

Trish kneaded the muscles in her lower back before bringing her coffee to the table. All this physical labor she wasn't used to had every muscle in her body aching. She pushed her mug aside and laid her head on her outstretched arms. Sleep. She really needed a good night's sleep. One not filled with dreams or anxieties.

Neither Craig nor his mother had brought up the two subjects that troubled Trish. Had Craig truly believed his brother's birth brought on his father's early death? All that grief over such a beautiful little boy. And Craig said he didn't want children based on that. He'd make a perfect father. Why couldn't he see that?

Trish agonized with a desire to say something but didn't feel she had the right. Yet her thoughts kept her up most of the night. That and physical pain.

"Harrison coming tomorrow to paint?" Craig asked as he sat beside her.

"Yes, but I'm not sure I'll have the energy to do much with him." Trish forced herself to sit up. "Where did I see those toothpicks? I need something to keep my eyes open." She reached for her coffee. It was cold. "Don't you ever get tired or feel the strain in your back?"

"Of course. Mom does yoga, and I do a lot of stretching exercises that help." He glanced her way. "But I've been doing this a while, whereas you just started last week."

Trish placed her free hand on her lower back and leaned into it. "I could really use a massage."

"Want me to give it a try?"

"Really? How do you expect to do that since we're no longer touching each other?" She made no attempt to keep the sarcasm out of her voice.

"Believe it or not, I can be trusted. Besides, I can give references." That smile in his voice made her pause. "I've become pretty good at getting the kinks out of my mother's back."

After glancing at the amusement in those blue eyes, she knew a massage wasn't the best way to go. Not since he'd become much more prominent in her latest dreams. She flinched as she rose, her muscles tightening. "Thanks, but I have some Aleve that should do the trick." She got herself a glass of water and the gel caps.

"Come on," Craig said when she didn't appear ready to follow.

She headed for the cot. "I'm going to lie down for a minute until the pills do their thing."

CRAIG LEFT HER to sleep. Why had he ever volunteered to give a massage? Obviously he had this crazy need to torture himself.

Thank goodness she had more brains than he did.

Get back to work and focus on something else.

He started at the top stair with a can of clear finish and a paintbrush. The pads on his knees helped keep the strain off them as he slowly descended each stair. A good half hour later he was on the fifth one down when he heard Trish behind him.

"Why did you let me sleep?"

He didn't turn around when she placed a hand on his arm. "Figured you needed it. You feel better?"

"Yes. And thank you. I feel a lot better." She sat next to him, adjusting her own knee pads. "When we finish here, let's take a break. I need to find a good restaurant for when Harrison comes tomorrow."

"I'd recommend The Country Barn. They also have dancing. But you don't have to go to the same place two nights in a row. I can make soup and grilled cheese tonight."

Trish retrieved her paintbrush and followed his rhythm. They worked so well together. Had she noticed?

"No, it's my treat, and dinner and dancing

sounds like a nice break from the smells and dust of this place."

No, dancing would never do. He was not about to risk holding her in his arms. "How about…" Craig stopped before he blurted out something even more intimate, an evening spent at his apartment. "I know another restaurant. Food's excellent. It's also a quiet atmosphere where you can talk."

"That sounds even better. There's a lot I want to talk about."

Did that mean she wanted to talk to him tonight or Harrison tomorrow? On several occasions, she had hinted at subjects Craig managed to avoid. "You have something you want to discuss?" he asked.

"Yes." They slipped down to the next stair still working as a team.

"With me or Harrison?"

"With you."

Craig moved down one more so he was lower than Trish. He looked up. "Something that's been gnawing at you for a while?"

"Yes." She moved down so they were on the same stair. "It's your life, but I…"

"Stop. You don't agree with me about not wanting children. I understand why they're important to you." He continued painting the stair. "Try to see it from my perspective. I could be dead—"

Trish grabbed his hand, the sticky substance on his brush covering her palm. "Drat," she said, pulling away. "You did that on purpose."

"Don't go up the stairs. The solvent's on the table in the downstairs hall." He didn't bother to deny her accusation. He'd have painted her lips closed if he thought that would stop her delving into his personal demons.

She clomped down the stairs, hitting each one with a determined stomp. Trish came back with the same amount of noise while rubbing solvent on her hand with one of her old dish towels. "We're going to have this talk, Craig. I can't sleep worrying about you and your mother."

"My mother? What's she got to do with it?"

"You don't know?"

He turned around, placing his elbow on the wet stair. He'd never discussed any of this with his mother, so he had no idea what Trish was talking about. "Let me have that rag." When she handed it to him, he rubbed the sticky substance off his arm, checked the stair and corrected the area he'd mussed.

"You planning to tell me or keep me in suspense?"

"Yes, I'll tell you. But let's get the staircase done first. We do better work without distractions."

Like he wasn't distracted now? What was she going to tell him about his mother?

"I'LL TAKE CARE of the brushes," Trish said when they completed the staircase. "You go home and clean up. I'll pick you up when I'm through here. Say in two hours?"

"You know where I live?"

Trish shook her head. Craig reached for his wallet, took out a business card, flipped it over and wrote on the back. "You can't miss it. Two-story brick. I'm on the second floor in the back. Why don't you come up in case I don't hear you beating on the horn?" His voice had lost its pleasant quality.

"Are you angry with me?"

"A little. But don't let that worry you. We'll unearth all my family secrets so you can sleep at night." He headed for the door and turned. "By the way, I like steak with lobster and anything else that's expensive."

Trish stayed under the shower much longer than usual. *Oh, the heat feels so good against my back and shoulders.* Steak and lobster. Really? Okay, so he deserved it for all his hard work. The house looked less like a work in progress with the finish line right around the corner. Craig could have several lobsters if he wanted.

After drying her hair into light brown fluff that floated around her shoulders, she added a touch of her favorite scent—Chanel No. 5. Craig said he liked it.

What should she wear? She had brought only one dress. It happened to have a swirly skirt with tiny colorful flowers on a black background and a black top with three-quarter sleeves. She should save it for tomorrow to go dancing with Harrison. As she began to hang it back in the closet, she wavered. Tonight was special, too. So was Craig. She put it on. After adding her black heels, she grabbed her red purse and Craig's card. Forty-four Bradley Street. Hmm, that wasn't very far at all.

The weather had turned nasty. Her black coat barely kept the chilling breeze out, and she still had no gloves. Trish started her Toyota, turned up the heat and headed for

Craig's apartment, barely keeping within the two hours she had given him.

His truck was in the area reserved for tenants. Trish parked on the street and made a mad dash for the entranceway, carried by a forceful wind. She ran up the stairs and down the hall to the very end, where Craig's business card was tacked to the door. She knocked.

"Door's open."

She came in expecting to find him ready to go. He stood in the large studio apartment still wearing what he'd been working in earlier.

"Sorry, but my brother called, and I had to stop and see him. I'll be ready as soon as I take my shower." He began pulling off his sweater. "Help yourself to water or soda in the fridge. Sorry I don't have your favorite— coffee. Maybe all that caffeine is what's keeping you awake at night."

While he was in the shower, Trish removed her coat and walked over to a wall of bookcases filled with architecture and reference books. When he was young, Craig had read voraciously, and they both spent a great deal of time at the library. He had a fantastic memory. Once read, everything stayed in his mind, so he didn't bother to keep books. Except...there was Shakespeare's *Hamlet*, Dickens's *Great Expectations* and Tolstoy's *War and Peace*. They had studied them together for her English class. Or was it history? Why had he kept these? What was he reading now?

Curious, Trish ambled around his room. A kitchen area had only one dish in the sink and a spotless countertop. A double bed, neatly made, was on the opposite wall, with a sitting area separating the two sections. Trish settled on the couch across from a fireplace and picked up the only item out of place. A thriller by John Sandford, *Stolen Prey*, with library markings. Trish put it back where she found it, preferring romances herself.

The water turned off. A few moments later, the bathroom door opened a crack, and Craig stood there wrapped in steam and a white towel, vigorously drying his hair with a smaller towel.

Someone knocked on the outer door. "Who could that be?" He poked his head out of the bathroom and said, "Could you get that?"

Trish pushed off the couch, her bones and muscles still stiff. "Sure. You expecting anyone?"

Craig shrugged, and Trish went past him

to open the door. He certainly looked nothing like the boy she remembered. When they'd gone swimming together during the summers, he was thin, without a single lump that could be called a muscle. That certainly wasn't the case today. She pulled open the door and faced…"Cyndi?"

"Trish. What are you doing here?"

Craig leaned past the bathroom door and stared at the two of them.

Cyndi looked first to him, then back at Trish. "Did I interrupt something?"

Wide-eyed, Trish shook her head. "Why don't I wait in the car?" She grabbed her coat and maneuvered past Cyndi. "Nice to see you again," Trish said as she slipped into the hall.

Trish ran as fast as her weary bones would take her down the stairs and out the front door. When she got to her car, she collapsed in the seat, started the engine and turned the heater on full blast. From her startled expression, Cyndi hadn't looked too happy finding another woman in Craig's apartment. *How is he handling that situation?*

She waited nearly twenty minutes according to the clock on her dashboard before Craig appeared with Cyndi. He walked her to the

Jeep parked in front of Trish's car, opened Cyndi's door and stood there forever in the swirling wind, kissing her. Trish pressed her teeth into her bottom lip. She tried closing her eyes to cut off the view, but every time she opened them, they were still in a clinch. She sank lower in her seat and focused on a pine tree's branch swooping around. It was cold out there, but the couple in front of her were heating up the whole neighborhood.

When he finally came to Trish's car, Craig had to bang on the window to get her attention. "Whew. That wind is a killer," he said when she'd unlocked the door. "She thought we had a date."

Trish sat there, staring at him. "Did you?" Had she interrupted his plans, forced him to go out with her when he really wanted to be with Cyndi? Maybe he felt obligated because she was technically his employer.

"No. She texted me asking to go out tonight. I never saw it."

"Well, you could have gone with her." Only Trish was happy he'd chosen not to. She wanted this time alone with him.

"And miss out on a free steak dinner?" He leaned closer. "With lobster." When Trish continued to stare, he motioned toward the street. Finally she put the car in gear and pulled out of the parking space. "Go down Bradley until Center then take a right. We're going to O'Malley's, the best steak joint in New Jersey."

CRAIG DIDN'T SAY any more, allowing Trish to concentrate on driving. She didn't look like a happy camper. Maybe that extended kiss with Cyndi had annoyed her. Wouldn't that be a kicker, if Trish really cared? He still did, even though it was useless with her engaged to Harrison. But during that kiss, Craig had realized how little Cyndi meant to him.

The whole episode, with Cyndi showing up unexpectedly, had turned into a sham. What was she trying to prove? And he felt sure she'd extended that kiss for Trish's benefit. Every time he tried to break away, she pulled him back. Why?

He glanced at Trish, unable to shake the unpleasant feelings Cyndi had created. Who would have thought that being pursued by the prom queen would become a turnoff? And now everyone considered them a serious couple, with a wedding in the future. No. That was not going to happen. He had to end it. How?

As they pulled into O'Malley's parking lot, Craig asked, "Okay if we eat first? I wouldn't want our discussion to ruin my appetite."

"Of course. I wouldn't want it to ruin mine, either."

Once they were seated, Craig perused the menu. "Should we get wine? I think they have a few hundred-dollar-per-glass varieties." Trish didn't flinch. "You want white or red?"

"Order what you want. I'll take iced tea. Alcohol puts me to sleep and red wine gives me headaches."

"So nothing's going to bother you? No outrageous expense?"

"If you think you're going to avoid tonight's conversation by being a pain in the butt—" she leaned closer "—you have no idea who you're dealing with. Have you any idea what I do for a living?"

He sat back. He couldn't remember her mentioning her job before, other than the fact that she worked with Harrison. "No. What?"

"I answer panic calls for a credit-card company. My coworkers call me the Queen of Calm. I handle people who've had their identity stolen, lost their credit cards, can't rent a hotel in a foreign country, need a hospital a thousand miles from home." She ticked off each one on her fingers. "Should I go on?"

Craig needed a different tactic… If only he could think of one.

The waiter came over asking what they'd like to drink, and Trish ordered her tea. Craig asked for any beer they had on tap.

"What? You're not going for that hundred-dollar glass of wine?"

"No. You scared me with all your highfalutin powers." He turned to her then, all the playful banter gone. "Why on earth would you want to do that kind of work? It sounds depressing."

"It pays well, and I never know what to expect, so I'm prepared to handle anything."

The waiter came back with their drinks and waited patiently while they decided on their order. Trish wanted the Cobb salad since most of her evening meals had consisted of takeout and pizza. She needed some greens. Craig ordered a six-ounce steak and a house salad, ranch dressing on the side.

"No!" Trish grabbed the waiter's arm. "He wants the best steak you have and lobster."

Craig shook his head. "Don't listen to her. My order stands as is."

Trish leaned on the table. "But…"

"You said you could handle anything. How about handling me changing my mind?"

Trish tossed her napkin on the table and glared at him. After a deep breath, she retrieved the napkin and placed it on her lap. "Of course. That's your prerogative."

"A toast?" Craig tapped his beer glass against her iced tea. "Who would have guessed that sweet young girl I knew would one day become the Queen of Calm? To us and a wonderful evening."

CHAPTER TEN

AFTER THEIR MEAL, Trish's thoughts turned to Noah. "Your brother showed me his 'room' under the table. I got to meet his stuffed toys, including his favorite, Butchy, named after his best friend."

That brought the smile she wanted to see. "Yeah, he's my best friend, too." Craig took a sip of beer and placed his elbows on the table, a look of total contentment in those blue eyes. *He really does love that little boy.*

"I tried replacing that ugly dog with a new one, and he wouldn't have anything to do with it."

"Is he like you?"

Craig glanced down at his beer. "In what way?"

"Intelligent, precocious?"

He looked up, his blue eyes searing through her again. "No. He's normal."

"Well, you were, too."

"No, I wasn't. I was a freak." Craig took

a breath before adding, "It never seemed to bother you, though, and I appreciated that. You were my best friend and got me through some pretty rough times."

Trish leaned closer and reached over to cover his hand. "I remember our childhood together as the most wonderful time of my life. Like when we went camping? Your parents were so much fun compared to mine. They gave me a childhood and showed me what a real family could be. That's what I plan to have with Harrison."

Craig pulled his hand free and reached for his beer. After taking the last sip, he lifted the empty glass to get the waiter's attention.

"I took Noah camping this summer. We did all the fun things you and I used to do. Flew kites. Played ball. Rolled around in the grass."

"Did that skunk ever come around?"

"No."

His new beer arrived and he picked up the glass.

"See? You'll miss all that if you don't have your own children." Craig's eyes narrowed, and any contentment she'd seen before disappeared. "I'm sorry. I shouldn't force my beliefs on you. I just hate the thought that you'll miss out."

He gave her a half smile. "I won't. I promise."

After a moment, she asked, "So, what was it your brother wanted this afternoon?"

"At first he just wanted to talk, tell me about his day. I mentioned I was going out, and he asked if I needed to shave. It's our ritual. We both lather up, and he uses a bladeless razor similar to mine." Craig rubbed his smooth jaw.

Something a father might do. She kept her thoughts to herself.

What had she hoped to accomplish tonight? Resolve her sleeping difficulties by solving his so-called problems? The situations she dealt with at work had formulas, policy dictates and learned responses that didn't apply here. She couldn't fix something he didn't consider broken.

"I'm sorry, Craig. I didn't mean for this evening to turn into a battle."

He smiled. "Shall we start again on some safe subjects?"

"Sure."

"I found out how to open the drawers on the secretary."

"You did?"

"Yes. I was looking for a note I'd left in there before you moved."

"Did you find it?"

"No."

"You're not just saying that because you don't want me to see it, right?"

He put down his glass and raised an eyebrow. "When did we stop trusting each other?"

Trish agonized a moment, realizing he was right. Before, they could talk about anything, tell their deepest secrets and know they were safe from ridicule or misunderstanding. "I'm sorry. I…"

Craig reached over and grasped her hands. "Don't. You're not at fault. I'm the one who snuck inside your house to check out the secretary. I did it because I wanted to find the note and definitely not let you see it. But I didn't find it. Who could have taken it?"

They held hands for a long time without coming up with any answers.

CRAIG GRIPPED HIS second glass of beer. This night had turned into one disaster after another, and he didn't expect it to improve.

"Would you like some dessert?" Trish asked.

"No. Are you going to delay this forever or get down to the reason we came here?" He waited a moment before adding, "My mother. You had something to tell me because it's preventing you from getting any sleep."

Trish nodded. "Did you know she thinks you blame Noah for your father's death?"

Craig's jaw dropped. "She what?" He sat up so suddenly, his hand tipped, and he nearly lost the remainder of his beer.

"The pressures from his birth led to your father's death. Isn't that what you think?"

"No!" he shouted. People close by turned and looked at them. "Could we take this somewhere else?" He pushed his chair back and prepared to get up. "Please."

"Yes. But I have to pay the check." Trish picked up the black plastic envelope that contained their bill, waved it around and looked for the waiter. Craig grabbed it from her, removed her credit card and replaced it with enough cash to cover the bill and tip.

"You can't do that. It's my treat."

"I'll add it to my bill."

She glowered, so that must not have gone over too well. As he helped her slip on her coat, he said, in an attempt to smooth the tension between them, "You look lovely to-night. Sorry I didn't say anything earlier."

He saw a flash of anger in her eyes, but it passed quickly. Not that he wouldn't hear about the bill later. Trish was primed for battle.

IN THE CAR, Trish asked, "Where should we go to talk?"

"My place?" Nothing romantic could happen there if she was screaming at him in righteous anger.

"Fine."

When they reached his studio apartment, Craig removed her coat, again enjoying her perfume, but he didn't mention it. She hadn't appreciated his belated compliments before, so why start another battle? He removed his parka and began rubbing his hands as Trish took a seat on the couch.

"Winter decided to come tonight. All right if I light a fire?"

"That would be nice." When he grabbed a remote control, Trish said, "Let's not watch TV."

He pressed the remote and a fire blazed in the fireplace, followed by warmth fanning toward them. "Surprised?" he said, grinning at her.

"Is it real?"

He shook his head. "No. It's electric, but it adds to the atmosphere and provides heat. Okay if I turn off the overhead light so we can enjoy the ambience?"

"Sure." She giggled and pulled a crocheted throw his mother had made from the back of the couch. She wrapped it around her legs.

Craig flicked off the fluorescent light in the kitchen area and turned the table lamp on low before taking a seat next to her.

"Have you looked at the fireplace in my living room?" she asked. "It would be nice to build a fire in there."

"I checked it out, and you shouldn't. The cement has deteriorated. All the smoke would end up drifting through the house. It can't be used until that's repaired."

"How expensive is that?"

"Very, especially with all the other repairs that need to be made. How do you like my fireplace? You could install a unit like this and seal up your chimney. It would be less expensive, and you can get the version with the sound of crackling logs."

"I'd probably go that way if I planned to

keep the place." Trish pulled the afghan up to her shoulders and snuggled close to him. "We'll give the person who buys the place that option."

He didn't want to say anything that might spoil the moment, but he did want to know about his mother's accusation. "Why does my mother think…what you said?"

Trish moved even closer. Was she doing this on purpose to make him lose focus? Because he was certainly having a hard time keeping his mind on the topic.

"Did you know your mother thought she couldn't have children after you?"

"No. She told you that?"

Trish twisted around and leaned against his shoulder. "Yes. The doctor told her it was impossible. It was a total shock when she became pregnant. A pleasant one because they both wanted a child."

"She told you that, too?"

"Yes. You're the one who didn't want him because…" She yawned, and he feared she wouldn't continue. In a fading voice she added, "…it stopped you from getting a degree in architecture."

He tensed as she relaxed against him. Was that it? Had he somehow taken his destroyed dreams and transferred his anger onto his mother?

"It never stopped me from getting a degree. I was so young and felt intimidated taking classes with people much older than I was. I used my scholarships to get my bachelor's degree in math online."

"But you never followed your dream to become an architect. I hate that you threw that dream away."

Should he tell her? Craig hadn't told anyone that he'd applied for more scholarships and grants. If a few things panned out, he could be going for his architectural degree starting the coming spring semester.

No, he'd keep that to himself. A typical Trish response of joy and hugging was out of the question now. And it was exactly the response he'd want. He sighed.

Trish's breathing was slow and steady. Had they settled whatever was bothering her? Must have if she was sleeping. Craig pulled the afghan over himself and rested his head on Trish's. *Might as well enjoy the moment.*

CRAIG AWOKE TO a vibration on his waist and realized his pager had gone off. A fire! Any moment the horn would start to alert the town. He pulled free from her warmth, brought her legs onto the couch and attempted to make her more comfortable.

He slipped out of his apartment without waking her. With any luck, she'd still be asleep by the time he got back. Their talk must have helped her relax, but it hadn't helped him. Sitting there, holding her in his arms, listening to her breathing, his own lungs filled with her scent. He had to be out of his mind getting himself in these situations that were nothing more than pure torture.

He arrived at the firehouse within minutes and quickly dressed in his turnout gear. Even though he wasn't actually fighting the fires, he needed protection.

"What is it this time?" he asked several of the men as they suited up.

"Chimney fire."

He and Luke, one of the firemen, headed for the truck. Craig carried his Nikon DSLR camera along with a leather bag containing the attachments for close-ups.

"Yeah, with the temperatures dropping, we can expect a lot of these," Luke said. As they took their seats behind the driver, Luke gave him a nudge. "You and Cyndi break up?"

The evening's happenings flashed through

his mind before Craig answered. "Why do you ask?"

"Saw you over at O'Malley's with that cute chick." When Craig didn't respond, Luke continued, "You forgot already? Tall with light brown—"

"Yeah, yeah. That's Trish Lowery. I'm working on her house." Thank goodness they arrived at the fire quickly so nothing more was said. Everyone went to the tasks they'd been trained for the moment the truck pulled up to the house. Sparks flew in a Fourth of July explosion from the chimney. Craig glanced at it, noting how fire could produce some beautiful sights that could quickly turn to devastation. He began snapping pictures while the men went on with their duties.

"Luke, get some water on that roof before a spark takes hold," the captain shouted. Within minutes the fire was out. They finished containment and headed back to the firehouse. After restoring the fire truck to readiness and changing out of their turnout gear, the men congregated in the lounge.

"Anyone want a beer?" Luke asked as he went behind the bar.

"No, I'm going home." Craig waved from the door.

"You got someone waiting for you?" Luke asked with a laugh.

Yeah, I do, Craig thought as he headed for his van.

But when he pulled up to his apartment, Trish's car was gone.

CHAPTER ELEVEN

TRISH AWOKE FROM a dreamless sleep. *Where am I?* Slowly she rose to a sitting position and watched the flames dancing in front of her. A fireplace? She looked around and recognized Craig's apartment. A noise had awakened her. The fire horn? Back when she lived in Riverbend, the sound had never disturbed her, but lately she heard it every time it went off. Craig must have gone to the fire.

She got up, folded the afghan and placed it on the back of the couch where she had found it. The clock on the microwave said 5:05 a.m. She'd slept for nearly seven hours, and what she remembered... Had Craig held her or was that a dream? A delightful, warm, fuzzy dream similar to the other ones she'd had this week when she managed to get any sleep.

Trish caught her breath. Harrison planned to arrive by eight for breakfast. She had to get back to her house. With a quick check, she found the remote and turned off the fire-place. Yes, she liked that. Something she definitely planned to consider for when she and Harrison had their own place. *Wrapped in each other's arms in front of a warm, cozy fireplace.*

But for some reason she couldn't manage to keep Harrison's face in the picture. The image kept turning into Craig with some very contented blue eyes.

THE DOORBELL RANG right at eight. On time as always. Trish reached the door before Harrison could ring a second time. "Come in," she said when she opened it, expecting a kiss or some kind of embrace. Instead he walked past her, checking out all the areas she and Craig had worked on. Trish sighed but didn't say anything.

"You're making progress. This staircase looks great. Never would have believed it was a blond wood. What is it, oak?" Trish nodded. "Bet the house can go on the market by Christmas." He came back, grasped her face between his hands and kissed her. Pulling away, he said, "Do I smell bacon?" *Obviously my Chanel No. 5 isn't working its magic.*

"Yes." Grabbing his hand, she drew him into the kitchen.

Harrison glanced around. "What, no handyman this time?"

"No. It's just you and me."

When they were nearly finished with the farmer's breakfast she'd prepared, a mixture of scrambled eggs, potatoes, bacon and onions, Harrison reached across the table and grasped her hand. "You realize I haven't seen the rest of the place. You never showed me this fantastic attic where you and the handyman... What's his name?"

"Craig."

"Where you and Craig used to play."

"We can't go up there yet. Craig and I just finished sealing the staircase, and it's still tacky. Let's check it out after we finish painting. It might be dry by then. I'd like to take down all those boxes that are stored there. You want to help?"

"I'm at your service, my dear." Harrison pushed away from the table. "Let's get started." He took his work clothes into the downstairs bathroom and changed. When he came out, he wore a stained T-shirt and jeans that had seen better days. She wore some old clothes of her grandmother's, baggy slacks and a gray sweatshirt with several holes. He raised an eyebrow when he saw her but didn't make a comment.

Harrison looked up to the second floor as they entered the hallway. "What did you finish up there?"

"The bathrooms."

"Get rid of those ugly tubs?"

"No."

Harrison frowned. They went into the living room, rolled up her grandmother's Persian rug and left it in the center of the room along with the secretary. Next they placed newspaper on the floor to catch any spatter, outlined the areas they didn't want painted with tape and began painting the living room with long-handled rollers. By noon the pale green walls were finished. Harrison wrapped his arm around Trish's shoulders and admired their work. "Isn't this the same color I have in my condo?"

"Yes. I loved it when I saw it there and thought—why not? It's perfect for this room." She grinned at him, expecting a kiss. Instead he released her, leaned over and began picking up the newspapers they'd placed on the floor.

"You going to make some lunch or should we go out?"

"Everything's already in the kitchen."

"Okay, I'll come there as soon as I take care of this."

Trish appreciated his help. They worked well together on so many levels, and she felt quite pleased with their accomplishments. So what if he wasn't naturally cuddly the way she was. He did have his moments.

She took out the ham and his favorite American cheese and began making sandwiches. Deli mustard, some lettuce and tomatoes on rye, and they were all complete by the time he came into the kitchen.

"Would you like soup?"

"Nah, I'll have a bigger meal when we go out tonight. Where should we go? They have anything special in these sticks?"

"There's The Country Barn. It has excellent food and dancing." Her attention momentarily turned to the fire horn blaring, and she checked the clock. It was well past twelve, so it wasn't the noonday blast.

"What's that noise? Some emergency warning to take cover?"

"No, the fire horn. We have volunteer firemen here, and…" Trish caught a whiff of smoke. The fire must be close.

Within moments the area rumbled from

heavy fire trucks, their lights flashing and sirens blaring as they came down the street. When they halted in front of her house, Trish ran to her front door.

"It's near here. It has to be. What's that roaring noise?" It sounded as though it came from her house.

She opened her door just as a man in a white jacket with neon reflector tape and a white fireman's helmet came to a halt in front of her.

"You two get out of the house. Now!" he shouted. "Anyone else in here?"

Trish shook her head, stepped back and almost landed on Harrison's shoes. He clasped an arm around her to keep her steady. They headed for the porch as several men in black followed others right up her newly finished staircase.

Speechless, Trish watched firefighters outside hitting her dried grass with brooms, trampling their feet on her lawn and spraying it with water.

"What is going on?" Harrison asked, gripping her shoulders.

A harsh voice grabbed their attention as one of the men stomped from the living room to the entranceway. She recognized

Craig when he pulled off his black helmet. "You trying to burn the house down?" He glared at Trish. "What part of 'you can't use that fireplace' did you not understand?"

Wide-eyed, Trish stammered, "Wha-what are you talking about?"

Craig didn't bother to answer as the man in the white hat came out and shouted orders. "In here," he called to several men who tramped across her clean floor. He motioned a few to follow him while several others flew up the staircase.

Someone shouted, "It's out." Several men clomped down the staircase after that announcement, leaving footprints on the sticky substance.

Trish stood immobile on the porch, wishing someone would explain what was happening. Was her house on fire? Craig came out of the living room again, carrying his camera, his free hand on his hip. "You can't burn newspaper in the fireplace, Trish. What didn't burn down here went straight up the flue, ignited the creosote inside the chimney walls and went onto the roof."

Trish caught Harrison backing away. Had he started that fire? He must have. But casting blame around wouldn't help anything. She should have told him the fireplace didn't work.

Trish called on all her reserves and quietly said, "Thank you. It won't happen again." Keeping her eyes cast down, she asked, "Can I come back in? It's freezing out here."

Craig waved her in. Trish walked past him into the living room to observe the damage. Soot and black water covered areas of the floor, soaking the Persian carpet. More soot by the fireplace had been tracked everywhere. What looked like clouds of gray made patterns over the areas they had just painted.

She turned to see who had followed her. "The roof was saved," Craig said in a much more soothing voice than he'd used earlier. "Fortunately, we were having a cleanup at the firehouse, so our men were already there when someone reported sparks coming from your chimney." He put his arm around her shoulders. "You okay?"

Trish didn't trust her voice. She nodded.

"I'm sorry I lost my temper," Craig continued, turning her around so that she faced him. "I just hated to see this…after all the work we did here. I was afraid you would lose your house."

Still not willing to say anything, she pressed her face into the hard surface of his jacket. His arm went around her back, drawing her close. She sniffled several times before catching herself. *The Queen of Calm doesn't cry... not even when her house nearly burned to the ground.* Tears suddenly puddled against Craig's jacket, and he patted her back. "Come on. Let's get away from this mess and go back to the kitchen."

TRISH HADN'T STARTED the fire. Was she taking the blame for it, though? They found Harrison, the arsonist, busy washing dishes. He turned as they entered, soapsuds up to his elbows.

When Harrison spotted them, his expression mellowed. He wiped his hands and arms before reaching for Trish. After a few hugs and some whispered words of comfort, he directed her to a chair. "I'll take care of this," he said to Craig. "I'm sure you've got plenty more to do. Should we contact the insurance?"

Craig nodded. "I can recommend a cleaning service. Have it here immediately."

"Yes, please. I don't think I have the stomach to clean that mess right now." Trish sat hunched over the table in the rattiest sweat-shirt Craig had ever seen. Besides several holes, it had splotches of green paint from the ruined living room.

Harrison sat next to her, pulling her against him and giving Craig the evil eye over her head. Craig shrugged and headed back to his men. He had plenty of pictures to take before leaving. One of the trucks had already started to drive away. Once on the lawn, Craig circled the house, looking for any other possible damage, recording everything with his camera. They'd lucked out. He hated to imagine what might have happened if they'd gotten there a few minutes later.

And to think Harrison wasn't going to take responsibility for any of it.

HARRISON RAINED KISSES on her cheek and forehead, whispering how sorry he was. "I never should have burned those papers. You forgive me, don't you?"

"Of course. You didn't know the fireplace wasn't working." She tried to sound calm, reassuring, but she couldn't keep up the pretense. She felt stressed beyond anything she could remember. It wasn't like her to hold on to problems. They had lived through the trauma. The house hadn't suffered any real damages. Why couldn't she shake this feeling of distress?

He gripped her shoulders and pressed his cheek against hers. "I could have burned the place down. We could have lost everything."

"But we didn't." Trish adjusted her position to take full advantage of Harrison's cuddling. He held her, offering comfort, chastising himself for his stupidity. She would have preferred more quiet time with him, safe in his embrace to deal with the horror she'd just experienced, but Harrison pulled away.

"Come on. Let's do something to put this nasty incident out of our heads. Since the firemen used the stairs, we can go to the attic and take those boxes down." Reluctantly Trish got to her feet.

As they approached the staircase, Trish saw someone standing at the front door. She opened it to two women with an assortment of cleaning tools, including a wet/dry vacuum. "Hi. I was about to knock. Craig sent us to do the cleanup."

"That was quick," Harrison said as Trish invited them in.

"Damage is minimized if we can get to it right away."

"Thank you. Most of the mess is in there." Trish pointed to the living room and let her voice drop. Keeping an upbeat perspective at this point seemed like a waste of time.

As Trish and Harrison headed up the stairs, she visualized starting over. What if she couldn't redo the stairs? What if she had to cover them with another rug? What if…?

While Harrison checked out both bathrooms, Trish followed the trampled path into her grandmother's room. The fireplace in there had been blocked off with bricks years ago, so her room didn't appear to have any problems.

Harrison came in behind her. "Wow. That brass bed and the painted cabinet over there should add a good deal to the kitty."

"It's an armoire. Dave Henry said it was another priceless treasure. I remember climbing into it when I was little. My grandmother always seemed to find me. Probably because she knew that was my favorite place to hide when we played hide-and-seek."

"I can just picture it." Harrison went over to the dresser and began poking through some of Gram's personal items. "Did she have jewelry?"

Trish shrugged. "A little. She gave me the valuable pieces years ago."

"You still have them?"

"Of course. They're all safe in a bank vault." With a sigh, Trish turned back to the hallway. "I'll show you the way to the attic."

Harrison came over and placed an arm around her shoulders. "We'll get all those boxes down, and you'll feel better."

Sounds below indicated the cleanup had begun, but even that didn't make her depression go away. How would she ever fix everything? She headed toward the door to the attic when Harrison grabbed her around the waist and stopped her.

"You know, when we get our own place, we'll have a guest room." His eyes lit with pure pleasure, and he pulled her closer. "What if we filled it with your grandmother's bedroom furniture? Our kids can play in the armoire like you did. Would you like that?"

Trish collapsed against him, her depression suddenly gone. "Oh, Harrison. That would be lovely." She hugged him and covered his face with kisses. "Absolutely the best news I've had all day."

FINDING MARGE AND Gloria available to clean Trish's place was pure luck, Craig thought. They were the best, a team he recommended to anyone who needed a cleanup after a fire. Maybe they could relieve some of the pressure Trish would be feeling right now. All that time wasted on the staircase. At least the oak would survive.

After finishing the workday at the firehouse, Craig took a shower and prepared for the rest of his traumatic day—dealing with Cyndi. He'd rather be fixing some electrical problem in a dusty, unvented attic on a hot summer day, crawling through rat poop and spiderwebs. How was he going to break off their relationship?

The night before, they'd made plans to have dinner. He'd been trying to appease her since he'd already made plans with Trish. Should he say something to Cyndi before or after they ate? He still liked her and didn't want to hurt her feelings, yet he couldn't go on this way. Especially if she expected their relationship to lead to marriage eventually.

Craig put on his best pale blue dress shirt, gray pants and blue-gray suit coat. He decided against wearing a tie. Why go that formal? After reconsidering, he pulled the blue tie from the rack. His aunt Jenny had given it to him for Christmas last year because it matched his eyes. He could dress up for his last date with Cyndi. She deserved that much consideration.

When he reached her house, Craig walked briskly to Cyndi's door, wishing he'd considered a topcoat. The temperatures were already below freezing, and a light breeze made the air feel even colder. He rang her bell.

Cyndi greeted him in a peach bathrobe and fuzzy slippers. "Are you sick?" he asked once he entered the vestibule. She shook her head, grabbed his hand and pulled him to the living room couch. She sat down, and he followed suit, keeping a little distance just in case she really was contagious.

"We need to talk."

"Okay." He kept his voice level. "What about?"

"What's going on with you and Trish?"

His mind went blank. "What do you mean?"

"I came over the other night expecting to go out, and you broke our date to go out with her."

"We had no date. I never got your text."

"Oh, come on, Craig," she said. "Since she showed up, it's like old times, with you trailing her like some puppy dog."

Craig frowned but realized she might be right. He'd never hid the fact that he adored Trish.

"Okay, you're right to a point. I came here planning to break off with you. But it has nothing to do with Trish. You and I have nothing in common."

Her expression turned to openmouthed shock. Probably because no one had ever ended a relationship with her before. "You're breaking up with me? Why?" she asked, jumping to her feet and placing her fists on her hips as she looked down on him. "I'm no good anymore now that she's back in the picture?"

Craig stood and towered over her. "That's not it at all. She's getting married to someone else. There's nothing going on between us."

Cyndi looked miffed, and he wanted to make it up to her. "Why don't we go out tonight and have a good time?"

"And do what? Celebrate our breakup?"

"Yeah, why not? You get dressed and I'll take you to the restaurant of your choice." Even spring for steak and lobster if she wanted. He saw a smile beginning. He really liked her and saw no reason they couldn't remain friends.

TRISH BEGAN OPENING the boxes piled around the dining room while Harrison continued to bring more from the attic. "This should do it. The last of your family's treasures." He placed one more box on the pile before collapsing on a chair. "Anything of value? Or just more junk?" He leaned toward her, inspecting the hatbox she held. "You're throwing out those old clothes, right?"

Trish picked up the gray fedora and a straw hat covered in flowers. She and Craig had played dress-up on rainy days with so many of their friends. There were her grandfather's top hat, her grandmother's wedding veil and several other garments wrapped in memories and mothballs. "No, I'm donating them to the high school's theater group."

He bent over and kicked a box toward her. "What's all this?"

Trish pulled back the lid and looked at the miniature houses made from balsa wood, wire and bits of scraps. "Oh, my goodness. I didn't realize we still had these." She picked up one and examined it. "These are Craig's. He used to design houses, and we'd make them. Had a whole village at one point." She started to chuckle, then stopped when she saw Harrison's expression.

"Garbage?" he asked.

"No, of course not." She pushed the box to the side. "I'll see if he still wants them." Maybe it would spark him into going for his architectural degree.

Harrison shrugged and reached for the next box. "What about these Christmas lights?"

Trish pulled out a string of lights wrapped around a piece of cardboard. It was labeled in pen, Front on West Side.

"These are the lights I used to help my grandfather put on the roof every year. Just one more time, I'd love to see them on the house. Maybe I can get Craig to put them up."

"Don't bother." Harrison stood. "They're probably not even working anymore, and why pay the handyman to do that? Don't forget, what goes up must come down. A double waste of money."

She stretched to grab another box and pulled it toward herself. "Here are the Christmas decorations for our tree." She picked up the angel they used every year. Its dress had lost its stiffness and hung in a shapeless bulge of shimmering gold. "Wouldn't it be nice to set up the Christmas tree right here in the vestibule so it can be seen on the street?"

"No, it wouldn't. Stop fooling around with that and put it away. I'm going to take a shower and get ready for dinner. I've worked up quite an appetite going up and down those stairs." He jerked his thumb toward the attic. "You can go soak in one of those antique tubs you like so much."

Trish continued to unwrap and rewrap the delicate glass ornaments in tissue paper. She lingered over several Hallmark figurines with their dates pressed into the glass. She and Gram had shopped every year for the newest ones to add to the tree. With utmost caution, she took one from its wrapping. A flat pink glass angel with white wings. Gram had bought it the year Trish turned two because it reminded her of Trish. Digging deeper, Trish pulled out the one she had picked all by herself when she was seven. A crayon box with tiny white mice sleeping in it, their nightcaps in bright crayon colors.

Marge and Gloria had gone earlier, so Trish was alone with her memorabilia after Harrison left for his shower. There was nothing here she really wanted to keep except the Christmas bulbs and lights. Then again,

Harrison hadn't shown much interest. What could she expect? These were her memories, not his.

She might as well get ready to go out for dinner. Harrison would have to leave for his place right after since he had to fly out to Chicago early the next morning. Too bad he'd be missing Thanksgiving, not that he seemed to mind.

Would he visit his parents? Did they even celebrate holidays? Maybe not, if Harrison's disinterest in Veterans Day, Thanksgiving and Christmas were any indication. Well, she planned to change that. She'd keep these Christmas decorations for the tree she planned to have once they were married.

CHAPTER TWELVE

No one would've guessed that Craig and Cyndi had broken up. They held hands, hugged and kissed each other on the cheek, but their relationship was purely platonic.

Cyndi had dressed in a black sheath and red heels that added at least six inches to her height, although she was still tiny compared to Trish. And she wanted to go to The Country Barn for dancing. Which was fine with Craig. He hoped Trish wouldn't show up with her fiancé, but that was a chance he'd have to take. He'd given Cyndi the choice, and he wasn't about to take it back.

Only Trish did walk in with Harrison. She wore the same dress she had on last night, looking just as lovely. It brought back memories that burned in Craig's gut. Was she wearing the same perfume? Of course she was.

The two stood at the entrance, Harrison looking annoyed by the wait. They'd be out of luck if they hadn't made reservations. The band that frequently played on Sunday nights brought in regulars who loved to dance. Maybe with any luck, Harrison would decide to go somewhere else instead of lingering through the usual twenty- or thirty-minute wait for a table.

"You know," Cyndi whispered near Craig's ear, "we can tell her you and I broke up so the two of you can get back together."

Craig hadn't realized he'd been watching Trish and Harrison with such concentration. "That's her fiancé," Craig said, his voice barely audible. "There's no Trish and me and there never was." Not that he hadn't tried everything in his power to make that happen.

"Don't deny it. I remember the two of you back when we were growing up. You were inseparable." Cyndi stood and began waving. "Hi, Trish. Why don't you join us?" Cyndi's spontaneity had caused him more than a few uncomfortable moments. What more could she do tonight to embarrass him?

Harrison and Trish, his arm around her shoulders, started toward them. If only some catastrophe could save Craig from dealing with them and Cyndi—*a three-alarm fire would be the perfect excuse to leave.*

No fire horn blew.

Craig's manners kicked in, and he rose to welcome them as the two reached their table. Trish stood in front of the seat directly across from him. She smiled at Craig before turning her attention to Cyndi. "Thank you. We'd be waiting forever if you hadn't invited us. I'd like you to meet my fiancé, Harrison Morris." She patted him on the shoulder before reaching across the table and grasping Cyndi's hand. "And this is Cyndi Parker, a neighbor and classmate from high school. We were cheerleaders together."

"Cheerleaders? Really? You never mentioned that before." After seating Trish, Harrison sat across from Cyndi, who provided him with the welcoming smile that had stolen men's hearts and won her the prom-queen title back in high school. Would Harrison be immune?

"Well, it was pretty insignificant on my part," Trish said. "With only one year on the squad, I moved to Virginia and only cheered the teams from the sidelines."

When the conversation dead-ended, Craig

asked, "Did Marge and Gloria finish the cleanup?"

"Yes. They did an excellent job." Trish smiled and looked ready to add more when Harrison spoke up.

"How much is that going to cost us?"

Us? Craig waited a moment while his mind adjusted to "us." Now it was Harrison's place as well as Trish's? And she didn't even twitch. Was she the Queen of Calm, or had she merely accepted everything of hers also belonged to Harrison?

"The insurance should cover it," Craig said in hopes of ending the subject.

"But the insurance adjuster never saw it before the cleanup crew came in."

"Pictures. Everything was documented." Craig knew because he'd taken them himself while Trish and Harrison were in the attic.

Harrison turned to Trish. "What's our deductible on that?"

Trish patted his hand and looked a little like her perpetual calm had faded. "Let's not talk business tonight."

After the waitress came by and took their order, Cyndi asked, "Are you attending the play-off game at school? We could use some more support."

"What play-off?" Harrison and Trish asked in unison.

"The football team made the play-offs. All the past and present cheerleaders are strutting our stuff on the sidelines to back them."

Trish chuckled. "I haven't done anything like a cheer since high school, and I don't remember the routines."

"It's like riding a bike. And it's so much fun. Right, Craig? You'll be there, won't you?"

"You were a cheerleader?" Harrison chortled, pointing at Craig.

Cyndi laughed, too. "Don't be silly. All the past players come on the field during halftime, and we, the Riverbend Orange Wildcat Cheerleaders, give them our best rah, rah, rah. It's lots of fun. You should come see it."

Craig glanced at Trish. From her blank expression, he realized she never knew he'd signed up for football during his junior year. Not that he actually played.

"Sorry, but I'm driving back to the city tonight. Taking off for Chicago in the morning." Harrison placed his arm around Trish's shoulders and pulled her close. "But you should go, sweetheart, and cheer for all those football jocks." He brought his arm back and leaned on the table. "Football, Craig? I thought Trish said you were more of a nerd back in school, played chess and read all the time."

Trish sat up straighter, her eyes widening. Before she could refute Harrison's words, Craig said, "That was me, all right. We both changed our image when she moved away." The band had started to play, so he turned to Cyndi. "Care to dance?"

"No. I want to find out more about Harrison. You and Trish go." She dismissed him with a wave and leaned closer to Harrison. "So, tell me how Trish lucked out and managed to take you off the eligible bachelors' list." When Craig didn't follow through and immediately ask Trish for a dance, Cyndi waved them both onto the floor. Harrison didn't offer an objection, so Craig stood and reached out to Trish.

He realized as they walked onto the floor, they'd never danced before. Not in this face-to-face, arm-wrapped-around-her-body, pulling-her-close type of slow dance. And he liked it. For the first few chords, he filled his lungs and eyes with Trish, ignoring all the other sights and sounds around them.

"When did you become a jock?" Trish asked, destroying his musings.

"When you left, I had to find other outlets. Some friends convinced me to try out for football. I had a real growth spurt and became a tall, skinny player who could outrun anyone who came after me, so I wouldn't get tackled."

"You're kidding, right?" Trish chortled and pulled closer. "I always loved your sense of humor."

"Eventually I gained some weight, and it all came together in what you see now."

She moved away and caught his gaze. "I'm sorry for telling Harrison you were a nerd. He asked about you, how we knew each other, and…"

"Don't sweat it, Trish. I'm a nerdy jock with movie-star good looks. I just have to live with that." He pulled her back against his chest while they both laughed at each other's nonsense. *Just like old times.*

"So…what position did you play?"

"I didn't." Craig could see he wasn't going to get away without an explanation. "I suited up and did some exercises with the guys, but most of the time I sat on the bench." If only he could say he'd caught the ball, made a touchdown, been the hero of the day. That little bit of glory could have cost him his life, and he had no intention of telling her about it.

"You never played?"

He shook his head. "I took pictures. I was the historian, capturing all the players' fantastic feats. The pictures went in the school paper as well as the local newspaper."

"Well, that's something. I'm sure everyone appreciated that."

"Yeah, right. Life goes on," he said.

"So, do you plan to marry someday?"

Her question startled him. "Why? We're not on that other subject again, are we, because…"

"It's a yes-or-no question."

No, it wasn't. She had some trap set. Craig thought a moment. "Yes." As long as someone willingly accepted the short term of happily-ever-after. He couldn't promise more than that.

"Despite all your denials, I think Cyndi adores you."

He spun Trish around so she could see their table. Cyndi stretched across the table toward Harrison and gripped his hand. "Right now, you'll notice she adores Harrison. And when that peters out, she'll adore someone else. That's Cyndi. She's not happy unless she's the center of attention."

"Okay, so if she's not the one, when you meet the person you want to marry, she'll have to know your feelings about children."

Craig stopped so that people on the dance floor had to skirt around them. "You want to destroy this perfectly lovely evening?" When she didn't answer, he spun her around in a dance move then pulled her back in his arms. "I thought last night you managed to sleep without those nightmares of me ruining my life."

"Well, they came back today to haunt me."

He stopped again and studied her expression of total concern. "Okay, what do you suggest I do? Every time I meet someone new I should announce it before our first date? How about I have it tattooed on my forehead?" He was being ridiculous, but he couldn't get past this frustration. Why was his desire to not have children so important to her?

She glared at him. "Yes, that should do it. Have it written across your forehead in indelible ink. *I will never have children.*" As she spoke, she poked his forehead with her index finger before pulling away and heading for their table.

BY THE TIME they returned, their food had reached the table. Cyndi and Harrison were deep in discussion and didn't break away until Trish and Craig sat down.

"What were you two fighting about?" Cyndi asked.

Craig picked up his napkin and placed it on his lap. "Fighting? We weren't fighting." He glanced at Trish and hoped she'd follow his lead. "Right?"

"He didn't want to attend the Thanksgiving football game because it conflicted with plans he has with his family. I convinced him he shouldn't miss it."

No wonder I love her. She didn't betray anything we discussed. Craig watched her ease back into Cyndi and Harrison's conversation as realization sent an arrow through his heart. He did love Trish, always had and always would, even if she insisted on making the mistake of her life and marrying Harrison.

"You all right?" Cyndi asked, reaching over and gripping his hand.

Craig shook himself and smiled at her. "I'm fine." He looked at his plate and wondered what he had ordered. Salmon? What possessed him to order fish? He saw Cyndi laughing with Harrison.

"I told you he wouldn't like it." She reached over to Harrison's plate and attempted to switch the meals.

Craig held on to his plate. "No, that's a nice change." He watched with satisfaction as Harrison's expression took a nosedive. "Thank you for thinking of it." Before anyone could make a further attempt to change his meal, Craig cut into the pink delicacy and took a bite. "Mmm, good."

Trish's mouth was twitching, but she quickly controlled it and started on her own meal.

Harrison hadn't touched The Country Barn's specialty, spiced spareribs. He glowered at his plate. "Are we through playing childish games?"

Trish captured the waiter's attention. "Could you please bring another dish of salmon? I'm afraid there was a mistake. My fiancé didn't order spareribs."

The Queen of Calm. You're amazing,

Craig thought. Did Harrison appreciate the treasure he was getting? He certainly didn't deserve her.

CHAPTER THIRTEEN

HARRISON DIDN'T LOOK PLEASED, even though his salmon arrived almost immediately. And Craig would have preferred his spicy spareribs. What had gotten into Cyndi? Harrison was right; it was childish. Every now and then Craig caught her wearing a slight smirk.

When they'd finished the meal, Harrison asked Trish to dance. Craig would have preferred to sit it out, but Cyndi jumped up and headed for the dance floor. She'd probably make a scene if he didn't follow her.

He took her in his arms with no intention of bringing up the salmon disaster. But best-laid plans with Cyndi never worked out. "Did you see Harrison's expression? I thought he was going to throw those ribs at you." She started to laugh. "Can't believe Trish wants to get stuck with him."

Cyndi had that twinkle in her eye that usually meant trouble. She went on, "I can't understand why you don't stake your claim,

swoop her away from him. Want me to help?"
She started to step back, and he grasped her
hand so she couldn't break away.

"Don't. If we hadn't ended our connection
earlier, Cyndi, I'd be walking out right now.
Leaving you on the dance floor."

She relaxed against him, and he loosened
his hold. All too soon, Cyndi pivoted out of
his arms and headed for Harrison and Trish.
"Hi. Care to switch? I haven't had the pleasure of dancing with the handsomest man
in the room."

Trish walked over to Craig. "She never
stops, does she?" Trish said and stepped into
his dance embrace.

"Aren't you a little afraid she might steal
your man?"

"No, and there's nothing you have to
worry about, either, because she's not his
type."

"He told you?"

"Yes. She's an outrageous flirt." Trish
pressed her lips together. "I'm sorry. I'm
being catty. I shouldn't say things like that,
especially when she's your girlfriend."

"She's not. Cyndi and I ended our relationship hours ago. This is our last hurrah before
we go our separate ways."

"Oh, I'm sorry." She looked about as upset as she had when he told her he didn't want children.

"Don't fret about it. The decision was mutual." Harrison twirled Cyndi to the other side of the dance floor. She was probably plotting something that would turn Craig's hair prematurely gray. Why did he suggest this breakup date?

"Would you mind sitting this one out?" he asked. "I'm a little rattled after downing that salmon."

Once they reached the table, Trish took what had originally been Cyndi's chair. This way she and Craig could both face the dancers. "What time do the festivities start on Thanksgiving?"

"Eleven. That way everyone can get home for turkey and the football games on TV."

"Have you been to one before?"

"Yes." He sat up and moved a little closer so they could hear each other over the music. "Never did anything during halftime, though."

Trish leaned closer. "Well, I have no intention of doing the cheers. What do you say we stick together in the bleachers?"

"Like glue." He couldn't ask for anything better.

"What's your schedule for tomorrow?" she asked.

"Outside work. I need to scrape the house before we can paint it. You're sticking to white, correct?"

"Yes. Dave's still considering buying the place, and he liked that we're not making changes."

It looked as though Harrison and Cyndi had begun to drift closer to their table. "So, what are your plans tomorrow?" Craig asked.

"I'm packing all the china Dave wants for his shop and calling Reverend Meyer to take away more furniture. And if you could show me, I'd like to see how to work the different drawers on the secretary."

"Sure." He could see Cyndi more clearly now as they danced toward this side of the room.

"Do you still want to buy it?"

It took Craig a moment to reconnect with their conversation. The two coming off the dance floor didn't look particularly jubilant. "I want to but can't afford it. I could buy a car for my mother for what Dave says it's worth."

Trish nodded, her eyes focused on the two approaching.

"Come on. We're leaving," Harrison said without any preamble. He took out his wallet and dropped several bills. "This should cover our portion of the check." Harrison came around to Trish's side and started to practically lift her from the seat.

Craig got to his feet with every intention of preventing Harrison's manhandling, but the Queen of Calm went along without hesitation. They sped to the coat check with Harrison bent over, talking in her ear.

Craig collapsed in his chair and turned to Cyndi. "What did you do?"

TRISH USED EVERY ounce of control she could muster to keep up with Harrison and not lose her temper. She didn't understand what she'd done to make him so angry. Finally she pulled from his grip and stood in the parking lot. "I can't run in these heels. Will you tell me what's going on?"

Harrison stopped and turned to face her. "Why didn't you tell me?"

"Tell you what?"

"That you and Craig were lovers!"

Lovers? Had he been talking to her mother? She was the only one who ever came up with anything so ridiculous.

"What have you been drinking?" Her breath came out in puffs of vapor. "Let's finish this conversation in the car. I'm freezing."

He opened her door, and she scooted onto the cold seat. She definitely needed to stop by her apartment back in the city for gloves and a warmer coat. When Harrison entered, he turned the key and warmth filled the car, including the seat. She tucked her hands under her legs to pick up the extra heat.

"Cyndi said the three of you grew up together and you and Craig were never apart. The two of you..." Harrison hesitated. "When you and your family moved suddenly, everyone thought..." He sat back, obviously having a difficult time coming up with the right words.

"Everyone thought what?"

"You were pregnant and had to leave Riverbend."

Trish was incredulous. How had a rumor like that started? "Cyndi said I was pregnant?"

"Well, not exactly. She just hinted... Is it true?"

"Of course not. We moved because my father got a promotion. For heaven's sake, Harrison, when I moved Craig was thirteen, and we certainly weren't lovers." Wait till she got hold of Cyndi. She'd strangle her. Why would she tell those lies?

Harrison sat back and sighed. "She really had me going." He reached over and pulled Trish's hand free. His was still cold, so Trish didn't appreciate losing the warmth from the seat. "I need to get a clearer picture of this Craig and your relationship with him. You say he was a nerd, but he sure doesn't come off like a character from *The Big Bang Theory.*"

Maybe not now, but back then… How could she convince Harrison that she'd never thought of Craig as anything more than a friend?

CYNDI HAD DONE SOMETHING, said something to upset Harrison, but she wouldn't admit to anything. Oh, well, Craig would hear about it later from Trish.

"We should be leaving," Craig said. *Oh, please let this night end.*

"You go. It's way too early, and I want to dance." She studied the people on the dance floor while Craig silently fumed. He couldn't take off without her. Okay, so he'd dance some more.

He got up and offered his hand. "Shall we?"

They were halfway through the slow dance when Cyndi said, "The guy didn't have a clue."

Craig shuddered. "About what?"

"About you and Trish, of course. I told him how the three of us would play sometimes in her grandmother's attic. You would be the groom in the hat that folded, and she always had to be the bride with that veil." Cyndi huffed. "She never would let me be the bride."

Because I wanted to marry her, not you.

Craig considered this for a moment. Harrison couldn't possibly be upset by some kids playacting. "That was a long time ago."

"But then she moved." Craig looked down into Cyndi's face and watched her grin broaden. "I told him what some people… well, a lot of us…sort of hinted at, in fact."

Craig sighed. "What?"

Cyndi scrunched her features so she looked like a pixie. "That she maybe had to leave."

Craig shook his head to remove the cobwebs that had started to clog his brain. "What are you talking about?" He knew the reason for Trish's move. Her father's new job.

"The baby."

Craig stopped moving his feet and stared. "She was pregnant?"

Cyndi looked around at the people who had also stopped, totally unconcerned with the bomb she'd just dropped.

"You told Harrison that Trish had a baby?"

"Well, not exactly. But, hey, that's what a lot of us thought when she took off so sudden-like."

"I can't believe you'd say something like that."

"Didn't you want that engagement broken? Now the two of you…"

Craig walked Cyndi off the dance floor. "There is no two of us. There was no baby." He grabbed her purse and handed it to her. "I'm taking you home, and if you don't agree, I'll toss you over my shoulder fireman-style."

"Ooh, fireman-style," she said, pursing her lips.

After Craig dropped Cyndi off at her house, he drove by Trish's place. Harrison's gold Lexus sat on the driveway. Craig gave him an hour, but the car hadn't moved when

Craig drove by again. Reluctantly he quit trying to see her, went home and tried to get some sleep.

"I DON'T KNOW what else I can tell you." Trish poured Harrison a fresh cup of coffee. Although he insisted he needed it so he wouldn't fall asleep while driving home, she knew he really wanted to talk.

"So you and Craig never…?"

Maybe she could put a stop to this. While going through her grandmother's things, she'd discovered a photo album. Her grandmother had become very efficient in scrapbooking and had made a lovely book depicting Trish's life in pictures. The cover consisted of lace and satin ribbon in sunshine yellow. She reached over, removed it from the counter and placed it on the table in front of him.

"Here's Craig and me one summer." She pointed to the two of them smiling at the camera, their arms around each other in comrade fashion. "Craig moved into the neighborhood when he was nine and I was twelve, the year I reached my full height. I was taller than most of my teachers." The picture showed two skinny kids, certainly not the man Craig had turned into. "I was still taller than he was when I moved to Virginia."

Trish stood next to Harrison and flipped the pages. "Here. These are the other kids in the neighborhood. We played together." Trish pointed to a young girl quite a bit smaller than the rest of the group. "Here's Cyndi. She tried to make up for her size by being the life of the party. She hasn't changed."

Harrison closed the book and pulled Trish onto his lap. "I'm sorry." She relaxed against him and placed her arms around his shoulders. "Cyndi really pushed my buttons." He grinned at her before planting a welcome kiss.

"So, what I said before..." Although he continued to hold her close, Trish felt a distance developing between them. "I don't think you should stay here alone. It's not safe. You can stay at your place, or, for that matter, mine, since I'll be away for the next week."

"And do what? Commute here every day?" She stood up. "In case you haven't noticed, I still have plenty of work to do."

"In case *you* haven't noticed, Craig's no longer that skinny little boy." Harrison also stood. "I don't trust him."

"Do you trust me?" Harrison hesitated way too long before answering. "Because that's what it comes down to. Either you trust me or you don't."

He pulled her against him and nuzzled her neck. "I trust you. It's just dealing with everything this evening. That pregnancy bit. Oh, God," he said, pulling away and rubbing the back of his hand against his eyes. "I still can't get that image out of my head."

While he slipped into his topcoat, they walked to the front door. Harrison glanced at the boxes in the dining area. "You getting rid of those?"

"I'm contacting Reverend Meyer tomorrow to see if he wants anything in the boxes, including several pieces of furniture that Dave doesn't want."

"And the Christmas things. Those are going, right?"

"I'm looking through it all. Our children will be able to enjoy a tree filled with my memorabilia until they collect their own. I can tell them when I got each…"

Harrison shook his head. "Really? Let's start from scratch when we have kids. Make our memories with them."

Trish considered that for a moment, not

sure she wanted to toss her collection of ornaments. "Do you have any special Christmas memories?"

"My parents took my brothers and me on vacations during Christmas breaks. So my memories are of Disney, Hawaii and skiing."

He walked to the box containing the lights for the house. "Toss those, too. It's a waste of money paying someone to put them up. And I don't want you trying to do it on your own. You're not that little kid helping your grandfather decorate the house anymore."

She walked him to the door without agreeing. How could she? Christmas was important to her, and she'd always spent it with family at home.

After a quick kiss, Harrison headed for his Lexus. He waved. "See you when I get back. Stay safe." A moment later he was in his car driving away.

Trish felt deflated. How late was it, anyway? Sleep would never come when she had today's events swimming around in her head. She went back to look at her scrapbook. All that work, all the love that had gone into it. *Gram, I miss you. What would you do if you were me?* Someday she hoped to be the same loving grandmother her gram had been.

She changed out of her dress and put on the grubby clothes she'd worn to paint, including Gram's holey sweatshirt. Should she have another cup of coffee? Maybe Craig was right. The caffeine could be destroying her sleep. Oh, well, since she couldn't sleep anyway, might as well have another cup.

Would Craig be awake? She speed-dialed his number on her phone and almost hung up when she realized the time. Midnight. But he answered.

"I can't sleep," she said.

"I can't, either. Harrison leave?"

"Yes. I've got something to show you. Okay if I come over?"

"Sure."

CRAIG JUMPED OUT of bed and dressed quickly. What could she have to show him? How had her night gone after she left The Country Barn? Quickly tossing the bed back to its original state, he checked the rest of the room. He grabbed the architectural plans he'd started and dropped them in a dresser drawer. Maybe he should brush his teeth.

He'd just finished that chore when he heard a light tap on his door. He rushed to let her in.

"You sure I'm not disturbing you?" Trish asked, standing by the opened door. She glanced toward his bed. Thank goodness he'd remade it.

"Nah, come in. I was watching TV. Couldn't sleep if I wanted to."

"Right. Unbelievable day."

"Cyndi told me what she said, and I…"

"Forget it. Cyndi was being Cyndi. I brought you something."

"What have you got there?" She handed him a large cardboard box, and he placed it on the table. He helped remove her coat and saw the torn and paint-spattered sweatshirt, another item that was her grandmother's. He held on to one sleeve with two fingers and pulled. "Do you need that?"

Trish rubbed her arms and shivered. "It's warm."

"I've got something that might be warmer, and it doesn't have holes to let in the cold air." He went over to his dresser and pulled out a navy blue sweatshirt he'd outgrown. "Try this." He liked the idea that she'd be wearing something of his.

Trish removed the old sweatshirt and traded it for the newer navy one.

As he watched, his insides felt on edge. Maybe it was that salmon. He took the gray sweatshirt and placed it next to her coat. "So, what did you want to show me?"

She removed a bulky yellow book and set it beside the box. "We'll look at that later." A smile lit her face as she pulled out something else. "You remember this?" She held a model house on her palm. "Back when you wanted to design houses? I found them when we were cleaning the attic." After putting that one on the table, she took out several more.

Craig picked one up, and it fell apart in his hand. "I can't believe you found these."

"They represent all your creative talent. Something you should…"

"If you're going to start on me again, Trish…"

She sighed. "I'm not. I just wanted to give them to you. Harrison wanted me to throw them in the trash. I couldn't. We had so much fun making those, creating dreams—"

"Trish, don't." He tried making his voice menacing so she wouldn't continue. He still didn't want to talk about his college plans. Why bother when she wouldn't be part of them.

With a shrug, Trish picked up the yellow book, walked to the couch and took a seat. She patted the spot next to her. "Sit. I found this scrapbook going through Gram's things."

"Should I get something? A drink, maybe?"

She patted the seat again when he didn't comply quickly enough. "No, I had coffee before coming over, and you're probably right—it could be what's contributing to my sleeping problem."

He sat down, and Trish spread the book so it opened half on his lap and half on hers. "This is my baby picture."

"Cute." He leaned over to examine it more closely. "You were actually small at one time?" She whacked his arm, and he grinned. He expected that response from her, and he liked the familiarity. He rubbed his arm and pretended he suffered from great pain.

She flipped through the next pages, and he watched her grow from a toddler to the Amazon she'd turned into. She towered over everyone in the pictures except her parents. "Here you are." She pointed to the two of them, her arms around his shoulders and his around her waist.

Underneath the picture in neat script, her grandmother had written MUTT & JEFF. Trish laughed. "We could never get away from that nickname until you finally added a few inches."

Craig placed a hand on the page so she couldn't move it. Trish and him, the summer he moved to Riverbend. He tapped the photo. "That's the day you became my superhero, threatened to break Sammy Bentley's arm if he didn't stop picking on me."

"That little squirt." Trish chuckled and attempted to turn the page.

"I mean it. You were my hero and my best friend."

Trish became serious. "No, you were my champion. I was terrified I'd never stop growing, and you didn't seem to mind. I felt normal around you instead of like some overgrown weed."

"Okay if I make a copy of this?"

Trish tried to pry it loose. "Sure, but it seems permanently in place."

"That's okay. I'll take a picture." He pulled his iPhone out of his pocket and snapped a few photos. He could resize or edit them later.

"You want more?" She began slowly flipping pages, some with pictures of the two of them, some with shots of their neighborhood friends. He snapped several before she stopped and pointed. "Here's Cyndi. You want one of her?" He brushed his hand across the page, motioning for her to go on.

Craig stopped her again when she no longer towered over the other people in the photos. "Who's that?"

Trish chuckled. "I think his name was Chuck something. My first date after I moved to Virginia. We went to one of the school dances." She tried closing the book but he wouldn't let her. "You wouldn't be interested in these. They're all of me and the guys I dated."

"You're wrong."

"Really? You want to check them out?"

Craig grinned and gave her a nod.

When she came to the end, her graduation from college, Craig asked, "Did those boyfriends mean anything to you?"

"No." She smiled and said, "None of them asked me to marry them, if that's what you want to know."

"How come you never took me seriously?"

Trish closed the book and got to her feet. He stood, as well. "How could I? You were nine when you started proposing." She placed the book on the table and turned back to face him.

"And I'm twenty-three now." She no longer towered above him as she had in those early pictures. She looked away, and he placed his palm against her cheek to gently turn her back toward him. Trish moved her head almost imperceptibly and kissed his palm.

Heat raced through him. Without putting any more thought into it, he wrapped his arms around her and touched her lips with his own.

Then she kissed him back.

CHAPTER FOURTEEN

SANITY QUICKLY RETURNED and Trish moved
away, placing her fingers against Craig's
mouth so they couldn't kiss again. "I have to
go." He dropped his arms. "It was a mistake.
I shouldn't have come here." She turned and
searched for her coat. Where had he put it?
"It's late. I need to get home." She couldn't
stop talking. Couldn't stop babbling. What
on earth had gotten into her?

"It was a mistake," she said again while
the words repeated over and over in her head.

Trish got home somehow, totally on auto-
pilot. By the time she reached her door, she
couldn't recall how she'd managed any of it.
She headed for the small room behind the
kitchen, dropped her purse and the book on
the floor and flopped onto her bed.

That first kiss so long ago had never given
her a second thought. But this one... She
pounded her pillow and attempted to force the
image from her mind. It wouldn't go away.

TRISH AWOKE TO her telephone ringing. She groped for it on the floor and turned it on without first checking the caller ID. "Hello."

"Hi, hon. I'm boarding the plane now. Wanted to check with you about a few things." Harrison stopped. "You there, Trish?"

She threw her feet over the side of the bed and sat up. "Harrison?"

"Of course it's me. Who else do you know boarding a plane at this hour?"

Trish glanced at the clock on the nightstand. It said 10:00 a.m. in glowing red. How could it be? She'd slept this late? "Um, what did you want to check on?"

"Find out if Dave really intends to buy the house. You need to speak with a Realtor and find out exactly what it's worth. If he's not going to offer that amount, we should look into getting other buyers. Also…" He droned on. Something about the furniture, the Christmas decorations and Gram's bedroom furniture. Had he decided to get rid of it after telling her they should keep everything for their guest room? Trish held on to her head, not able to take in much of the conversation. He ended with "Have you thrown those models and the Christmas lights in the trash yet? Whoops. Sorry, I have to go. Turning my phone off now till I reach Chicago."

Trish fell back on the bed, still clutching her phone. Her head ached. What was that noise? She rolled onto her elbow and focused on the sound. Was something brushing against the house? Craig had said he planned to scrape away the flaking paint.

How would she face him after last night? It was the scrapbook's fault. She should… hide it? Destroy it? The kiss… She pressed her fists against her lips.

With great effort, Trish dragged herself up and went into the kitchen. Coffee. She emptied the grounds from the percolator and measured enough for a new batch. Craig walked past the kitchen window and waved. A moment later he knocked on the kitchen door.

"Hi. Anything you need help with before I get the scissor lift?"

"The what?" Trish took a seat at the table.

"I'm painting the house and fixing all the gingerbread. The lift gets me up and down and around so I'm not restricted by a ladder."

She supported her head with her hands while staring at the percolator. Craig dropped down in front of her. "You all right?"

"Headache." She started to stand up to get away from him. "I'll find some aspirin in the medicine cabinet."

"Don't." He reached into his jacket and pulled out a bottle of tablets. "The stuff in there is way past the expiration date." He pushed the bottle toward her. "Use this." Craig went to the sink and brought back a glass of water. "I'll be back later."

He was way too handy. Who carried aspirin around in their pocket? Too bad it couldn't help her heartache.

Trish decided to check all the medicine in the bathroom. Sure enough, everything was way past being usable. She cleaned out the cabinet on the first floor and went to the second. Up there, besides Gram's prescriptions, she found dozens of Gramp's, and he'd been dead for almost ten years. She tossed all the bottles into a plastic bag and brought them downstairs.

She was beginning to feel human again when someone knocked on her front door, a woman she didn't recognize. "Yes?" Trish asked as she opened the door.

The attractive redhead, dressed in a wool cape in forest green, grinned at her and stuck out a business card. "Hi, I'm Eugenia Ross. I understand you're selling this lovely house, and I'm sure we can connect you with the one buyer who will love it as much as you do. May I come in and see it?"

Not wanting to be rude, Trish invited Ms. Ross into the vestibule, where she could keep warm. "How did you find out about the house?" Except for people close to her, Trish hadn't told anyone about the potential sale. Why do anything until it was market-ready and Dave had made his decision?

"Harrison Morris told me. I was his real-estate agent when he found that gorgeous place on the Palisades."

"Yes, it does have an excellent view of the city."

Ms. Ross brightened. "Oh, you've seen it? We went through dozens of places till he found exactly what he wanted." She glanced around Trish. "What a magnificent staircase." She looked ready to sprint up the stairs, but Trish managed to prevent her.

"Thank you, Ms. Ross," Trish said, re-checking her card, "but I'm not ready to show it yet."

"But…"

Trish opened the door. "When I am, you'll be one of the first people I call." She stood in place, making any movement forward from the Realtor an impossibility. Finally Ms. Ross took the hint and stepped onto the porch. There were definite advantages to being tall.

Had Harrison mentioned he'd talked to a Realtor? He might have, but Trish couldn't remember. When they'd spoken she hadn't been fully awake. But she was now, and she didn't appreciate being blindsided.

CRAIG DROVE HIS van to Moody's to pick up the scissor lift. The more he thought about it, though, the more he doubted a lift would work. The ground in and around Trish's house might be level, but several spots were still soft. He didn't want that huge structure tipping.

"Hey, Max, I've been rethinking the scissor lift. Maybe a knuckleboom would be better. I can park it on the driveway or sidewalk and reach the areas I need to paint. What do you think?"

Max scratched his chin while he looked at the different pieces of machinery. "You need it for the gingerbread?"

"Yeah, all around the peak where it broke away. And then for some painting."

"How much painting?"

"The whole house. Trish said it hasn't been painted since before she moved, so that has to be ten years."

"Nah, you need scaffolding for that. I can get the crew over there today and get it started."

Max was right, but that meant the last project at the house would be done quickly. Once he finished, she'd sell the house and marry that...that arsonist.

They went inside, where his mother sat in the office. "Rachel, you want to get the paperwork started?" Max gave her all the information, then went back to the lumber area.

"How long have you been working for Max?" Craig asked.

"Always have. You and your father never gave me enough to do, so I keep track of his inventories, employee benefits, paychecks and anything else that comes along." She entered information into her computer, then reached over to the printer to take out a list of the items Craig needed. "You seeing Trish today?"

"Yes."

"What's she doing for Thanksgiving? Meeting up with Harrison?"

"I don't think so. He's in Chicago."

"If she's going to stay in town, invite her over for Thanksgiving. We'll be eating sometime after four."

"You want her to bring anything? You know she's going to ask."

"Does she cook?"

Craig shrugged. "Cookies?" That was all she ever baked for him.

"Whatever she wants to bring will be fine."

THE KNUCKLEBOOM HAD a trailer hitch so he could attach it to his van. He drove the folded contraption to Trish's and set it up on the driveway. She came out of the house still wearing the navy sweatshirt he'd given her.

"You ever going to take it off?" he asked, pointing to the sweatshirt.

"As a matter of fact…" She grinned and hugged herself, obviously not warm enough in the slight breeze. "Is that the scissor thing?"

"No. It's a knuckleboom, and you should get in the house, where it's warm. You could be coming down with something." He shooed her onto the porch and opened her door. "Your headache gone?"

"Yes. How come you carry aspirin around?"

"Need to be prepared in case someone has a heart attack." He hoped she wouldn't ask more questions, and thankfully, she dropped the subject.

"I went through the medicine cabinets as well as Gram's room and found a ton of pills. Is there any place I can get rid of them? I know they shouldn't go in the regular garbage."

"Right. I can take them. The fire department has connections." When they walked into the vestibule, Trish handed him a large plastic bag. "Are we going to talk about it?" He placed the bag near the door.

"What's to talk about? They're old prescriptions and…"

"You know that's not what I mean." Trish might want to pretend the kiss hadn't happened, but he couldn't. "I meant that." He pointed past her, and Trish turned to see what he was talking about.

"Yikes. There it goes." Craig ran into the living room with Trish right behind him. He caught her as she came around the corner. "Did you see it?"

Trish looked to her left and right and skimmed the ceiling with her gaze. "See what?"

"The elephant in the room."

Craig waited a moment while she collected herself and turned into the Queen of Calm. "You kissed me back," he said.

Trish turned away. "I called Reverend Meyer. He's coming over in a little while to pick up some furniture."

Craig gripped her shoulders. "Tell me the kiss didn't mean anything to you. I need to know. And don't lie to me. I can always tell when you're lying." Slowly she turned around to face him, but kept her eyes closed. "Unless you want me to rain kisses on you, Trish, you'd better open your eyes." She did but her mouth hardened.

"Your kisses have definitely… improved." She stared at him a moment, and he saw her lips moving as she attempted to let him down easily. What had he expected? After one kiss she'd suddenly realize she couldn't live without him? When had he become such an idiot? He turned away, about to leave, when she touched his cheek.

"Craig," she whispered. "I know you have feelings for me that go beyond friendship. But I...I'm engaged. I want things you can't...won't give me. I want a family, children. I want to be a grandmother one day, and you..."

Her voice intensified. "You get me so angry, Craig Cadman, I could hit you, and not just a tap on the arm. You don't want children and you know that's what I want. So why do you kiss me that way?" Tears ran down her cheek. She brushed them away.

He bent and pressed his cheek against hers, feeling the wetness seep into his skin. "What way is that?"

She gripped his arms. "Like you could be a husband and father and the love of my life." She sniffled. "And you can't."

He tried wrapping her in his arms, only to have her push him away. "Remember how you said we should back off from each other, not get cozy or friendly?" she asked. "Well, it's really hard for me not to be affectionate with people I know and love. And you're not helping one bit."

Craig didn't try to stop her as she stormed into the vestibule and headed for the kitchen. Her words resonated in his brain, and he couldn't control a smile. She loved him. She'd said it: *"people I know and love."*

Slowly his elation faded. Love alone couldn't help the problems they faced.

CHAPTER FIFTEEN

REVEREND MEYER AND his son had filled his truck with furniture and the items, mostly clothing, from her grandmother's dressers. Trish emptied the armoire and wiped it down so that it glowed. Such a lovely piece with painted flowers and filigree outlined in gold. Would she and Harrison have enough space for it?

When she went downstairs to get the itemized list from Reverend Meyer, she saw that metal knee thingamabob sitting in the driveway and its hinged arm bent toward the house. Trish went outside and watched Craig in the metal cage high above as he attached the gingerbread. "Looking good," she shouted. He waved and came slowly back to the ground.

"You have time to look at the secretary?" he asked. "I'll show you how to open the drawers."

"Sure. Want something warm to drink?"

He followed her into the house. "Hot chocolate would be nice."

"Sorry. I don't have any. Will coffee do?"

He nodded, took off his gloves and scarf and followed her into the kitchen. "My mother would like to invite you to the family gathering at Aunt Jenny's for Thanksgiving. You don't have any other plans, do you?"

"I'd like to join you but…" Trish scrunched her eyes and looked terribly guilty.

Was she still worried about that kiss? "Don't worry," he said when she held out the mug of coffee. "I killed the elephant, and he's mounted on the wall in my place."

"Poor elephant."

"Stop it, Trish." He took the coffee and winked as they walked toward the living room. "We both know you have no sympathy for the elephant."

"That may be true but Max asked me to your mother's place for Thanksgiving. I didn't think the invitation should come from him, so I lied and said I had other plans. Wouldn't want to show up and hurt his feelings."

"I'll handle it so he won't be offended."

"Okay. We're still going to the game, aren't we?"

"Sure." Craig pointed at the secretary. "Want to pull the writing board down?"

She did as instructed. "Hold on to the squirrel with one hand and the acorn with the other. Now move them." After a slight struggle, the carvings moved and the drawers came into her hands.

She giggled and nearly hugged him before remembering—she had to be more guarded. "Wow. Craig, look. They're all unlocked. What a clever man that Willard Williams was, and how clever of you to figure it out." She ran her hand over the polished mahogany. "This is such a lovely piece of history."

"Are you going to sell it?"

"I...I don't know. It's so large." She looked at him. "It should belong to you, Craig. Your apartment's big enough."

"No. I can't afford it, and you'll need all the money you can accumulate to pay my bill."

When he started to head for the door, Trish decided to suggest a compromise. "Could we do a little bartering here? You take the secretary as part payment?"

Craig came back and handed her the empty coffee mug. "'Fraid not. Every time I looked at it, I'd remember the elephant."

THE EVENING BEFORE THANKSGIVING, Trish considered what she could make for the festivities. She looked forward to spending time with Craig's family, especially little Noah, whom she hadn't seen since he showed her his "room." Craig had said she could bring cookies, but he didn't have any knowledge of her baking abilities. Cookies? Really? Pumpkin cookies had possibilities, but she decided to go with something more traditional. Pumpkin pie, one of her specialties.

But if all those medicines were past their prime, the flour and other cooking ingredients couldn't be any good, either. As she emptied the kitchen cabinets, she found her grandmother's recipe book. She looked up pumpkin pie and found one she'd often made with her mother back in Virginia.

Trish compiled a list of the ingredients she needed: flour, shortening, sugar, cinnamon, ginger and cloves. She already had the eggs, but she needed evaporated milk, cans of pumpkin-pie filling and some genuine whipping cream. Would salt go bad? Probably not, but she decided not to take the chance. She tossed the container and added salt to her list.

About to take another garbage bag outside to drop on the growing pile, she stopped when her phone rang. "Hi, Harrison. How's your day going?" she asked.

"It could have been better." He paused before adding, "Why wouldn't you let Eugenia see the house?"

It took Trish a moment before she made the connection. "You mean Ms. Ross?"

"Yes. She did such a wonderful job for me, and I thought she could help you, as well."

"Quite possibly she could." Trish took a few deep breaths. She smiled at herself in the hall mirror that Dave had left behind—something she'd learned while working with disgruntled customers. Smiling always helped her keep frustration out of her voice. "However, you and I never discussed it, and…"

"And what? You wanted to handle it yourself like you've dealt with Craig and Dave."

She heard anger in his voice and felt her own control slipping. "What's wrong with how I've handled Craig and Dave?" Had she actually handled them? They managed pretty well on their own without her supervision.

"I can't get into it now." *Then why did you bring it up?* She heard his heavy breathing. "I'm…I'm sorry. I'm taking my frustrations out on you, and I don't mean to."

Maybe he'd had a hard day and needed to vent. She could understand how irritating their particular job could get. "Everything okay at work?"

"Yes…and no."

"Could you explain? I'd like to help if I can."

"I was turned down on both those promotions in California. Overqualified. Can you believe it?"

"I'm sorry. Maybe—"

"But another position came up here in Chicago. I'm considering it. Chicago being my hometown and all, but…" He sighed. "My family lives here."

He'd never talked much about his family, and Trish had often wondered why he clammed up whenever she asked questions about them. She decided to try again. "You planning to see them this Thanksgiving?"

"I'm working tomorrow. It's one of the holidays I agreed to cover. You know the credit-card industry doesn't close down for holidays."

Yes, she knew that, but he hadn't really answered her question. "So, will you see them at all while you're there?" She couldn't imagine being in the same city as her parents and not visiting. Besides, Harrison also had brothers and other members of his family in the area. Wouldn't he want to catch up with them?

"My parents are having relatives over on Thursday, and I'm heading there after work. I suppose I should bring something. Any ideas?"

"How about flowers for your mother?" That suggestion had worked pretty well for Max.

"She has the place professionally decorated, so I doubt she needs flowers. Maybe wine. They can always use something to replace their booze." He sounded annoyed.

"I just wish this whole week was over and I could get back to you."

She appreciated his sentiment. "I miss you, too."

"Give Eugenia a call. She could be a real help in getting the house off our hands so we can get on with our lives. Love ya. 'Bye."

The call left her rather depressed, but she decided to shop for the essentials she needed for tomorrow's party. Just thinking about making the pie helped get her into a better mood. On second thought, she decided to make some cookies, as well, and added those ingredients to her list. And she also had to do some shopping for herself. She had no intention of going outside one more time without gloves.

EVER SO SLOWLY, Trish had emptied a lifetime of living from her grandmother's house, which equaled a huge accumulation of countless "stuff." Although not exactly a hoarder, her grandmother had kept almost everything she ever owned, plus ancestral items from her family as well as her husband's.

Dave Henry had taken a good portion of the antiques and managed to sell some of them at his different venues. Most of them sat in storage in the barn. The rest were listed on the internet, waiting for interested buyers. And there were many. Her grandmother had had some very special treasures.

Reverend Meyer came again and took the rest of the items Dave didn't want. The three stacks in the barn had dwindled to just Dave's items. The trash had gone into the Dumpster that Trish had rented and stored beside the barn. She still had the bed in the small room behind the kitchen, her grandmother's bedroom furniture and the secretary. Boxes of personal items waited under her cot. She'd saved that for last and expected to bring most of it to her own apartment. On Thanksgiving morning, Trish grappled with what she still had to do while she rolled the remaining pie dough.

Two pumpkin pies sat on the counter, sending their glorious aromas throughout the first floor. This would probably be the perfect time to have people view the house. Hadn't she read that certain cooking odors helped sell homes? Pumpkin pie had to be one of them. She'd just finished putting the leftover scraps of dough in her grandmother's fifty-year-plus oven when someone knocked on the kitchen window. She looked up to see Craig.

"Come in," she called and waved him toward the back door.

"Oh, man," he said after he opened the door. "You can cook?"

She offered him the plate of pumpkin cookies. He took a bite out of one. "Harrison has to be the luckiest man in the world." Craig walked over to the pumpkin pies and took in a deep breath of satisfaction. "Are these for later?" He looked about ready to poke one, so she swatted his arm. He raised an eyebrow but didn't say anything.

"Sorry. Old habits," she said.

"Yeah, some habits are hard to break. You about ready to go? I think it's better if we walk to the high school. Traffic and parking can get pretty hairy at the football games. And dress warmly. There's a chill in the air, and we could get snow."

The timer went off and she pulled the last of the extra piecrust from the oven. Craig's hand came toward the tin. "Watch it, Craig. It's hot."

He picked off a piece of crust and dropped it, shaking his fingers back and forth before dipping down to grab the crust again. When he dropped it a second time, he brought his fingers to his mouth, blew on them and looked as though he might go for another piece. "Don't you ever learn?" she asked, swatting his arm. "Here. I'll put some on a plate and you can take it with you."

WHEN HIS FINGERS COOLED, Craig gave her the package he'd brought. "For you." She traded it for the plate of broken piecrust. Her eyes lit as though he'd given her something extraordinary. "It's mittens and a hat. You lose most of your heat through your head, so I figured you could use them." When he'd seen them in their local drugstore, a special because they were in Riverbend's school colors, he immediately thought of her. She always seemed to be so cold.

She started toward him, then stopped. "You are so sweet," she said, then threw her arms around him and gave him a genuine hug. All too soon she pulled away. But they'd connected. Maybe he hadn't ruined their relationship with that kiss. Even now his lips tingled thinking about it.

He sampled the piecrust, warm and delicious, then packed the broken pieces into a bag along with several cookies for a snack at the game.

When they went out the door, he collected the two padded stadium seats he'd left on her porch. "These will help keep the cold from creeping into our bones."

Trish wore her new knit cap, an almost fluorescent orange, and placed her new mittens over gloves she had purchased. She could have said she no longer needed mittens, but that wasn't Trish. The Queen of Calm would never hurt anyone's feelings and belittle his gift.

"I'm really hyped up about this," Trish said, tucking her arm through his as they headed toward the high school stadium. She carried a woolen blanket in case they needed more warmth.

After greeting several of their friends and neighbors, they found seats in the center of the hometown bleachers. The Orange Wild-cat rivals, the Blue Centurions, had a smaller set of bleachers across the field, and their supporters spilled out on either side.

Trish was adjusting her stadium seat and placing the blanket over their legs when she turned to Craig. "Have you told people about me wanting to sell my house?"

"I may have. Why? It's not a secret, is it?"

"No. It's just…" She sighed. "Harrison sent a Realtor to see the house, and…" Trish sighed again.

"And what?" Craig leaned closer to hear over the crowd's noise.

"I ungraciously sent her packing."

"You? Ungraciously? Really?" He chuck-led, trying to picture the Queen of Calm being bad-mannered. "Why? You haven't contacted any other Realtor, have you?"

"No. But if I sell to Dave, and I'd really like to, there's no reason to work with a Realtor. Why pay her for a sale I've made on my own?"

"What was Harrison's reason for sending her?"

"He says we need to find out the true value of the house."

It had to be the first time Craig actually agreed with the man. "That makes sense. At some point you'll need to find out what it's worth." Why was she so reluctant to do that? He hoped she had decided to keep the house, but that was wishful thinking on his part.

They sat watching the band marching below, and he noticed a few people he recognized, including Cyndi in her old cheerleading outfit.

"I didn't like her," Trish said.

He was about to ask why when Trish stood and grasped the blanket when it nearly fell on the people in front of them. She frantically waved her arm and hollered to Marty and his wife, Mary Ellen.

"You have any room up there?" Marty shouted.

Trish shook her head. "Sorry." When she sat down again, she replaced the blanket and tucked it around his legs as well as her own. "We're packed in here like sardines."

"Why didn't you like her?"

"Who?"

"The agent Harrison sent to look at the house."

Another long pause. Trish spoke so softly, he nearly had to place his ear against her mouth to hear. "She wore a wraparound coat exactly like mine. The one I left back in my apartment."

Craig pulled away and watched her closely. "Well, I suppose by any standard that's a perfectly good reason to dislike someone."

She giggled before going back to the somber expression she'd worn since she started talking about the Realtor. That couldn't be the extent of her reasoning, could it? Something to do with a similar coat?

"Is it possible she stole it?"

She rolled her eyes. "Of course not. It's just…" Trish scowled a moment before coming back to whisper, "How crazy are you about seeing this game? I'm freezing."

She probably needed that coat she had become so concerned about.

Craig swung the blanket off his legs, stood and twirled it over his head in a sweeping arc. "Hey, Marty. Want these seats?" Marty looked up, delighted, and started to climb the steps.

"Let's leave the stadium seats for them." Craig headed down the bleachers, the blanket in one hand, and forced a path between the spectators. With a glance over his shoulder, he saw Trish coming down right behind him.

"LET'S HEAD TO your apartment, okay?" Trish said when they reached the ground. "It's closer than my place." She couldn't believe the weather. Even with all the warm bodies around them on the bleachers, the cold had numbed her. Her black coat, even over several layers, wasn't warm enough. If only she had the one she'd left in her apartment—but who could've known the weather would turn so cold?

"Sure. We'll warm up there before heading to my mother's."

"I need to get the pies." A stiff breeze blew into her face, and she gripped Craig's arm for warmth and stability. Icy particles nipped her cheeks. "Is that snow?"

"Yeah. Feels like it." They both ducked their heads to avoid the biting wind. The football game would go on through any kind of weather for all those die-hard fans. Trish wasn't one of them.

When they reached Craig's building, Trish ran up the stairs and over to his door. She waited not too patiently for him to unlock it. The moment she entered the apartment,

Trish went for the remote and turned on his fireplace. She stood there for several moments with her mittens braced against the heating unit.

"Oh, that feels so good. First thing when I get back to my apartment in Queens, I'm going to get a fireplace like this." She pulled off the mittens, gloves, hat and scarf before unbuttoning her coat. Craig helped pull it away, exposing what had once been his navy sweatshirt.

"Why would you do that? Aren't you and Harrison buying some house or condo together? It might come equipped with a fireplace." He took her cold-weather clothing as well as his own and tossed them on the bed.

"You're right." Trish sat on the couch and covered her legs with her blanket. "You have anything warm to drink? Some hot cocoa would really be wonderful right now."

"What, no coffee?" Craig walked over to his Keurig coffeemaker.

"Cocoa is fine. Too bad I left all the cookies and piecrusts at my place."

Craig returned, shaking the bag he'd carried since they left for the stadium. "No, you didn't. I took them with me." After setting up a TV tray with a plate for their dessert, he went to his coffeemaker to get her the cocoa.

"So," he began once he took the seat next to her, "let's get back to that coat and the Realtor you dislike."

"I have a question for you." Trish turned toward him and took a bite of one of the cookies. "Can you smell my perfume and recognize it again even on someone else?"

HAD SHE DROPPED the subject of the Realtor? He studied her before deciding to answer. "I think I'll always connect you with that scent. Don't know about the rest of your question."

"I told you Harrison gave me the perfume, didn't I?"

Craig nodded.

"But I didn't tell you why?"

He shook his head. Craig took one of the pieces of piecrust and sat back against the couch cushion. Did he really want to know? He had no desire to connect something he enjoyed with Harrison.

"You have a very nice aftershave on. I've noticed it before. Are you able to smell it?"

He sat up. "When I first put it on, sure, but after…"

She grinned and nodded in agreement as though he'd said something brilliant.

"What's your point?"

"People can't smell themselves. I put the Chanel on because I like it. Then it disappears for me, but I can smell your after-shave."

Craig picked up the TV remote. "Okay if we watch one of the football games while we talk?"

Trish snatched the remote and tossed it on her side of the couch. "No. This is important. When that Realtor, Eugenia Ross, came to my house, I could smell her perfume. It's supposed to be vanilla something or other, but it doesn't smell like vanilla. It's more of an overpowering fragrance. Something I don't like at all."

Craig rubbed his chin then placed an elbow against the back of the couch. Why was this so important to her? "I can smell the Chanel. You smell lovely. And no, I can't smell the Calvin Klein Euphoria I put on my face." He took in a deep breath to show her he was trying to understand. "Sorry, but I haven't the slightest idea what you're talking about. What does this lady's perfume have to do with you?"

"Harrison gave me a bottle of her vanilla perfume as a Christmas gift. I hate giving a gift back, but I told him I can't wear that perfume. My mother is allergic to it. Mom gets migraines and can't stop sneezing. If she doesn't get away from the smell, she can have an asthma attack. That's when Harrison asked what he could get for me instead, something that wouldn't send people to emergency care. I told him Chanel No. 5."

Craig bent over and placed his head in his hands. "If you don't get to the point, Trish, I'm going to get that TV remote, even if I have to wrestle you for it." She didn't respond immediately, and when he looked her way, her chin wobbled. Was she about to cry? He sat up. "What's going on?"

"I think Harrison's cheating on me," she said in a choked voice.

Craig sighed. *At least now she might send that arsonist packing.* But Craig doubted Harrison's exit would come easily. "Explain. I'm not following your logic."

"Six months ago, he bought his condo, using that Realtor. She was wearing the same perfume he once bought me." She bit her lip. "And she was wearing a copy of my blue coat. He said he liked it. It matched my eyes.

And now she has one in green, and it…it matches her eyes."

"So you think there's something going on between the two of them?"

"Yes. Why else would he tell her to look at my house?"

"That's something you'll need to discuss with him."

CHAPTER SIXTEEN

CRAIG DIDN'T UNDERSTAND. How could he? But Trish knew the possibility existed. Harrison might have had some fling with the green-eyed redhead. The first chance Trish had, she'd confront him.

She handed Craig the remote, and the two sat back to watch a football game. For the most part, Trish ignored the game and watched the flames darting about in the fireplace. How could something so artificial look so real? Besides that, it was comforting. Or maybe the comfort came from sitting next to Craig.

Had she overreacted about the real-estate agent? Of course. She was being silly, turning her suspicions into full-blown jealousy. Coincidences—that was all they were.

She reached for one of the piecrusts and finished her cocoa, then realized Craig hadn't gotten his drink. "You forgot your cocoa."

She tossed the blanket aside and went to the Keurig to get his drink. Someone knocked on the door. *It can't possibly be Cyndi, can it?* When Craig started to get up, Trish waved him back. "I'll get it."

Trish opened the door to Marty and his wife, both looking as though they'd walked through a blizzard.

"You wouldn't believe the change in the weather," Mary Ellen said as she walked in, dusting snowflakes from her coat. "We're returning your seats." She pointed to Marty, who dropped the stadium seats by the door. The moment Mary Ellen spied the fireplace, she walked directly to it and embraced its warmth. "Oh, please, can we stay here awhile? Our car is in gridlock with everyone trying to get home."

"Sure." Craig came over to take her coat. "Want coffee or cocoa to warm up? Marty, what about you? A beer?"

"That would be great." Marty removed his jacket and joined his wife in front of the fireplace. "You're a godsend. I don't remember a storm like this coming on so quickly." He glanced at the TV before taking a seat on the couch. "Hey, the Giants. Who's winning? Will you look at them playing in the snow? The storm must be coming up from the south."

Mary Ellen joined him on the couch, and she motioned for her husband to move to one end so Craig and Trish would have space. "So, Trish," Mary Ellen began when Trish sat beside her, "what have you been doing? Marty said you're staying at your grandmother's place."

Before Trish could reply, Mary Ellen continued, "I always knew you and Craig would get together one day. No way could Cyndi keep his interest with you back in town. The two of you getting serious? You can tell me. I can keep a secret."

"No, she can't," Marty said, accepting a beer from Craig, who also handed his hot cocoa to Mary Ellen.

The two men grinned at each other. Trish extended her hand to show Mary Ellen her ring. "I'm engaged."

"Oh, you little rascal!" Mary Ellen squealed and grabbed her hand. After a quick look, she reached up to grip Craig's sleeve. "I never knew you to be such a fast worker." Immediately she turned her attention back to Trish. "When's the wedding? My triplets would make the cutest flower girls."

"I'm marrying Harrison Morris sometime in the spring," Trish murmured, "and the wedding will probably be in Virginia, where my parents have a home." Okay, so she'd lied about the wedding date and her parents' home. Her nose didn't suddenly grow. But she needed to quash this rumor before it took flight. The fib managed to bring Mary Ellen's ramblings to a halt.

Craig took the seat next to her. He grinned and lifted his beer in a toast. "To the Queen of Calm."

AFTER COLLECTING THE two pumpkin pies from Trish's place, Craig and Trish headed for his aunt's house. The precious cargo lay securely between their seats. The snow continued to astound them as it accumulated and covered everything in white.

"I'm heading to New York tomorrow to see someone about my CAD program. You know, the one I used to fix your roof. I could use some company, and we could stop by your apartment and get your coat."

"You going by train? I hate driving in snow."

"No. The van has all-weather tires." Even so, Craig drove slowly. Their headlights barely made it possible to see the streets.

"I'll think about it." But he already knew

she'd say no. It didn't take long for her to come up with a reason. "I can use my grandmother's camel-colored coat. It's warm, and my other one is way too dressy for what I have to do around here."

That ancient coat was full of moth holes, but he didn't mention that. He knew the real reason. She needed to keep her distance from him, and he understood why. Despite their best intentions to avoid contact, that magnetism kept drawing them together.

"You sure you don't want Mary Ellen's daughters in your wedding? They're really cute." The proud parents had pulled out several pictures before they left for their own Thanksgiving celebration. Craig received the usual response, a soft whap from Trish's gloved/mittened hand. "You don't agree?"

"They're adorable. But no, I don't think I want Mary Ellen involved in any way with my wedding." Trish started to laugh. "Nothing changes. I come home after all these years, and I'm right back in high school. No one's changed. Cyndi's still the biggest flirt. Mary Ellen will dig out any dirt she can find and broadcast it. She practically had the two of us married to each other." Trish continued to chuckle. Craig didn't see the humor.

"What about me? Have I changed?"

Instead of replying in the same lighthearted tone, Trish turned thoughtful. "I think you have."

Obviously not for the better.

Craig pulled into his aunt's driveway and parked behind Max's truck. "I'll carry the pies. Can you handle the rest?" Trish had brought the makings for whipped cream, not satisfied with squirting it out of a can or scooping it from a container.

"What about the other packages you have?" He had several bags of chips and other items for TV snacks.

"I'll make a second trip. Be careful getting out. Everything's slippery." Craig managed to retrieve the pies and open his door. He took a careful step...and went flying. The pies in their traveling containers disappeared under the van. Before he could get up, Trish stood over him and offered a hand.

"You okay?" When he didn't reply, she got on her knees and brushed his face with her new mittens. "Can you get up? Did you hurt your back?"

"The only thing that hurts is my dignity." He placed one hand in the snow and pushed himself to a sitting position. "What happened to the pies?"

"They're safe." She bent over and pointed under the van.

Trish covered her mouth with one hand, her shoulders shaking with silent laughter. "Right now, lady, you are in grave danger of getting your face pushed in snow." Before he could get to his feet, a cold ball of fluff hit him directly in his nose. He reached out and grabbed her hand. Her mitten pulled off, and he tossed it. Fortunately, the neon orange would be easy to find. When he finally got a good grip on her arm, he pulled her to the ground and held her while he tried to gather some snow. He scratched around with her giggling beneath him until he had a handful.

He propped himself above her, staring down at her slightly opened mouth. Was she waiting for a kiss? Were those blue-gray eyes daring him to try it one more time? Instead he rubbed the snow against her face. She had to be freezing, but she continued to giggle and didn't try to wiggle out from under him.

For several moments they stared at each other, their breaths coming out in clouds that quickly dissipated. Craig felt an ache that had nothing to do with the cold. He rolled away and started to get up.

"You all right?" Max shouted as he approached in galoshes. Something Craig should have considered instead of his leather-soled loafers.

"I think so. We lost our dessert under the van. You have anything long so I can pull it out?"

"I'll get something." Max disappeared, came back with a rake and managed to capture a pie. It was less than circular inside the plastic container. "Looks ruined."

"Don't worry about it," Trish said when Max handed it to her. "We'll just cut it up and smother it with whipped cream."

"I'll get the other one." Max went around to the opposite side of the van and pulled it out. "This one looks okay, and I'll make sure it arrives safely in the house." He held it possessively as he came over to Trish. "You'd both better get inside, where it's warm. You look like a pair of snowmen. What were you doing, wallowing in it like a couple of kids?"

"We were making snow angels," Trish said as she headed for the house.

Max shook his head with a "Yeah, right"

and aimed a look of disbelief at Craig. "You got more in the van?"

"Yep. I'll get it." Craig reached inside and pulled out the grocery bags filled with munchies. With any luck, he could get back to watching football. And erase some of those images of Trish.

"WELL, HOW'S MY favorite little Pilgrim?" Trish asked when Noah greeted her at the door, wearing a handmade black paper hat. "I love it. Just like the real thing."

He held out another black hat with a gray Pilgrim buckle glued to the front.

"Is this special hat for me?"

Noah nodded and reached for her hand. "I made one for you and one for Butchy." He pulled her toward the kitchen as Max and Craig came in the door. The moment he saw his brother, Noah released her and ran to him, leaving Trish to go on by herself.

"Hi, Rachel. Thanks for having me over," Trish said when she reached the kitchen. "This pie should be served first. It sort of had an accident when Craig came out of the van. Do you have a bowl so I can whip the cream?" Trish placed the pie on the counter along with many other desserts, including a pecan pie. "Everything smells so delicious. You must have been cooking for days."

Rachel handed her a bowl. "Jenny helped. I sent her to rest and watch the football game. It was sweet of you to make the pies."

Noah walked in with Craig, who was wearing a black paper hat way too big for him. "We're all Pilgrims, and we're gonna eat turkey just like they did."

"These are so nice. Did you make them all by yourself?"

"My teacher helped."

Trish began peeling off her outer clothes, her black hat resting on her eyebrows. Craig came over to help. "I can take all this so it's out of the way, Pilgrim." Craig pushed his hat back, but it continued to dip on his forehead. "We probably won't find your other mitten until next spring." After helping her out of her coat, he added, "Sorry about that." But he didn't look sorry at all. In fact, he looked rather silly with his hat constantly dipping into his vision. He disappeared behind a door and came back empty-handed.

He picked up Noah. "Does this little guy know how the earliest Thanksgiving started?" He winked at Trish and pushed his hat back.

"The Pilgrims wanted to play football, so

they invited everyone to play," Noah recited with a big grin.

"And who won?"

"The Pilgrims!" Noah collapsed against Craig's shoulder in giggles.

"You been teaching him American history? A version not taught in schools?"

"Of course." After flipping Noah head over heels to the ground, Craig asked him, "So, you want to watch football?" Craig handed him a bag of potato chips. "Take this to the living room. It looks like they've run out of munchies."

"Don't you dare," Rachel shouted. "It's almost time to eat, and I don't want you ruining your appetites." She brought a dish of hot string beans to the table. "Craig, help me put everything out. I'm having Max slice the turkey once we sit down. Noah, you go wash your hands." She turned to Trish, who had all the ingredients ready for the whipped topping. "Why don't you wait on that until we're ready for dessert? There's no more room in the refrigerator, but it can go outside until later. It's certainly cold enough."

After placing the bowl with the whipping cream outside the back door, Trish looked around at the full table. A golden-brown

turkey, orange squash, whipped white potatoes, candied yams and green beans made
splashes of color on the tablecloth patterned
with oak leaves.

Rachel smiled, a look of pure pleasure on
her face as she removed a bouquet of orange,
yellow and deep red chrysanthemums mixed
with fall leaves from the table. She placed it
on the sideboard and gave an extra smile to
Max, whose cheeks became a bright pink.

Rachel turned to the group assembling in
the dining room, waved a hand at the table
and took a seat. "Let's eat."

Jenny and her husband, Arnold, both in
Pilgrim hats, took seats on one side of the
circular table, with Max and Rachel opposite them. Noah sat between Trish and Craig.

"This is Thanksgiving, so we'll start the
meal with gratitude for all our blessings."
Rachel grasped the hands of the men on either side of her, and the rest of the table followed suit. "We give thanks for the food and
the friends we have sharing it with us." She
glanced at her sister. "And for the generos-
ity of relatives who provided a place for us."

Jenny leaned across the table, still holding
hands with Arnold and Trish. "Thank you,

my dear Rachel, for your boundless energy and all this great food."

Max cleared his throat. "Okay if I say something?" Everyone nodded approval, including Noah, who stared wide-eyed at Max.

"I want to thank you. Every one of you." He turned to Rachel. "And you, not only for inviting me to this wonderful celebration but also for brightening my day every time I see you at the lumber company." If possible, his features actually appeared to get pinker before he looked away.

Trish pushed up her Pilgrim hat and noticed the two had squeezed hands, although she couldn't tell who initiated it.

"My turn," Arnold said. "Since our kids flew the nest, Rachel and Noah have put life back in this house. You're both always welcome here…especially when you can cook like this. I've gained at least ten pounds since you moved in."

"Closer to twenty," Jenny added, giving her husband a nudge. He bent down and kissed her cheek.

Trish watched them all, enjoying the essence of family. Did Craig see any of it? Her own contentment fought with sadness for all that he'd be missing without having kids of his own. When she looked his way, he said, "Your turn, Trish. What are you thankful for?"

"I'm thankful for having met Pilgrim Noah—" she nodded at him "—and meeting Max and renewing old friendships. I feel overwhelmed. All of you have been so welcoming and helpful. One day I hope to celebrate like this with my own family." She turned to Noah. "And what are you thankful for?"

For several moments, Noah grinned at them. Then his features turned serious. "I'm getting a leg." Everyone started to laugh.

Max stood with knife in hand. "I guess I'd better get started on this," he said and began carving the turkey.

As they passed the food around and piled the feast onto their plates, Trish wondered why Craig hadn't offered anything during the handholding. Didn't he have anything to be thankful for?

CHAPTER SEVENTEEN

AFTER THE MEAL and the pumpkin pie, Trish helped Jenny and Rachel with the dishes. Most went in the dishwasher, but the pots and pans required extra work. "One thing I always liked about you, Trish," Rachel said, "even when you were twelve years old, you always helped out. And that pie is to die for. When did you learn how to cook?"

"In college. I took several cooking classes as electives."

"Did you want to be a chef?" Jenny asked.

"Oh, no. I just wanted to cook for myself and one day for my family. Harrison, my fiancé, likes several dishes I make."

"Maybe that's why he proposed," Jenny said with an added smile.

Trish thought about it a moment. "No, I think it's more because we share the same ideas about marriage and family. I want several kids, and he does, too." Her thoughts turned to Craig's put-downs of such ideals, but she didn't mention them.

Max had walked to the sink with several dishes from the living room.

"There's little more to do here, Trish. Why don't you and Jenny go join everyone in the living room? Max can help me finish up."

Max took Trish's dish towel and shooed her away.

"I'm not too interested in football. Besides, I hear Arnold snoring," Jenny said when they reached the stairs. "I think I'll go to my room and read."

Trish headed back to the living room, although she really had no interest in football, either.

"Care to join us?" Craig stood by the cleaned-off dining room table with a battery-operated lantern and a large brown sheet over his arm. Noah stood next to him with his welcoming smile.

"We're remaking Noah's room, minus the animals. We can show you how to play chess." He turned to Noah. "Right?" The two gave each other a high five.

"Yeah. I'm going to beat the pants off ya," Noah told Trish.

"Whoa, there, young man. You don't say

that to a girl." Craig tossed the sheet over the table while Noah crawled under, carrying the lantern and a box under his arm. "You coming?"

Trish walked over. "You're teaching him chess?"

"Why not? I taught you, and he's at least as smart."

Craig held up one end of the sheet while Trish ducked under. "It won't be much fun for him if you never let him win."

He crawled in after her. "I let you win on several occasions."

"You had to or I wouldn't have played with you anymore." With two adults, the area seemed a great deal less roomy than it had before. Noah already had the board set up on the floor and had begun to put the pieces in their proper places.

"I hate to be a party pooper, Craig, but that isn't the same chess game you and I played."

Craig made a point of checking out the "Chutes and Ladders" board. "Looks like chess to me."

After they'd played for a while, Craig tried to adjust his position. "This gets a little cramped. My leg went to sleep. Okay if we take it up top and play on the table?"

Noah scowled. "I like it here."

Craig glanced at Trish and began to rub his face. "You know what? I forgot to shave today. I think I'll go take care of that now."

Immediately Noah abandoned his game and pushed past her. "I'll get the shaving stuff."

"You're one devious character," Trish said as Craig followed his brother.

"That I am." Craig grinned. "I'd invite you to watch, but it's really a man thing. You wouldn't be interested."

Trish crawled after him. "Who said? I'm watching."

"No, you're not."

When they reached the bathroom, Noah already had several items on the counter: a bladeless razor, shaving cream and an after-shave lotion. He stood on a plastic bench and leaned against the sink. When Craig beat her to the room, he closed the door.

Trish whacked it with an open palm. "Let me in."

Craig peeked around the door. "You can't come in. This is men's business. No girls allowed." But he didn't close it.

She had a perfect view thanks to the partial opening and the mirror. Craig squirted shaving cream into Noah's hand, then a good helping into his own. Noah imitated every step as Craig spread the substance around his own face. He then took out a regular razor from the top shelf of the cabinet for himself.

"I could help," Trish said, wanting a chance to be part of the duo. She made eye contact with Craig through the mirror.

"You're not going to cry, are you?"

The thought hadn't entered her mind, but she decided to go with it. Trish forced a sniffle and made weeping noises.

"Girls!" Craig said in total disgust. He pushed the door open and came close enough so that some of the shaving cream came off on her cheek.

When she tried to wipe it away, he grabbed her hand. "Anyone entering this domain has to shave." He turned back to Noah. "Right?"

"Yeah." Noah grasped the shaving cream and handed it to him.

"You're kidding, right?" Trish rolled her eyes, only to have Craig brush her other cheek with his and leave a mess of white cream.

He winked. "While I shave, why don't you do the honors and shave Noah? It's not a good idea for him to keep it on too long."

When Noah handed her the bladeless razor, Trish took a seat on the edge of the tub. Craig finished his shaving at the sink, and Trish quickly shaved Noah. After running a facecloth under the tub's faucet, she wiped his face as well as her own and dried both with a soft towel. "You look so handsome."

"Yep. I am. And I'm really smooth." He patted his cheeks.

Trish pressed her cheek against his. "Oh, that is so smooth. I love a man with smooth cheeks."

Craig came over with aftershave on his hands. He rubbed it around Noah's face. "Try it now." Trish did. "Better?"

"Absolutely. You smell so good, I could eat you up." She enfolded Noah in her arms and kissed him. He accepted her attention with giggles before pulling away.

"Now it's his turn." Noah pointed to Craig and yawned.

Trish tried slipping past Craig, but he caught her arm. "You stepped in it, Trish. Check it out." He tilted his face toward her.

She ran the back of her hand along his cheek with the realization she shouldn't be doing this. He watched her with eyes that looked so inviting, so thoughtful. Her breath caught when he grasped her hand and drew it across his lips.

"Smooth, very smooth," he said.

Everything about him shouted danger. Trish yanked her hand away.

"Problem?"

"I don't play with fire."

He leaned close to her ear and whispered, "Yes, you do, and one of these days, you'll get burned." He turned to Noah and picked him up. The boy's eyes were already at half-mast after a busy day. It was close to his usual bedtime. "Come on, big guy. You need to get to bed."

Noah twisted away and reached for Trish. "Okay if I take him?" Craig transferred the boy to her waiting arms. He felt so solid and oh, so smelly with all that aftershave. She hugged him close. "Show me where to go."

They were halfway up the back stairs when her phone rang. As soon as she reached the top, she returned Noah to Craig. The boy was too far into dreamland to protest.

"I'll take it from here." Craig slipped into a bedroom while Trish retrieved her phone.

"Hi, Harrison. How was your Thanksgiving?" No answer. She checked the phone to see if she still had a connection. "Hello, Harrison, can you hear me?"

"I have a question for you." He paused. "You free for the next few days?"

"Sure. We pretty much fin—"

"My parents want to meet you."

"Really? I—"

"I'm making reservations for you to fly out here."

"But, Harrison, that's so expensive…"

"No problem. I'll use my points. Which airport do you prefer? Newark or LaGuardia?"

Trish hesitated. Would he interrupt her again? This was all too fast. "Um. LaGuardia. It's close to my apartment. But it's snowing here. A major storm. The airports could be closed."

"It's snowing here, too. I'll let you know which airport to go to. If it's Newark, you can stay at my place before the flight."

"No," Trish said, raising her voice and finally getting her mind wrapped around the present problem. She couldn't go anywhere without fresh clothes, and she needed all the warm outfits she'd left behind in her apartment.

"No? You're not going to come?"

"I'll come, but only if it's from LaGuardia." Trish took a seat on the top landing. "Can I bring anything? Something for your parents?"

"No. I told you they don't need anything. Their only interest is in meeting you, my fiancée. And I hope you had your fill of turkey. My mother probably won't go the whole Thanksgiving route twice in one week." He sounded annoyed. With her or with his mother?

"Is something wrong?" She heard a TV in the background.

"My mother lit into me for not bringing you. All my brothers and their wives and kids were there. I had no idea she planned anything that elaborate. And now she wants everyone back on Saturday so they can meet my fiancée. You'd think she declared war on Canada. Everyone had plans. It's a mess."

"I won't come if it's going to cause problems."

"Don't say that, please," Harrison said with a catch in his voice. "I promised you'd come."

A hand lightly squeezed her shoulder. Trish moved to the side so Craig could go down the stairs. Instead he sat next to her.

"Who's that?" Craig asked, pointing to the phone.

"Harrison."

Craig nodded, crossed his ankles and relaxed against her, his elbows on the landing. How on earth was she supposed to have a private conversation with him sitting there?

"Do you mind?" she asked, not bothering to keep the annoyance out of her voice.

"You have someone there?"

Trish returned her attention to the phone. "Yes—Craig. I'm still at his mother's."

"Why?"

She gasped, realizing she'd never told Harrison she'd be spending Thanksgiving with Craig's family. "She invited me over for Thanksgiving."

"Give him the phone." His tone of voice told her that would not be a good idea.

"No. You call me back after you check on planes out of LaGuardia." She disconnected without saying goodbye, way too annoyed by the turn of events. She turned to Craig. "He wants me to fly to Chicago to meet his family."

"When?"

"Sometime tomorrow. He'll call me with the details."

"He snaps his fingers and—"

Trish placed a hand over his mouth. "Stop. I've about had it dealing with all this testosterone."

Craig took a deep breath and leaned back on his elbows. "I can drive you to the airport."

Trish got up and started down the stairs. "No. I'll probably have to go tonight." He stopped her when she got to the bottom stair.

"You are not driving. I told you I need to go to the city tomorrow. We'll go ahead tonight, and I'll drive my van, which has the proper tires." When she started to protest, he added, "It's not negotiable."

"Can you stay the night?"

"You have a couch or a recliner?"

Trish nodded. She'd have no problem putting Craig up. But then another thought struck her. What kind of arrangements had Harrison made for her in Chicago? She couldn't stay with him in his hotel room. Any presumed impropriety on Harrison's business trip could get them both fired.

TRISH STAYED IN the van while Craig stopped at his apartment and took what he'd need for the trip. Ten minutes later, he got back in with a small suitcase and a garment bag. He'd changed into winter boots.

As they circled out of the parking lot, Trish tapped her fingers on the window and watched the snow fall. She really didn't want to fly to Chicago. What if Harrison had been cheating on her? She had no desire to confront him about it in Chicago. Under different circumstances she would have loved to meet Harrison's family, but from what he'd said, it sounded as though she'd end up in a war zone.

"Do you have any idea when this storm will be over?"

"The snow's getting lighter and the plows are out." Craig turned in to her driveway. "You need help?"

"No. I've been living out of my suitcase, so it won't take long to pack."

Despite her not needing his assistance, Craig followed her in. "While you're gone, my mother and I will finish the painting."

"That will be terrific. Why don't you take the key?" She still hadn't found a suitable place to hide it. "I can settle with you tonight, if you want. I won't be coming back to stay, just to get my car and some personal things of my grandmother's." Craig sat on the cot while Trish packed clean clothes into her suitcase. "Do you want cash? I can get it from the ATM and give you a check for the rest."

"Wait on that. My mother handles all the bills, and I'll have to add anything we do while you're away." He looked so forlorn, slumped over, holding his head in his hands. She felt terrible having him drive her in the storm, but she had no idea what else she could do. The trains were probably on a holiday schedule, and she didn't look forward to arriving in the city after midnight. She'd never get a taxi. Taking the subway to Queens and trekking to her apartment in the storm was the only other option.

Craig stood and reached for her suitcase. "Anything else you want to bring?"

"No." On the way through the kitchen, Trish slowed. "I'm not replacing the older appliances. Dave said they give the place ambience. And they still work."

She paused to take it all in. She'd had so much fun making those pies. She'd miss it. Trish pressed her lips together and blinked back some unexpected tears. She'd miss everything. Not just the house but also her grandmother, her friends, Craig.

"Is Dave definitely going to buy the place?" Craig said by her ear.

"I don't know." Her voice cracked, and she rushed to the door.

Craig stopped her, pulled her into his arms and held her without speaking.

CHAPTER EIGHTEEN

TRISH WAS PLANNING to leave for good. The next time Craig saw her she might be married to Harrison, or at least have wedding plans finalized. Thinking about that pretty much destroyed Craig, but he couldn't do anything about it. Instead he held her, comforted her and filled his lungs with her scent.

"We better go," Trish said, and he loosened his grip. "Thank you. For everything." She kissed him on the cheek, turned and went out the door. After locking it, she handed him the key. "I'll text you when I need it again."

Once in the van, they limited their talk to the swirling snowflakes that made the drive difficult. He slowed even more after hitting an icy patch. They traveled down Route 17 until he reached Route 4, which took them over the George Washington Bridge. The storm dwindled within the city limits, and they made it quickly across Manhattan Island into Queens.

"It's the tall building on the right." They went into the basement to Trish's empty parking space. "I'll let the manager know you have the right to park here. Otherwise you'd get towed."

"A parking space in the city? You must pay a fortune."

"I do, but there are times I really need a car. Once Harrison and I get a place, we hope to have a double garage."

"You're still planning to buy something in the city?" Trish turned weepy again. "Sorry," he said. "It seems like everything I say sets you off."

"It's not you. Why hasn't he called? If driving here at this hour turns out to be a false alarm, I will personally strangle him." They headed toward the elevator with their luggage.

When they reached her door, she opened it to a room smaller than his studio apartment. "You have a bedroom where I can put your suitcase?"

Trish twirled around, arms outspread. "This is it, my little spot in heaven." She pointed to an alcove that contained a single bed. "You have a choice between the futon and the recliner. Personally, I'd take the recliner. The bathroom's that way."

Her phone rang. "Finally." She took it over to the bed and sat there while Craig searched for a place to hang his garment bag.

"LET ME GET a pencil. I just got to my apartment."

"Don't bother. I'll text you all the information. You're going out of LaGuardia tomorrow at 11:00 a.m., arriving here at 12:48. Remember Chicago's in a different time zone. I tried getting you on the return flight with me, but that didn't work. You'll be flying back to LaGuardia on Sunday."

"Where will I be staying?"

"With me, of course."

"You know that's against company policy. We could both lose our jobs."

"So don't say anything."

"What if it somehow comes out?"

"Make up something."

"I'm the world's worst liar, Harrison. We've been walking this tightrope since you asked me to marry you. We can't blow it now."

"What do you suggest?"

"Get another hotel room for me."

"Women!" His voice came out in a huff. "Between you and my mother—"

"I don't have to put up with this. Cancel my reservation. I'll meet your family another time."

She disconnected the phone and fell back on her bed. What was the matter with him? They'd been discreet, never doing anything that indicated they were a couple. They could get married with no problem once they no longer worked in the same department. But that wouldn't end until she took on her new responsibilities. Now he wanted to destroy that?

She could sense Craig staring at her. "Don't say it," she said, not bothering to look at him. "I've gone from the Queen of Calm to some raging witch, and if I hear a peep out of you, Craig Cadman…"

"You have an extra blanket and pillow?"

Trish sat up. What was the matter with her? She had a guest who had gone out of his way for her through a blizzard. For nothing, as it turned out. The least she could do was make him comfortable.

"I do. I'll get them for you." She opened her grandmother's hope chest, the gift she'd received from Gram when she moved to the city, and drew out a blanket and pillow. She brought them over to Craig, who sat on the futon. "What's it going to be? The chair or the futon?" Craig nodded toward the chair.

In one easy motion, Craig grabbed the blanket and pillow, plopped into the chair and pulled the blanket over himself. "You want to tuck me in?" He started to chuckle. "Or not."

"This is not funny."

"Sure it is. I bet—" he looked at his watch "—in five minutes he'll call you back with the arrangements you want."

Twenty minutes went by while Trish got ready for bed in flannel pajamas and a warm, fuzzy blue robe. She carried the phone in her pocket, just in case. After brushing her teeth, she dabbed a bit of Chanel by her ears, all the while expecting the phone to ring. Nothing. When she came out of the bathroom, Craig was asleep. At least, she thought he was. He snagged her hand as she walked by.

"You never asked why I was going to New York."

Trish took a seat on the edge of the futon, close to him. "Aren't you going there to sell your CAD program?"

"Hopefully, but I'm also going for some

advice from a friend. I've applied to several architectural colleges to get my degree."

"Oh, that's wonderful." Trish clapped her hands, then brought them up to cover her mouth. "Where do you want to go?"

"Pratt in Brooklyn or New York Institute of Technology on Long Island."

"And you have scholarships, right? You were brilliant in high school."

"I've applied for grants, and I'll keep looking for anything that can help."

She had to do something. Make a connection. Let Craig know how proud she was that he planned to fulfill his dream. She attempted to give him a hug and fell awkwardly on top of him. When she tried to pull away, he held firm, inhaled deeply and pressed his lips against her cheek. "You always wear your perfume when you go to bed?"

"Habit. I didn't realize..."

He chuckled. "You are the world's worst liar. But then, you know that." Those blue eyes seared into hers, and she snuggled closer. "You never could lie. One of the many things I love about you." He kissed her cheek again.

"But you managed to lie."

"Never."

"You said you and Noah were playing chess and you weren't."

"We were teasing you."

Trish closed her eyes. What had started as an uncomfortable position felt increasingly cozy, and she didn't want to leave. When his lips brushed hers, she surrendered to his kiss with a longing she never anticipated and couldn't control. He responded with the same urgency.

Her phone rang.

Immediately Trish pushed away, suddenly aware of her surroundings. She stared at Craig, her hand braced against his chest, wondering if she really wanted to answer the phone. Craig reached in her robe's pocket and handed it to her without commenting. For several moments she stared at it before connecting. When she did, Trish moved to the futon. Harrison had already begun speaking without waiting for her to say hello.

"You're staying at my parents'. No conflict there since I'll remain at the hotel. I'll pick you up at O'Hare. It would have been better at Midway, which is closer, but...oh, well. Dress appropriately for the weather and bring something nice to wear for a fancy restaurant. My mother is not into casual." He paused. "I'll send you the text with all the info."

"Wow," Craig said, moving out of the chair and walking past her. "Sounds like you've got plans." He disappeared into the bathroom.

CRAIG GRIPPED THE edge of the sink and stared, unblinking, at the wall. What had he done? It wasn't all one-sided. She had... He straightened and looked at his image in the mirror. *Be honest with yourself. She'd had a blow to her self-esteem from that jerk. That's all it was. A cry for understanding and...*

He looked at the partially opened medicine cabinet. Chanel. Maybe it *was* a habit, not a desire to tempt him into kissing her. And he certainly had been tempted. *Face it, Cadman. You've been lying from the get-go. You want children. Trish needs to know the real reason why you won't let it happen.*

She had retreated to her bed. He'd never get to sleep, and he doubted if she'd be able to, either, despite her attempt to tunnel under her covers. *Too many elephants in the room.* Craig walked to the window. The storm had passed and the white below reflected the moon bathing what might be a small park. "Snow's stopped."

"Turn off the light and go to sleep."

He left the shade opened on the window, turned off the light and settled under the blanket in the recliner. "Can't sleep." After a moment's pause he added, "I need to talk."

He saw the faint movement on her bed as she tossed off the cover. "What about?"

"You're right. I lied."

She readjusted and pulled the covers over her head. "It's not important. I'll get over it."

"I lied about not wanting children."

Trish sat up like a zombie coming out of its grave, grabbed her blue bathrobe off the bed and slipped it on. She moved past him, turned on the light and went into the kitchen area. "I'm making coffee. You want anything?"

Craig pulled the blanket over his shoulders like a cape and took a seat at her tiny dining table. "You have hot chocolate?"

"Yes. But I'm making the coffee first."

Her coffeemaker sat on the counter by the sink, stove and refrigerator, all in miniature. "I didn't realize space in Queens was so limited," he said. "Couldn't you find an apartment with more room?"

Trish brought her coffee to the table and went back to make his hot chocolate. "When I came here, I had limited funds, thanks to paying cash for my car. I needed something close to Gram's nursing home and my work. This place suited my needs. Still does."

"So…how have you been able to pay me? Your grandmother leave you enough or did you take out a loan on the house?" He accepted the hot chocolate from her and added, "None of my business." He didn't want to hear that Harrison had contributed.

"It's not a secret. Gram saved a lot more than a house full of furniture. She gave everything to me, her only grandchild. My father, her only child, didn't want any of it, including the stocks and bonds."

"So you're rich?"

"I'm comfortable."

"Harrison know that?" Okay, so he was probing too much. But everything about the guy made Craig's hackles rise. Or was it nothing more than pure jealousy on his part?

Trish curled her hand around her cup and leaned toward him. "Tell me why you now want children." So she planned to ignore his question about Harrison.

"I didn't say that."

Trish partially stood, still gripping the cup. In a second he could expect to get hot coffee in his face.

"Sit, sit," he said, motioning her to retake her seat. "I'll explain." He took a sip of his hot chocolate and burned his tongue. *Great.* "Any children I father could end up with a heart condition."

Trish plopped back in her chair. "Oh, will you cut it out with this heart-condition business. Just because your father had…"

"I have a congenital heart problem, an arrhythmia, and I'll eventually need a pacemaker. It was discovered when I had a physical for the football team. That's why I ended up taking pictures instead of playing."

Trish sat back. Obviously not impressed. "Oh, sure. And the fire department said, 'Come join us. We don't care about silly old heart problems.'"

"I'm not a fireman. I go to fires to take pictures. Some end up in the newspapers and some are used for insurance purposes, like what I did at your place." He sucked on his tongue a moment to relieve the burn. "If I so much as lift a hose, they won't let me in the firehouse again."

Trish leaned on the table. "Are you serious?"

"Yes. Scout's honor." He lifted two fingers.

"Stop it, Craig. You were never a scout." She looked away, still not believing him.

Craig took out his wallet and handed her his medical card. After studying it, she gave it back. "Is that why you carry around aspirin?" He patted his shirt pocket and nodded.

The Queen of Calm didn't appear troubled by his confession. But he knew she'd never get to sleep tonight if she downed that coffee. Craig pulled her cup away and substituted the cocoa. Trish took a sip without appearing to notice the change. She stared at the cup for a long time before looking at him again.

"Are you unhappy?"

How on earth was he supposed to answer that? The woman he loved was going to marry someone else. Of course he was unhappy. "What's your point?"

"Do you wish you were never born?"

"Of course not."

"But you wish your parents never had Noah?"

"No, I adore Noah. You're missing the whole point. People shouldn't have children when they can pass on medical problems. When I was born they didn't know, but they knew all about the possibility when Noah was conceived."

"So Noah has heart problems, too?"

Craig hesitated. "I don't know."

Trish stood and began to pace. After a few circles around the small room, she came back to the table, pushed the cocoa toward him, picked up her coffee and tossed it in the sink. "I'm going to bed." She turned off the light before coming over to face him. "Personally, Craig, I think you're an idiot."

He sat there a long time while he finished his cocoa. An idiot, really? Most people who learned about his condition felt sorry for him, which annoyed him no end. He wasn't an invalid and didn't need special treatment. It just required extra attention to details on his part to keep himself healthy.

He walked over to her bed. "Do you know what to do if I have a heart attack?"

"Press a pillow to your face and count to a thousand." Her voice came out unnaturally harsh, and he recognized the reason. She had been crying. He sat on the bed and tried massaging her shoulder.

She sat up, twisted around and hugged him, getting his neck and cheek wet. "I don't want you to die. I want you to live to be a hundred and have a wonderful life with a dozen kids just like Noah."

His sentiments exactly. He changed the subject. "I have an AED unit in my van. You know what that is?"

Trish pushed away from him and put her pillow against the wall to support her back. "A defibrillator. I learned how to use it at the nursing home." She crossed her arms over her chest and watched him. "Why did you wait till now to tell me you really have a heart condition?"

"You weren't taking me seriously and I—" he took a deep breath, then headed for the recliner "—I had begun to believe you and that Pollyanna attitude could make anything possible." He wrapped himself in the blanket. "We both have a busy day tomorrow. If your plane leaves at eleven, we should probably get to the airport by nine."

But he wouldn't be able to sleep.

"You mind telling me how that defibrillator is going to help you?" she asked. "You can't use it on yourself."

"The moment I feel a strange sensation in my chest, I'm going to run down to my van, get the unit, bring it back here and give it to you so you can zap me with electrodes."

"Yeah, and then I'm supposed to start the mouth-to-mouth resuscitation."

"Exactly. Even a heart attack has its perks."

Trish chuckled. Just what he wanted to hear. Her laugh always made him feel good.

"Right. And if I wasn't here, you'd hand it to someone else and give them directions on how to use it."

"That's the plan."

"Well, your plan stinks." He heard the catch in her voice again.

"If you don't stop this ridiculous conversation and get some sleep," he said, "I'm going to…"

"What?"

"Take this blanket and pillow and sleep in my van." He punched the pillow.

"Come over here, Craig. I really need to hug someone right now."

"Not if you're going to cry all over me."

He heard her choking back tears. "I won't. I'm the Queen of Calm. I…I can handle anything."

Yeah, but could he?

CHAPTER NINETEEN

CRAIG AWOKE TO unfamiliar smells. Someone was cooking in his apartment. When he opened his eyes, he saw Trish standing at her stove. She still wore that blue robe, something that probably belonged to her grandmother. Anyone else would have taken that inheritance and blown it on bigger digs and a better wardrobe. Instead, she'd given a good portion of it to Reverend Meyer and his charities.

Craig rose from the recliner and folded the blanket. "Okay if I take a shower?"

Trish jerked around and gasped. "I didn't realize you were awake. Sure. There are towels on the stand over the toilet. I'm making pancakes. You can eat pancakes, can't you?"

Craig took his overnight bag and headed to the bathroom. "Don't start."

"What?"

"Don't treat me with kid gloves. I'm not an endangered species."

She followed him to the bathroom door, holding a spatula. "You want to watch me shave again?" he asked over his shoulder.

"Oh, get over yourself, will you? I only asked about the pancakes because that's all I have. If you want milk, juice, eggs, bread or bacon, we have to eat somewhere else."

"You have maple syrup and butter?"

"Yes."

"Then I'll take the pancakes." He closed the door, glanced at his image in the mirror and considered punching it. He didn't share his condition with many people, afraid they'd treat him differently. Typical of Trish, though, she wouldn't let him wallow in self-pity. She hadn't hugged him last night because she felt sorry for him. In fact, along with the hugs, she'd given him a lecture on how to get on with his life. He'd been quite relieved to finally get back to the recliner.

When he came out of the bathroom all washed, shaved and refreshed, he found her dressed in what looked like a business suit, blue pants and a matching jacket over a white blouse. "You look nice," he said, taking a seat in front of a stack of pancakes. Except for those two times she'd worn a dress, he hadn't seen her in anything but grungy work clothes.

"Thank you." She glanced up and smiled. "So do you. Who are you going to be talking with?"

"An architect friend. We're going to discuss which college I should attend. I plan to pick his brain."

"You know, if you decided to go to Pratt in Brooklyn, this apartment might be a good choice for you."

Craig looked around at the minuscule space. "You're kidding. How would I ever fit a drafting table, let alone all my computer paraphernalia, in this postage stamp?" He tried the pancakes. "Delicious. Are you all packed?"

After a deep sigh, Trish took a sip of her coffee. "I suppose so. Harrison said his mother isn't into casual. Probably means she doesn't like pants, but I'm not going out in this weather in nylons and heels. I packed them along with several dresses."

After they finished breakfast, Trish stacked the dishes in the sink. "I'll leave these for the maid." She retrieved her suitcase and headed for the door.

"You have a maid?" Craig said, joining her with his own belongings.

"Yes." She grinned and pointed to herself. "Me."

"You know, Trish, it's okay to spend some of that inheritance on yourself." *You don't have to spend it all on Harrison.*

She started to laugh, something that always lightened his mood. "Like I need a maid for my tiny place."

"No, I mean a larger apartment. Maybe a new bathrobe."

"You don't like my bathrobe?"

"It looks like another relic of your grandmother's."

"Shows what you know. Your mother gave it to me for my twelfth birthday." Before he could respond, Trish said, "It still fits and keeps me warm. I'm like my grandmother. I don't replace something if it's not broken."

When they reached his van, Trish asked, "Are you planning to park in Manhattan?"

"I'll have to. I'm heading to The Village."

"That's a nightmare. You know today is Black Friday, and everyone will be shopping."

"Yes, but I'll have to park somewhere." Originally, before driving Trish to her apartment, he'd planned to stop at a Park and Ride in New Jersey and take the bus into the city.

His briefcase held everything he needed, including the USBs with all his CAD information.

"Why don't you keep it here? I'll show you where to get the subway, and you can stay in the apartment tonight. My bed's more comfortable than the recliner, and there are fresh sheets in the hope chest." She handed him her key.

"Thanks. I'll consider it." Then again, prolonging his stay at her place might not be the best idea.

TRISH PICKED UP her ticket and headed to the waiting area for her American Airlines flight. She stopped and bought a magazine. Maybe reading about other people's problems would help her forget her own. That was pretty much how she survived her job. As long as problems such as identity theft and lost credit cards weren't directly related to her, she could handle the worst. But entanglement in her own problems...

After reading the same paragraph several times, Trish gave up. If only she could see the future, see what it held for her. When she tried to visualize a life with Harrison, things weren't as clear as they'd been before she went to Riverbend.

This trip could be an eye-opener, as well. For once, she'd be able to see Harrison dealing with his family instead of people in the corporate world, where he excelled. She hoped to meet his nieces and nephews and see Harrison play with them. He'd said he wanted children, but she'd never actually seen him with any.

When Trish boarded the plane, her thoughts turned to Craig and all that he'd be missing. He was so good with his little brother. But at least Craig would follow his dream of becoming an architect.

Harrison would probably ask about her progress in finding a Realtor. She'd made none, because she didn't consider that a priority. Had he worked with Ms. Ross to sell his own property? She definitely planned to ask. Just how friendly had they been?

How could they invest in any place around New York City with him considering a position in Chicago? No rush for either of them to sell until a final decision was reached about where he would end up working. And exactly what did that mean for her? Would she be able to find work equal to her newest job or would they get married and start immediately on a family?

Once her plane landed at O'Hare, Trish tossed the magazine and headed for the baggage area. Totally unfamiliar with the Chicago airport, Trish hoped she'd be able to connect with Harrison with as little hassle as possible. As soon as she had her bag, she'd try calling him. Carrying her warm blue coat over one arm, she reached for her luggage on the carousel. Someone nudged her aside and snatched it. She turned to see who would do such a thing.

"Harrison?" She hadn't expected him. Certainly not holding a large red heart balloon with the words I LOVE YOU written in white.

"Thought your plane would never land." Harrison gripped her elbow, leaned over and kissed her. "I've been desperate to see you."

"Hi," Trish said, taking a step back. Although she was happy he'd found her in the busy airport, his over-the-top behavior was a little unsettling. Did he really need such a large balloon declaring his love for all the world to see? It wasn't Harrison.

"You'll need that coat," he said as they headed for the garage. He helped her get into it and gave her another kiss on her cheek. Being separated from her for several days sure brought out his amorous side. Why did something she'd longed for seem so unnatural?

Once they reached his car, a rented Prius rather than another Lexus, Trish asked, "How's the snow here? It was totally unexpected in New Jersey."

"Typically Chicago. The lake effect."

"I'm not creating problems for your parents, am I, staying with them?" She hated the thought that she might be putting them out. Maybe that was the reason Harrison seemed so different.

"A little late to be concerned about that. They're expecting you, and they have plenty of room."

If they had plenty of room, why wasn't he staying with them? The red heart bounced around in the backseat, reminding her that she hadn't thanked him for it. "You surprised me with the balloon. I really appreciate the sentiment."

"Glad you like it, but I can't take the credit. My niece suggested it."

"Oh, I'm looking forward to meeting her

and the rest of your relatives." Good. At least he had a close relationship with his niece.

He sighed. "You will. I wanted to show you a little of Chicago before we head to my parents'. It will give us some private time to talk. Have you contacted any Realtors?"

Trish didn't like going into subjects that could produce tension. She sensed any joy from his earlier greeting had begun to slip away.

"No. Have you contacted anyone about your place?" she asked.

He raised an eyebrow. "No. Why would I?"

"You were going to sell your condo so we could combine our funds."

"I'm leasing, Trish. Sorry, if I gave you the idea I owned my place."

She was sure…

He continued praising Chicago while he drove, but she couldn't shake the feeling something was wrong. Hadn't he said Ms. Ross helped him find his condo? Once they reached the lake, he stopped and said, "Look at that. Lake Michigan. Isn't it gorgeous?"

Whitecaps played on its surface. She couldn't see anything attractive about the water under the cloudy skies that threatened more snow. Trish wrapped her coat tighter around herself. Was it the unpredictable weather or Harrison's remark about the condo that made a chill grip her?

After listening to his travelogue for a while, she decided to find out exactly where things stood. "Will you be able to contribute anything when we buy a house?"

"Would you like a spreadsheet of my finances?"

Trish didn't know what to say. From the tone of his voice, he seemed to think she'd turned into a gold digger. "No. But I think we need to discuss this whole business at some point."

"Let's save it for now." He continued the drive, pointing to another area. "I'm getting off Lake Shore Drive and heading over to my parents' place. They live in Hyde Park, actually in a section of the University of Chicago." He concentrated on driving for a while before adding, "That's supposed to impress you, give you an idea of how my family's sitting on enormous wealth."

Again, his tone surprised her. Why was he suddenly defensive?

"How much money you or your family have is immaterial. I want honesty between us." She gripped the lapels of her coat. "And I need to know exactly what is going on with you and that Realtor, Eugenia Ross."

"What?" Harrison glanced at her a moment before he began to chuckle. "You're jealous!"

Trish shook her head.

Harrison pulled over to the side of the road and put the car in Park. He leaned on the steering wheel and grinned. "Yes, you are."

"Is there any reason I should be?"

For a few seconds he continued to grin, and her discomfort increased.

"Absolutely not, but let me enjoy the moment." He reached over and kissed her cheek, caressing her face while he talked. "I haven't even seen Eugenia in over six months. I admit, I saw her a few times while I was looking for a place to live, but nothing ever clicked between us, and by then you had my full interest." He pulled back. "I kind of like it when you're green-eyed with jealousy. It shows how much you really care." He put the car in gear and pulled into the street.

Trish sat back, annoyed. She wasn't a moneygrubbing green-eyed monster, was she? *Let it go*, she cautioned. Harrison said his interest in Ms. Ross ended more than six months ago, about the time Trish and Harrison started dating. *Accept that and let it go.*

After traveling through the college, he stopped in front of a three-story brick building in what appeared to be a group of residential houses. He waved a hand at the building. "This is where I grew up. Built in 1906 and under continuous renovations and upgrades since then. One of the reasons I had no desire to live in your grandmother's old house."

They sat for several minutes staring at the house while he talked. "You're about to meet the great and all-knowing Dr. Mitchell Morris, the renowned biology professor— retired—and fisherman extraordinaire. We'll be lucky if he's awake and sober. And one cannot forget the great and worldly Dr. Maureen Morris, also retired."

Trish wasn't sure if she should comment, but the more he talked, the less comfortable she felt. "Is your mother a medical doctor?"

"On occasion. She has tried doing heart transplants, but the patients always die."

Trish stared at him, stunned. "What are you talking about? Your mother is a heart doctor?"

Harrison chortled. "No. Her doctorate is in

history. She publishes on a regular basis, but I'm sure you haven't read any of her books. Few have."

"I don't understand. There's no way I can relate to the problems you have with your parents if you don't explain."

"And your parents are so perfect?"

"No. We disagree on a lot of things, but I don't go bad-mouthing them. It's like you want me to dislike your parents as much as you do before I've even met them."

"I'm sorry," Harrison said in a more subdued tone. "I've had a miserable week. I can't possibly make you understand what it was like growing up with two demanding intellectuals."

She hoped they'd have a chance to talk more. She really did want to understand the dynamics of his family. How would his experiences affect how he'd be as a husband and father?

Harrison opened his door, and Trish watched him come around to open hers.

She felt uneasy, not sure of what to expect. How much antagonism would his family have toward her? An excruciating cold wind pulled her coat open as she got out of the car. She followed Harrison while strug-

gling to pull the folds of the blue coat together. It felt as though Chicago was telling
her she wasn't wanted. Not exactly the best
omen.

CHAPTER TWENTY

CRAIG LEFT HIS truck parked safely at Trish's apartment and followed her directions to the subway. The company interested in his CAD program had used it several times with his guidance. Now they wanted to purchase the license and pick his brains about other projects. They'd asked him to come up with a price, and he had, one that would cover his expenses for room and board when he went back to college. His grants were intact, so he didn't have to worry about tuition.

He took the subway to Union Square and walked a few blocks after getting off the train. The air, although crisp, didn't promise any more snow. Most of the accumulation from last night had melted, with a few plowed piles restricting parking. Good thing he'd left the van in Queens.

Craig had visited the office of Gene and Gerald Enterprises on 6th Avenue a few times before, but never to talk with the CEO.

Craig avoided the elevator and went up the two flights of stairs to their office.

"Is Mr. Rogers available?" Craig asked the administrative assistant. They'd met before, but he doubted if she'd remember him. "I'm Craig Cadman, and I have an appointment with Gene."

The well-dressed older woman gave him an endearing smile. "Yes, Mr. Cadman. He came in specifically to meet you. So nice to see you again." She rose from her desk and directed him to Mr. Rogers's office. After a soft knock, she opened the door. "Gene, Craig Cadman is here."

Craig walked over to a large mahogany desk. The man behind it stood and reached across to take Craig's outstretched hand. "This is great. Take a seat. I was expecting someone a little older but, hey, today even kids in kindergarten are skilled with computers."

They talked about Craig's patented CAD program, which Gene had been using—on a trial basis—for a while. "You mentioned wanting to license your program. I'm interested, but only if I can have you on retainer to handle any problems and potential improvements." After more discussion, they shook hands again. Craig left with Gene's promise to buy his program.

Barely able to tamp down his delight, Craig skipped down the steps and out of the building. He wanted to share his enthusiasm. With Trish. Of course it had to be Trish. He came to a complete stop. People began bumping into him, so he moved to the side.

Trish wasn't part of his life. When would he accept that fact? He couldn't believe how important her opinions and responses had become in the last few weeks. He'd never be able to share with her again. She was committed to Harrison, meeting her future in-laws in Chicago, planning her wedding. Craig pounded his fist into his palm.

Get over it. She's gone.

"I'LL GET YOUR LUGGAGE from the car once you meet my parents," Harrison said. After ringing the doorbell, he pushed the door open. "Mother," he called out, "Trish arrived."

A woman with lovely silver hair came to greet them, her arms outstretched. "My dear. How wonderful to finally meet you." After a substantial hug, Maureen helped Trish out of her coat. "Harrison, will you take care of this for me?" She handed it to her son, who disappeared into another area.

"You have a lovely home," Trish said, looking at the flower arrangements on the sideboard. Beyond she could see highly polished antiques and a cabinet filled with fine bone china.

"Come, sit down," Maureen said after taking Trish into a warm, paneled living room. "Would you like something to drink? Have you had lunch?"

When Trish shook her head, Maureen grasped Trish's hands and said, "What's the matter with that boy? It's nearly two. You must be starving." She turned away and called out, "Greta, could you come here a moment?" Thanks to the new time zone, it was actually closer to three for Trish, and she had begun to feel quite hungry.

A woman close to Trish's age came in. She wore blond braids wrapped around her head and a peasant-style blouse. "Please make some sandwiches for our guest. Use yesterday's turkey. And soup. Trish isn't used to our windy city." As an afterthought, she added, "And make something for Harrison."

Maureen rose. "Come on, dear. We can eat in the kitchen." She continued to talk while she directed Trish through the house. "Harrison told us about your grandmother's place, and how you're selling her furniture. Henry's Antiques. I looked it up on the internet. Lovely, priceless treasures. Why aren't you keeping them? They'd be perfect for when you and Harrison get married. When will that be, by the way? I hope you won't wait too long. I'd really like to have more grandchildren before I die."

Maureen continued her monologue while Greta brought a plate of turkey sandwiches on whole wheat and a large porcelain cauldron of noodle soup to the table. "Would you like tea or coffee?" Greta asked in what sounded like a German accent. She began ladling out the soup.

Harrison took a seat opposite Trish and reached for a sandwich from the large plate. "I washed my hands," he said, the words directed at his mother.

"Oh, for goodness' sake, Harry. Will you stop that?" She turned to Trish. "He used to come in from playing and never wash his hands." Maureen closed her eyes and took a deep breath, then gave her son's hand a quick tap. "You're giving poor Trish here the wrong impression of us." Maureen rose with the poise of someone at the queen's table. "You two enjoy your lunch, and if you need anything else, please ask Greta. I need to make a few phone calls."

When she had gone, Harrison said, "She's not making any calls." He turned to Greta, who cut up vegetables on the central island. An array of copper pots hung above her. "Am I right, Greta? She just wants to escape."

Greta met his gaze, but she kept any opinions to herself.

Harrison turned back to Trish. "You have any idea how many times I've told her not to call me Harry?"

Trish chose to follow Greta's example and not say anything.

"Can you guess where Greta's from?"

"Germany, maybe?"

"Good guess. My mother employs students from the university, but they need to have an ethnic air. She prefers her help to wear their 'native' clothes. The braids may be real, but the accent isn't. Greta speaks better English than most middle-class Americans."

Trish shifted in her seat. Talking about Greta in front of her that way seemed rude.

"So, what do you think of my mother? Remind you in any way of the witch in *Snow White*? Don't accept any shiny apples from her."

"She's quite nice." *You, on the other hand...* Why was Harrison acting this way? His mother had been gracious, helping to relieve Trish's apprehensions. Now her tension had come back doubled.

Harrison tossed his napkin on the table, picked up his sandwich and started for the side door. "I'll get your luggage, and then I'm heading out. You can come with me or not. Your choice, but I'm leaving right after I finish this sandwich." He took a large bite before heading to the car.

CRAIG WALKED TO Washington Square, not really paying attention to the sights or noises of New York. He passed New York University, where he could have applied, but he'd decided against it. Craig wanted to live close to any school he attended, and Manhattan rents and parking would break him. He hoped his friend Victor Bertram, an architect and mentor, could help him decide which school to attend.

At first Victor had recommended they

meet at the Village Underground, but Craig said no. He'd been there before and knew they'd never be able to talk. Besides, it probably didn't open until the evening, when they had entertainment. They'd decided on Nunez's Pizza, located near the university. Since students had no classes that Friday, they might actually find a seat and be able to have a conversation. Craig found the tiny storefront with no problem, but it was filled with students—who had no classes to attend.

"Hey, you made it." Victor stood and directed Craig to a chair. He'd shaved his head the moment his blond hair started to thin, and he looked a little older than his forty years. "I already ordered the pepperoni and green peppers. While we're waiting, I can help you decide between Pratt and NYIT."

"I've pretty much decided on Pratt. Since I already have a bachelor of science in math, I can get my master of architecture in three years. It would take four years to get a bachelor of architecture at NYIT."

"Then what am I here for?" Victor pushed over a bottle of beer.

"I need your opinion on whether or not I'd be missing out on a lot of basics by not going through the bachelor course."

"Your BS is in math? That's an excellent foundation."

"Yes, but most of my schooling was on-line. I was too young to start college when I graduated from high school. Now I'll be older than most of the students with a lot less school experience. First time in my life I've been older than anyone."

Victor started to laugh. "I don't believe this. Since when did you start doubting your abilities? Man! You've got more experience than half the people I know. Computer programs, photography and a contracting license. You did excellent work on my projects, by the way, and I've given your name to several people." Victor sat back, no longer laughing, but his smile continued to grow. "So, what's really bothering you?" He slapped the table and pointed at Craig. "Woman problems?"

Craig didn't say anything, but he could feel the heat rising up his neck. He shook his head and looked away. When the waitress smiled at him, Craig turned back to Victor. "No. Not really."

"Oh, come on," Victor said, leaning closer. "You met someone?"

Craig shook his head again and tried to think of how he could change the subject.

"I see the signs, kid. You've got it bad. What happened?"

Okay, so he'd tell Victor something to stop his prying. "She's engaged to someone else."

"So, do something about it. Women have been known to break engagements. Get out there and show her you're the better man."

Craig rubbed his eyes and began chuckling. Victor had no clue. "Trish…"

"Her name's Trish? What's that stand for? Trisha, Patricia?"

"It's Trish, and I'm not what she wants. Could we drop this?"

"No way. Wait till I tell my wife. You know she's been trying to hook you up with someone from the get-go. She'll give this Trish—"

Craig slammed a fist on the table. "Don't. She's marrying someone else, and that's the end of it."

Victor backed away, his palms in the air. "Okay, okay, man. Sorry." He moved to one side while the waitress placed their pie on the table.

She turned to Craig. "Can I get you anything else? Another beer?"

He hadn't even touched the one Victor had given him. With a glance in her direction, Craig said, "No, thank you. This will do."

Victor reached over and tapped the woman's shoulder. "Listen, sweetheart, this fellow just lost his girlfriend. Anything you could do to help him?"

"Sure." She bit her lip and watched him a moment. "I get off at two. Coffee?"

Craig took a slice of the pizza. "Sounds wonderful, but I have to pick up my wife and kid at the museum. Noah loves those dinosaurs. Maybe another time." He looked up and smiled.

When she left in a huff, Craig turned to Victor. "You try that again and you'll be wearing this beer."

TRISH WENT LOOKING for her coat. If only she had taken the hat Craig had given her. Not that neon orange would go with the blue, but at least it would keep her warm. When Harrison came in with her suitcase, she walked up to him. "Okay. We're heading out. I told Greta to tell your mother. What time do you expect to come back?"

With a shrug he said, "Whenever." He smiled and looked as though he planned to kiss her. She moved away before he could get that close. She went out the door into a fierce wind, her hair flying around her face. Harrison was right behind her and opened the passenger door of his rental.

They didn't talk while he drove. After a few minutes, he pulled into a side street and put the car in Park. "This area was known as White City at one time because of its numerous lights, although some would say because of its segregation. A World's Fair was held here in 1893. Most of the buildings burned down two years later. But one left standing was made into the Museum of Science and Industry, one of the largest in the world. My mother published a history of the fair, and I helped with some of the research."

He stopped talking and looked at her, possibly expecting a comment. Trish barely took any of it in, still consumed with what had happened back at his mother's.

"This was my sanctuary," Harrison continued. "Whenever I had problems at home or at school, I'd come here to the museum. Often several times a week."

Trish turned to face him, realizing this was the first time he'd shared anything about his family life. "What problems?" she asked.

"I'm the fourth son. My older brothers, who you'll meet tomorrow, all have their doctorate degrees. I'm the black sheep, and I've been reminded of that on a daily basis." He paused. After clearing his throat, Harrison said, "I never fulfilled the family goal. I didn't get my doctorate. Made it through my master's, what most people would consider an achievement, but since I quit after that, I failed to fulfill my mother's dream."

She had no idea he'd had such an extensive education. "What field were you in?"

"Communication."

"Well, that certainly helped you at work. You're great at—"

"I didn't achieve other family goals, as well. I never married. All my brothers married and started families. My mother always insisted that I should, too. So now I can finally make her happy. And you, too. You want all those children."

Trish felt numb. Was the cold seeping in? Snowflakes swirled around the windshield. "You never wanted children?" she asked, her voice barely audible above the car's engine.

He remained silent. Finally, after taking a deep breath, he turned on the windshield wipers and dusted off the accumulation.

"Yes, I want children. At least, I think I want them. It's expected of me and important to you, but frankly… I can't picture myself with kids."

"How do you picture yourself? I mean, ideally, what do you see yourself doing, say, five years from now, or even ten?"

"Ideally?" He sat back and watched the windshield wipers. "I know what I *should* say, sitting next to my fiancée in the midst of an argument. But…" He turned and gave her a woeful smile. "As you'll probably hear from my family later on, I'm not too good at doing what I should do."

"I didn't realize we were arguing. I thought that for once, we were actually talking. I'm not marrying your family. I—"

"Oh, yes, you are. You marry me and you get all my baggage. A mother I love but often can't stand to be around, three brothers who never do anything wrong and their beautiful wives who pop out gorgeous babies every two years. I've been asked over and over, 'Why can't you be like your brothers? They finish what they start.'"

Trish could feel his pain but had no idea what to say. She wanted children. Maybe it was too much to ask for. Neither Harrison nor Craig wanted them as much as she did.

"I never finished that food Greta put out," she said. "Could we get something to eat? Let's keep talking. I feel I'm finally seeing you."

He put the car in gear and moved slowly onto the street. "Oh, that's not a good sign. Finally seeing the true me?"

"It's a very good sign. I don't want to marry a stranger. For that matter, I may have secrets to share, as well."

"Do you snore when you sleep?"

Trish chuckled, feeling a little less panicked. "I don't."

"Really? I'm looking forward to finding out."

CHAPTER TWENTY-ONE

IT WAS CLOSE to six o'clock on Friday when Craig reached Trish's apartment. He was gripping her key in his pocket, pressing the metal points into his palm. He'd debated during the entire subway trip whether or not he should use it, sleep in her bed and dream of holding her in his arms. He decided against a restless night of unfulfilled yearnings. Why torture himself? The sooner he accepted Trish was gone, the sooner he could start thinking of his future.

After returning the key to her super, Craig called his mother, who invited him to dinner. Good, because they had a lot to discuss: his plans to attend Pratt, the dissolution of the handyman business and his brother's health. Had Noah inherited the same heart problems as Craig and their father? When he pulled into his aunt Jenny's driveway, he saw Max's truck. That was for the best, because he had to sever some ties with Max, as well.

Craig greeted his aunt at her door and pulled her into a bear hug. "I hope you have leftovers from yesterday." The moment he released his aunt, Noah propelled himself at him. Craig reached down and picked him up.

Noah wiped sticky hands against his cheek. "You need a shave."

When Craig rubbed his nose against Noah's, also sticky, he said, "You may be right, but let's eat first. Any turkey legs left?"

Noah scowled. "Nah. The turkey only had two."

"Next year, let's get a turkey with four legs."

Noah nodded. "Then all the men can have one."

"What, no legs for the ladies in the family?" Rachel came over with a wet washcloth and wiped Noah's hands. When she finished, Craig took the cloth and scrubbed his brother's face as well as his own.

"S'okay," Noah said. "I'll share mine with Trish."

Craig took a deep breath and pressed his lips together. He noticed all the other adults did the same.

"Did she make it to Chicago okay?" Rachel asked.

Craig piled his plate with sliced breast meat and a large helping of stuffing. "Yes. She sent a text. Said the wind could blow a person away."

Rachel rotated her shoulders as though she'd felt a chill. "Looks like winter has settled in for keeps here. Anything happen with your CAD program?"

"Yes. It's sold."

Rachel gasped and clapped her hands. "Enough to cover your room and board?"

"And then some. Gene Rogers is paying me a retainer that can help you out, since I'll be closing the handyman business."

"She can work full-time for me now." Max reached over, gripped her shoulder and placed a kiss on her cheek.

Rachel's face went pink, and she glanced around the room, catching Craig's gaze. He looked away and kept his amusement to himself. Another elephant had entered the room.

"I've decided on Pratt. I'll need to find an apartment before the semester starts in January. Know anyone who'd be interested in my place? I used to think it was small before I saw Trish's apartment—it's half the size of mine."

"But when she gets married..." Rachel

hesitated. "She's getting something else, isn't she, since she's not keeping her grandmother's place?"

Craig nodded.

Max passed him the gravy. "Is her house finished inside? The crew completed the outside painting before the storm hit. They're taking the scaffolding down Monday."

"I'll be painting inside until the work is done, maybe two or three more days."

"Sounds like you've got it under control. Oh, and I'd appreciate you returning the knuckleboom. I've got an order for it the middle of next week."

"Sure, Max. And, Mom, figure out her final bill. Trish wants to take care of it when she comes back from Chicago."

"She coming here to Riverbend?" Rachel asked.

"Just to pick up her car and some personal stuff of her grandmother's." Craig placed a few green beans on Noah's plate. They immediately came back onto his. "By the way, Mom, did you give Trish a blue bathrobe?"

"Years ago. Why?" His mother had a twinkle in her eye. She probably thought...

"She wore it last night. And it's...seen better days." The pile of beans on his plate had grown. Noah sat next to him, tittering. "Oh, my favorite." Craig began shoveling the beans into his mouth while Noah tried to contain himself. When Craig finished, he said, "No more. I've had my fill of string beans until the next Thanksgiving." He glanced up to see his mother moving the plate of beans out of Noah's reach.

"What about that bathrobe?" Rachel continued to give him an all-knowing look.

"I thought if she's still around this Christmas, it might be nice to replace it with something…"

"Something more feminine, maybe with a little lace?"

Craig shook his head. "She's always cold, Mom. Something full-length in fur would be better."

Lace wasn't what he had in mind. Especially when he'd never be able to see her in it.

AFTER CRAIG AND Noah shaved, Craig put his brother to bed. His beard was never that pronounced, and three shaves in two days had taken a toll.

They read Dr. Seuss's *Horton Hears a Who!*, with Noah correcting Craig anytime he drifted from the print on the page. Maybe

Noah was following in his brother's footsteps and could already read. Craig had been at a second-grade reading level when he was four. He hoped any similarities between the two stopped there.

When Craig went downstairs, he found his aunt and uncle watching TV in the living room. His mother and Max sat shoulder to shoulder at the kitchen table, skimming a magazine together. They looked up and put some space between them when Craig took a seat.

"Okay if I interrupt?"

Rachel stood and walked to the stove. "Nothing to interrupt. Would you like some tea?" She reached for the kettle and placed it over the burner.

Craig eyed Max, who squirmed in his seat. "Anything you want to ask me?" Craig said, leaning both arms on the table.

Max managed to control himself and pressed his lips together. "Like what?"

"Well, since I'm the eldest male in the immediate family, maybe you'd like to get something off your chest."

Rachel came over and began massaging Max's shoulders and neck. "There are times when he can be a real pain in the backside," she said, speaking to Max but directing the words at Craig.

Max took Rachel's hand and guided her to the chair. Once she was seated, he clasped her hands but kept his eyes glued on Craig. "I would like to ask the elder man of this family to allow me to make this beautiful woman—" he glanced at Rachel "—my wife."

Craig swatted the table with his palm. "It's about time!" Rachel and Max smiled, before she fell into Max's embrace. He kissed her on the cheek, then made a point of turning her face so he could kiss her quite possessively on the lips.

"You could be getting more than you bargained for, *Dad*. I'll be going back to college and hitting you up for spending money." Craig rubbed his fingers against his thumb. "And I predict Noah will be starting college, as well, probably next year. He can already read *Horton Hears a Who!*"

Rachel started laughing. "I have such smart boys."

"Well, you won't get money from me," Max said. "I expect my architectural *son* to take care of me and my bride as soon as he gets his degree."

"Serious for a moment." Craig walked over

to Rachel and Max and wrapped his arms around them, pulling them into a three-way hug. He kissed his mother on her cheek. "I couldn't be happier for you." As much as he wanted to talk to his mother about Noah, Craig felt it wasn't a good time. Why spoil their joy?

WITHIN MINUTES OF their arrival back in the house, Greta asked if they'd like to finish the food they'd left. Since they hadn't stopped to eat, Trish was still hungry. Greta had the sandwiches in front of them, along with bowls of hot soup, the moment they sat down at the table. Greta excused herself so they were alone in the kitchen.

"So, what secrets are you going to share?" Harrison asked.

"I haven't been totally honest."

"About what?"

"I don't want to sell my grandmother's house. At least not now."

"What do you plan to do with it? I told you my feelings. I'm not about to live in another old house. Dave may think those antique tubs are lovely, but I think they're hideous. We have five bathrooms here, and two have those tubs." Harrison shuddered.

"I can lease it and keep it in the family. Maybe our children will want it one day."

"As landlord, you'd be responsible for its upkeep. How will you do that if we move to Chicago or somewhere else? It's a drain, Trish, on all of our resources."

"My friend Rachel talked about turning it into a bed-and-breakfast. She and her son could live there. I'd keep the mortgage and…"

"Who's Rachel?"

"Craig's mother."

Harrison pushed away from the table, walked to the counter and leaned against it. "Craig the handyman?" He didn't look happy.

Trish nodded, but before she could say anything more, Harrison came back to the table and took his seat. "What's going on with you two?"

"Nothing." Certainly nothing like what his tone suggested.

"In case you haven't noticed, the guy has a crush on you, and I don't like it." Harrison stood and said, "That puppy-dog expression of total adoration gets a little tiring when it's directed at my fiancée."

Trish held up her hand. "Stop this right now. Craig is going back to college. Noah,

Rachel's other son, will be the one living with her."

Harrison dropped back in his seat and moved closer to her. "You don't deny he adores you?"

"Craig has been asking me to marry him since he was nine. At least a dozen times. And your proposal is the only one I've ever said yes to. Why can't you accept that I chose you, and I'm marrying you?"

Harrison put his elbow on the table and pressed his head into his hand. "I do. I do." He looked at her again and smiled. "Since he was nine?"

She nodded.

"What's Craig the handyman going to do in college? Never mind. I don't want to know. Just as long as he spends the next ten years there and away from you."

Greta came back into the kitchen, and they dropped their discussion. "How do you like Chicago weather, Greta?" Trish asked.

Greta smiled. "Love it. Reminds me of home. I'm hoping to get a chance to go skiing. Probably around Christmastime when school lets out."

Trish brought their empty dishes to the

sink. "Oh, I can do that," Greta said and looked guiltily toward Harrison.

"Don't be silly. I…"

Harrison came over and whispered in Trish's ear. "She's the maid. You want her to lose her job?"

Had Harrison lost his mind? Why would Greta be fired for…?

Trish turned to see Maureen standing in the doorway. "Greta," she said, in a voice that exuded authority. "Have you finished preparing for tonight's supper?"

Harrison watched Trish and raised his eyebrows. She leaned against him and whispered, "I will not accept any shiny apples."

He whispered back. "Promise? I wouldn't want to lose you."

"Promise."

"Come on. I'll show you to your room."

They took a boxy staircase made of dark polished wood to the second floor. Nothing as grand as the curved oak in her grandmother's house. "You'll be staying in what used to be my room." He opened the door, one of many in the wood-paneled hall. "Not that you'd know it. My mother removed anything that reminded her of me and replaced it with antiques. I wouldn't sit on the Sheridan chair.

It's been known to collapse whenever anyone over twenty pounds uses it. My mother usually re-glues it with a paste made from flour and water that never really works."

"I've used some very good wood glue I can recommend."

"No. She doesn't believe antiques should look like new and be serviceable. They're supposed to look old and used and be as useless as dust bunnies."

Could that be true? Trish had begun to wonder about his mother's judgment. Maybe Harrison's opinion of her was on the mark.

Harrison placed her bag on the bed. "You can use the closet here—" he pointed to another door "—and the bathroom with one of those tubs you love is there." He reached for her and wrapped his arms around her shoulders. "I'll give you some time to freshen up. If my mother follows her usual routine, we'll meet in the library for a drink at six before dinner." Deliberately and quite sweetly, Harrison hugged and kissed her. Maybe things could work out for them after all.

"Don't be late. And it's formal. I have to go back to my hotel for my suit."

Formal? Did his family do that all the time? She had come prepared for only one special occasion. Thank goodness she'd brought her full-length dress she usually wore at Christmas.

Trish sat on the bed with her phone. She smiled when she saw Craig had sent a text.

Sold the CAD. Found your other mitten. Let me know if you need a ride from the airport. LYWAM Imperfect H.

It didn't take Trish long to decipher the code: Love You With All My Imperfect Heart.

Trish sighed and erased Craig's note in case Harrison ever looked at her phone messages. After several false starts, she sent one back to Craig.

Congrats on the sale. Won't need a ride. Thanks.

For several moments, Trish gripped her phone and stared at it. She wanted to say so much more. She missed him. She hoped he'd enjoy his classes, and she wanted to share every new thing he learned. Would he ever design a special house for her? If he did, she'd sell her grandmother's house so she'd have the money to pay for it.

A soft knock on her door startled Trish. "Yes? Who is it?"

"Greta."

Trish rushed to the door to let her in.

"I brought you fresh towels. Would you like me to draw a bath?"

Trish tried to take the towels, but Greta sidestepped her and put them in the bathroom. Trish wasn't used to any kind of servant, especially one who wouldn't allow her to do anything on her own. When Greta went to the footed tub to turn on the water, Trish stopped her.

"Thank you. I prefer not to take my bath now." Not wanting to hurt Greta's feelings, Trish followed her into the bedroom. "You have a lovely blouse. Is it really what you wear back in Germany?"

Greta gave a neutral smile. "No. I wear modern clothes like you. Dr. Morris requires this." She glanced at the luggage sitting on the bed. "Should I unpack your bag?"

"No. Thank you. If I need any help, I'll give you a call."

Alone again, Trish unpacked her bag and hung her dresses in the closet. With nothing to do until she had to dress for dinner, she decided to call her mother. "Guess where I am?" she said, once her mother answered.

"Well, I hope you're not on the roof putting up Christmas lights like someone else I know." After a slight pause, her mother said, "You aren't, are you?"

"No. I'm in Chicago, meeting my future in-laws." Trish heard the exasperation in her mother's voice. "Why are you so upset?"

"Oh, I'm sorry. I shouldn't be so irritable but your father..." Her mother continued, totally ignoring what Trish had said about Chicago. "That man decided to deck the RV with Christmas lights. All the people at the campground are doing that." Her voice rose. "And he keeps blowing a fuse!"

"Can he hear you?"

"I certainly hope so." Her volume increased. "Tom, your daughter's on the phone. Come in and speak to her." Her voice softened. "Keep him on the line while I try and figure out what he's doing wrong."

Trish spent the next few minutes talking to her father, answering questions and assuring him he didn't have to pay for her wedding. She planned to handle everything herself.

"I found Gram's Christmas lights. Would you like me to send you some?"

"Nah. I bought those white ones that look like icicles. Toss the others. They're probably not good anymore."

"I thought it would be nice to decorate the house one more time."

"Don't you do that! I hated it every time you went on that roof. Alice, you hear that? She wants to put the Christmas decorations on Gram's house."

Her mother came back on the line, and they both told Trish every horror story they could think of to discourage her from decorating her grandmother's place. *You'd think I started a war.* It took a while, but Trish finally managed to calm them and disconnect.

She spent the rest of the afternoon preparing for the formal dinner. The antique tub had rust stains around the drain. The water came out fast and hot, but the stopper didn't work, and the water quickly leaked out. Nonetheless, she managed to make the best of it. Once she was through, Trish added a dab of Chanel under her ears.

Her simple sheath in red wool should keep her warm and be dressy enough for any occasion. After putting her hair up with fancy clips, Trish slipped into black heels and grabbed a lacy black crocheted shawl that had been Gram's. It not only provided warmth but also gave an elegance to the simple lines of her dress. Taking a deep breath and a positive attitude, she headed into the hall and went searching for the library. She met Harrison at the bottom of the stairs.

In her heels, they were nearly the same height. He drew her into an embrace and nuzzled her neck. "You look lovely and smell divine. Is that the perfume I gave you?"

"It's the Chanel I had you buy. Remember? I couldn't wear the one you gave me."

"Right." He took in a deep breath and kissed her neck. "I like this one even more."

He'd better. She didn't want him thinking about the perfume Ms. Ross wore.

He hooked her arm and headed for another room. "I believe my parents are expecting other guests."

"Your brothers and their families?"

"No. Just some friends. They want to show you off."

When they walked into the library, a room filled with bookcases that reached the high ceiling, Trish noticed a faint odor of decay.

Probably due to the thousands of books cramming the bookcases. Harrison's mother came over to them and grasped Trish's hand. "I want you to meet my soon-to-be daughter-in-law, if I can get Harry to finally set the date," Maureen said. Trish felt Harrison's arm tighten against hers, but he didn't chide his mother about the nickname. Trish felt nervous laughter bubble inside her as she thought of Craig's nickname. How would Harrison like being called Butchy? She managed to control herself, but her apprehension didn't leave.

"These are our dear friends Betty and Frank Bremerton. I should say Dr. Frank, the only medical doctor in the room." Maureen stepped aside, gripped another man's arm and brought him into the group. "And this is my husband. Dr. Mitchell Morris." Mitchell handed Trish a glass of red wine.

Great. All she needed was to add a massive headache to her unease.

Trish accepted the glass graciously and looked for someplace where she could pour it out. Harrison leaned over, kissed her by her ear again and whispered, "I'll get you something else after the toast."

She smiled at him, grateful that he remembered red wine always gave her migraines. It was going to be a long night, but at least she could count on Harrison.

CHAPTER TWENTY-TWO

WHEN THEY ENTERED the dining area, another wood-paneled room, Trish and Harrison took seats across from the two guests, the Bremertons. Maureen sat to Trish's left at one end of the table, and Mitchell was at the other end. A maroon runner connected Harrison's parents.

"So, you're in medicine?" Trish said to Frank Bremerton. "Do you have a specialty?"

"Yes. I'm a heart surgeon."

Immediately Trish thought of Craig and felt her dread increase. Should she bring up his condition? Why pursue the topic? She wouldn't run back to Craig and report what this man said. And for all she knew, anything she heard might make her worry more about Craig's condition. She turned to Betty. "Do you also work in the medical field?"

Trish moved to the side and allowed Greta to place a portion of meat on her plate, something that smelled of vinegar. The dish, a faded blue with wisps of darker leaves scattered across the porcelain, had a tiny chip on the edge. Glancing around, Trish noted hers wasn't the only imperfect plate. Why hadn't they used the china she'd seen in the china cabinet?

"Oh, my, no. I'm a stay-at-home mom. My son is nearly nine."

"And he's brilliant," Frank added. "He's at the top of his class and quite possibly will be skipping ahead a year." Betty smiled at her husband and patted his hand.

"Isn't that wonderful?" Maureen said. "A future doctor."

Again Trish was reminded of Craig. "That comes with its own challenges," she said. She accepted more food from Greta, this time white asparagus, and thanked her.

"What do you mean?" Betty asked and looked at Trish as though she'd said something insulting about their only child.

All the people around the table as well as Greta waited for her reply. She glanced at Harrison and wasn't sure she should continue. He'd already mentioned his annoyance with anything relating to Craig. At the moment, though, he seemed more interested in removing some cloves from his gravy. He pushed them to the side of the dish.

"So you think we should hold him back?"

"Like she would know," Maureen said. "Trish hasn't had any children yet, and she has no idea what that entails."

After taking a calming breath, Trish decided to dive in. "But I do know. My best friend is a genius. He has photographic memory and hasn't lost a chess match against adults since he was ten. After skipping two grades, he graduated when he was fifteen. During that time, he was younger and shorter than most people in his classes and was bullied. It's not an easy life to be smarter than everyone else."

Harrison continued to play with the cloves. Had he even paid attention? Of course she hadn't mentioned Craig by name.

Betty leaned toward Trish. "What happened to him?"

Trish felt energized. Talking about Craig and his achievements always made her feel that way. "He aced every class and was offered countless scholarships but used them to get his degree online instead of attending a regular college. He finally grew several inches and got his contracting license so he could work with his father as a handyman."

"So he never used his potential, his brains?" Maureen asked.

"He earned his bachelor of science in math, and now he's going for his master of architecture."

Greta looked as though she might want to add something to the conversation. After glancing at Maureen, however, she went back to her task and began dishing out some red cabbage. More vinegar and cloves.

Harrison grasped Trish's hand. "Eat some of your food before it gets cold. It's German sauerbraten."

Trish looked up to Greta. "How wonderful. I learned how to make spaetzle and sauerbraten in one of my cooking classes." She took a bite. The vinegar nearly took her breath away. She'd had sauerbraten before and knew this wasn't the best. She scooped up some of the spaetzle, a bland noodle, to help relieve her taste buds. "Wow. This is amazing. How long did it take you to make it?"

Greta glanced at Maureen before answering. "I'm not the cook."

Maureen chuckled. "No, we get our authentic food from a German restaurant."

"Oh, I'd like to know their name." *So I can make sure I never go there.*

Trish asked for another helping of spaetzle so she could finish the meal. After serving the food, Greta went back to the kitchen. When she was out of sight and hearing, Maureen leaned closer to Trish. "We don't talk to the servants while they're working."

Trish sat back after the reprimand and wondered what twilight zone she'd wandered into. She glanced in Harrison's direction and caught a fleeting smile.

Conversation flowed easily while they ate, although Trish noted Harrison and his father continued to eat their food and drink German beer without comment.

When they had finished, Maureen invited everyone back for another drink in the library. Harrison placed an arm around Trish's shoulders. "I've got to get back to my hotel, and I'd like to say good-night to Trish before I go." He started for the staircase, maneuvering her in that direction.

Trish twisted away. "It was nice meeting you," she said over her shoulder before Harrison guided her up the stairs and opened the door to her room.

"So what do you think?"

"Of the food or the people?" Trish took a seat on the bed, not willing to risk the Sheridan chair. Harrison sat next to her. He took her hand in his and began playing with her engagement ring.

"I was thinking more of the conversation. That passionate speech about your friend."

Was Harrison angry with her? "What about it?"

Harrison got off the bed, ran his hand through his hair and walked several feet away before turning to face her. "Remember when I told you how his mooning over you bothered me?" He held up a palm facing her when she started to rise. "Well, it's pretty much the same thing when you talk about him and light up like a Christmas tree in Rockefeller Center."

Harrison scratched his head and looked away. When he did focus on her again, he said, "This engagement is like a dam holding back your true feelings. If we call it off, your feelings could run free. We could see where they head."

Trish stood, putting a tentative hand out

to him. He grasped it and pulled her toward him.

"Would you run to him?" He paused. "Maybe you'd like to accept one of his proposals."

"There's no going back to Craig." Not when she had no chance of a future with him.

"Oh, but you have thought about it? While you spent all that time in Riverbend?" Harrison waited a moment before adding, "During the time you've been engaged to me?"

When she didn't reply, he stepped away.

"You've pretty much answered my question." He pressed his lips together before adding, "I can't go on this way with someone who isn't committed to me. I need 100 percent of your loyalty. If you can't give me that—we shouldn't get married."

Trish had never felt so alone. Was this it? Were they breaking up? She felt an urgent need to grasp something, to ensure that she wouldn't fall. Trish adjusted the shawl around her shoulders to ward off a sudden chill and hugged herself. She wanted comfort, some physical connection with another human being, and she realized she didn't want it from Harrison.

Trish walked back to the bed and sat down, her hands clutching the comforter. "You're right. I guess I haven't given you 100 percent." She realized she had no desire to marry Harrison, and she began removing her ring. "I'm so sorry if I hurt you." She held it out to him. "It wasn't my intention. I really thought we could make a life together."

"No, keep it," he said when Trish tried to give it back.

She shook her head, walked over and dropped it into his jacket pocket. "The dam is shattered." Trish didn't attempt a further explanation.

They both knew she'd never ask for the ring back.

Trish couldn't stay at his parents' house now that the engagement was broken. Nor could she stay at his hotel. Thankfully Harrison understood. "I'll drive you to the airport," Harrison said after she changed her clothes and packed her bag. "If you have trouble turning in your return ticket, I'll pay any expense."

"Whatever it is, I can handle it. I should thank your parents before I go."

"Absolutely not. The witch will burn you with her acid tears."

"Don't be silly."

"Have I been wrong about her so far?"

Trish hesitated. She'd never met anyone like his mother before, and she didn't understand some of her weird practices. Who served their guests on old, chipped china or kept furniture in a guest's room that could fall apart? But she did want to say goodbye to Greta.

"I'll sneak into the kitchen and let Greta know we're leaving."

"No."

"But…"

"No. Greta understands her place, and she won't be offended by our leaving."

"That's an awful thing to say. 'Knows her place.' Isn't Chicago in America? We don't treat people that way."

"Trust me. I'll explain once we're on our way." Harrison ushered her quickly out the door and into his car. It had already started to snow.

Trish couldn't see how anything he said could possibly make sense, but she wanted clarification. "Okay, explain."

"My mother hires students each semester to do housework, some minor cooking and serving meals at her parties. They get room and board, plus a garage to keep a car. No one stays here for more than a semester because either my mother can no longer tolerate them or they can't tolerate her. She has a reputation as... Well, you've seen her. Greta puts up with what you might consider humiliation, because my mother pays well and gives excellent references. Some of these students have dealt with a lot worse before coming here."

Trish shook her head and focused on the falling snow. "Thank you," she said in a resigned tone.

"You understand, then?"

"No, but...thank you for inviting me here. This whole thing—" Trish flung her hand out "—is totally beyond what I'd ever understand if I hadn't seen it. And you're right— I wasn't just marrying you. I'd be marrying the warts and all. Are your brothers...the same as your mother?"

Harrison didn't speak for a moment as he took the exit for O'Hare. "They seem normal enough. But one thing's for sure. I'm not taking any promotion that gets me within a thousand miles of Chicago. As it is, I'll hear about our breakup as one more thing I didn't finish."

Trish reached over and grasped his arm. "I'm sorry."

He stopped at the curb, put the car in Park and went for her luggage in the backseat. When she joined him, he pulled her into an embrace. "Find what will make you happy, Trish." After a quick kiss, he turned and went back to the car.

Trish watched until she could no longer see his taillights in the snowfall.

CHAPTER TWENTY-THREE

TRISH FELT NUMB. Finally on a plane back to LaGuardia, she couldn't make any sense of the past few weeks. All her life, from the moment she'd received her first doll, she'd seen herself married with children. When she and her friends played together, she wore her grandmother's veil and married...someone. Usually Craig, but before he'd moved to the neighborhood, she'd married Marty or any other boy who came by for Gram's cookies.

And now her life's plans had fallen through.

Harrison expected her to run off with Craig. That wasn't going to happen. Just because she loved Craig... She'd finally admitted it. The thought that he could die... Leave her... No, she wasn't going down that road. Ever.

After landing at LaGuardia, Trish took a taxi to her apartment complex, woke the super for her key and spent a sleepless night. Early the next morning, she dressed in jeans and a sweatshirt over her T-shirt, donned a black

winter jacket and orange hat, and headed for
the train to Riverbend. Since Craig had the
only key to the house, she sent him a text to
meet her at her grandmother's place. She'd pay
off what she owed him, see if Rachel might
want the house for a bed-and-breakfast and
say goodbye to Riverbend. Forever.

"WHERE IS HE?" Craig knew she'd returned
to Riverbend because he'd responded to her
text.

Trish walked back and forth in front of
the house. At least the sun had started to
warm the early morning air, and they had no
chance of snow. She checked all the windows
on the ground floor and found everything
shut tight with no option to get in without
smashing glass. Darn. Should she stay here
or walk over to Rachel's house and talk to
her?

Several other houses in the neighborhood
now had strings of Christmas lights. Her parents would have a fit if she decided to put
up lights. For that matter, so would Craig
and Harrison. They'd all told her to stay off
the roof. However, Craig hadn't removed the
ladder.

She walked over to it, debating. What would

it hurt to see if the hooks for the lights were still up? She'd tossed the old lights in the Dumpster, but she could buy new ones. Something that looked like icicles.

She sent another text.

I'm checking out the roof.

Maybe that would get Craig in gear. No way would she spend the whole day waiting for him. She'd go up the ladder, check out all the hooks and get down before he arrived.

Once on the roof, Trish saw the hooks were hit-or-miss. If she decided on lights, she'd need more hooks, possibly from Moody's. She sat with her legs bent, her arms wrapped around them, and rested her chin on her knees, looking at the expanse below. Trish knew every house, and, for the most part, every person who lived there.

Craig's van pulled into the driveway below and screeched to a stop. He bolted out and looked up at her. "Trish, come down here immediately!"

Testosterone. What was with these guys who figured they had a right to tell her what to do? Trish scooted toward the ladder, sliding on her seat. The motion propelled her faster than she intended. She fell on her back, her arms flailing. All the while she heard Craig screaming. Or was it her? With a wrenching twist, she flipped onto her stomach to get a grip. On something. On anything. Her arms lashed. Her feet pounded against the shingles. Her toes went over the edge.

CRAIG WATCHED IN horror as Trish scrambled to stop her plunge. His shouts did nothing but intensify his own panic. When her toes caught in the gutter, she stopped. He thought for sure his own heart had stopped, as well. He caught his breath and ran up the ladder.

"Don't move. I'm coming up. You stay put." His voice rasped out in one warning after another until he managed to get on the roof above her. "I'm going to pull you up. Let me do the work." He gripped her arms, pressed his feet into the shingles and slowly pulled her away from the edge. Once they were on higher ground, Craig enfolded her in his arms and pressed his face against her neck. Thank God, his Trish was safe.

He was going to kill her!

"How many times have I told you not to come up here?" She squirmed a little, but he held firm. "You're never coming on this roof again. Do you hear me?"

He heard a squeaky reply. Great. She was crying. Well, she should, after the scare she'd given him. He pulled her tighter.

"I can't breathe."

Craig let her adjust her position but made sure she remained trapped in his arms. She didn't seem to mind, as she curled against him. "Were you trying to give me a heart attack?"

"Oh, Craig. I'm sorry." She looked at him with utter dismay. Why on earth had he said that? "Are you all right?" She tapped his chest, right about where his heart pounded.

"I'm fine. How are you?"

"Scared to death." She pressed her face into his shoulder. "I'm so glad you're here." Her voice broke, and the tears flowed uncontrolled.

Craig kissed her cheek, tasting the salt. If he hadn't been… "Relax. You're safe now."

Why was she here? He hadn't believed it when he'd received her first text. Wasn't she supposed to fly in tomorrow night from Chicago? Come to Riverbend sometime the following week? When her crying turned to

hiccups, she began wiping her wet cheeks.
Time to get off the roof.

"Can we go down now?" He nudged her
in the direction of the ladder, only to feel her
stiffen. "We can't stay here, Trish. Come on.
I'll help…" She grabbed on to a metal pipe
sticking out of the roof and wouldn't budge.

Okay, this would require more drastic
measures. "If you won't cooperate, I'll have
to call the fire department." He took out his
cell phone and held it in front of her so she
could watch him punch in 911. She whacked
his arm, and whoosh, his phone went flying.
He reacted just as quickly with a lunge after
it. If Trish hadn't held him in a death grip,
he'd have jumped up and followed his phone
over the side.

Craig collapsed against her, his energy
drained. "What do you suggest we do?"

"Stay here and hold me."

Like he had any choice.

Actually, once he relaxed and his adrena-
line dissipated, he enjoyed breathing in her
essence, kissing the salt from her cheek,
straightening that ridiculous orange hat. He
could spend a lifetime holding her like this.

He glanced around, wondering if anyone
would spot them up here. That OSHA or-

ange hat might grab someone's attention, but only if they looked up. Then he noticed the knuckleboom sitting in the driveway.

Craig sat up, and her clutch tightened. "You see that?" He pointed to the knuckleboom. "I can bring it right to the roof's edge and get us off." She wasn't about to let him go. "Then again, I could start kissing you and bring in a whole herd of elephants."

"Shut up about the elephants!" Her eyes were still wide with fear. Craig's attempt to lighten the mood finally sank in, and she added, "Craig Cadman, I will shower you with kisses if you get us down safely. How will you get that thingamabob over here?"

"It would help if you'd release me so I could move." He had to pry her arms loose. "You stay put and hold on to that pipe. I'll get the knuckleboom."

"Can it hold both of us?"

"Yes. I'll be right back." He moved away in cautious, tiny stages toward the edge. Once he had space between them, he increased his pace and made it to the ladder. Not bothering with the rungs, Craig pressed his feet on the vertical supports and slid down the sides. The moment he hit the ground, Craig ran to the knuckleboom.

It took precious time to maneuver it into place and chock the wheels. But once that was done, he climbed into the cage, used the controls and brought it even with the roof. Trish hadn't moved. "You ready?" She still didn't move.

How did he expect her to get in the cage? Trish tried a few tentative movements toward it and slipped. She tightened her grip on the pipe. This unexpected fear of heights had destroyed any rational thought. She wiped at tears again.

"Stay there." He held up a hand to indicate she shouldn't move. As if she'd even consider it. "I'm coming to get you." He had the top of the cage a good foot higher than the roof. With an agility she hadn't expected, he managed to hop onto the roof and crawl toward her. If he thought she'd do the same kind of acrobatics, he was out of luck.

When Craig reached her, he didn't try to pry her away from the pipe. Good, because right now she probably had the strength to pull it free and whack him with it. He sat next to her, leaning on his elbow, and smiled.

"Remember on Halloween, when Mr. Flurry wouldn't come to his door, and we toilet papered his house? None of us knew his wife had just gone to the hospital." He readjusted his position. "Our parents made us spend the following day removing toilet paper."

Trish brightened. "Gram had me write a note of apology that everyone signed."

"I remember. Mrs. Flurry framed it. Had it on her living room wall."

"And Mr. Flurry sprayed us with his hose anytime the neighborhood kids went past his house. Whatever happened to Mr. Flurry after his house burned down?" She pointed to the vacant lot next to his aunt Jenny's house.

"He moved away and sold the property to my aunt."

They watched the activity on Center Street. "I used to ride my bike up and down that street a dozen times a day," he said. "See those kids over there? A whole group just like us horsing around."

"Friendships that lasted."

"Great times. Remember riding your bike down Center and over on Franklin?"

"Yes. Once I skinned my knee when my foot fell off the pedal and dragged beneath it. Cyndi helped me into the house and hijacked my bike. A month later the scab finally healed. It took quite a bit longer before Cyndi returned the bike."

"So many memories," Craig said with a sigh.

"Wonderful memories."

After several more minutes, he cleared his throat. "So, why are you here?" he asked as though they didn't have a single care. If this was his attempt to calm her, it was beginning to work.

"I wanted to see if any hooks needed replacement in case I want to put up Christmas lights."

That answer made him frown. "I meant, why are you in Riverbend?"

"Harrison and I broke up."

Craig sat upright. "Really?" Those blue eyes burned into her. "Are you okay with that?" Did he want to know if she was brokenhearted? Because she wasn't. Actually, she felt relieved. Until Harrison said their engagement was holding her back, she hadn't realized how much it was.

"It hasn't totally sunk in." Talking about the whole crazy experience made it begin to feel real. "I had my life planned. Now I don't know what to do."

"You'll figure something out. Something a whole lot better."

"I suppose."

"Oh, um, let's see about getting you to the cage. I'll go first." He extended a hand toward her. "So, the marriage's off?"

Trish grabbed his hand. "That's what breaking up usually means."

"Who did the breaking up?"

"It was mutual."

Before she realized where they were, Trish's feet touched the metal cage. Craig released her hand and slowly dropped into the cage. It moved. She froze. "Don't look down. Come closer and I'll lift you in." She closed her eyes. "That's it. A little more. Got you."

And she was in his arms. Safe.

Once they reached the ground, Trish asked, "Was that some firemen's technique, getting me to think about something else so you could get me down?" It certainly worked.

"Not really. I just wanted to know why you were here before we both fell to our deaths."

"Give me the key. I'll go inside and make coffee."

Craig pulled her house key from his pocket. "Don't make any for me. I need to get this knuckleboom back." He walked over to the ladder. "And I'll take care of this."

AFTER TAKING DOWN the ladder, he placed it along the side of the garage so it was out of the way. All the while, he kept thinking, *She's free!* He controlled a desire to click his heels together and do several cartwheels across the lawn.

When he returned to the knuckleboom, he found Trish still standing there.

"Are you going to Moody's?" she asked. "I'll go with you. I need to talk to your mother."

"Your jacket's ripped." He pointed to the large L-shaped tear. "Maybe you'd better fix that."

"Nah, I'll buy myself a new one." She came closer. "I haven't thanked you properly."

He didn't trust that look. If she planned to fulfill that promise of showering him with kisses…he'd best be out of here while he could still focus on what he needed to discuss with his mother.

"No need to get a new jacket. I know you're handy with a needle. Fix it. Your grandmother wouldn't toss something away if it could be saved." Craig concentrated on folding the knuckleboom in place and securing it to the back of his van. He turned back to Trish, who stood with her arms folded over her chest, watching him.

He had to keep everything neutral until he knew for sure what he could say to her. Something of a permanent nature, definitely, but he wasn't sure exactly what.

"I'll be back in a little while. Maybe we can do lunch."

TRISH WALKED BACK in the house feeling as though her life continued to spiral down. Craig didn't want her to thank him. Odd, since he'd never turned down kisses before. Maybe her being available was a turnoff. That hurt.

Well, she wouldn't sit around and wait for him. She was taking hold of her life. The past twenty-four hours had done a number on her. Meeting a bizarre history professor, being dumped and nearly falling to her death. She wanted to talk to Rachel about making Gram's house into a B and B.

Trish pulled her grandmother's sewing basket from under the bed. Not with the intention of using it. No. Craig's remarks about keeping the jacket irritated her. She planned to give away not only the jacket but also the sewing basket. She already had her own and didn't need a duplicate. She'd drop it off at Reverend Meyer's thrift store after seeing Rachel.

About to get in her car, she heard a phone ringing. It wasn't hers. When she realized it could be Craig's, she followed the sound. Sure enough, she found it sitting on top of one of the bushes. By the time she reached it, the ringing had stopped. She stared at the picture on his lock screen. Her face. When had Craig taken the photo? She must mean something to him if he had her picture on his phone.

Why couldn't she figure this out?

Trish returned to her car and drove to Moody's. Craig's van was nowhere in sight.

CHAPTER TWENTY-FOUR

BEFORE GOING TO MOODY'S, Craig stopped at his aunt's house to see if his mother might be there. He found Aunt Jenny and Noah playing cards in the kitchen. As usual, Noah launched himself at Craig the moment he saw him.

"Butchy! You want to play 'Go Fish'? I'm beating the pants off Aunt Jenny."

Craig carried him back to the table. "I thought I told you that's not a nice thing to say about girls."

"Aunt Jenny's not a girl."

Craig winked at his aunt. "Is Mom here?"

"No. She took off with Max."

Craig dropped Noah back in his chair. "I've got to see her."

Noah looked at him, disappointment written all over his face. "Me, too."

Craig bent down and kissed the top of his head. "Not now, little man. I've got something I need to do. When I'm through, I'll come back for you." He glanced at his aunt. "They'll be at Moody's?" When she nodded, he reached over and kissed her on her cheek. "Got to run."

His uncle came in and said, "Jenny and I've been thinking you might be able to help us."

Craig stopped. Uncle Arnold rarely asked for favors. "What do you need?"

Aunt Jenny walked over, entwining her arm with his. "Now that your mother plans to marry, we thought…" Arnold looked at Jenny as though he wanted her to continue.

"They'll need a place to stay," Jenny said. "Obviously our place is too small to take him in, and his apartment is no bigger than yours."

"But," Arnold continued, "your aunt and I have wanted to move to Florida and sell this place. Do you think Max would be interested?" He looked hopeful. "If we had you make some improvements?"

"We'll need upgrades, no matter what, if we want to sell."

"Sure," Craig said. "I'm nearly finished over at Trish's. Why don't you approach Max, and we can decide what needs to be done?"

Craig shook hands with his uncle and took off for Moody's.

He pulled into a spot near the rental equipment used by construction crews. Max came over to the van just as Craig opened his door. "You finished with the knuckleboom?"

"Yes. But I need to speak with Mom. Is she inside?" He headed for the office at a near run with Max right behind him.

"What's so dang important?"

"Trish is back," Craig said over his shoulder.

"I know. She's inside talking to your mother."

Craig turned around and stopped. "She is?" How did Trish get here so quickly? Why hadn't she stayed at her house and sewn her jacket? He needed a private talk with his mother, and he couldn't do it with Trish there.

"Come on," Max said, tapping Craig on his shoulder. "Let's see what the women are up to."

When they reached the office, Craig hesitated. Trish sat in one of the leather chairs in front of his mother's desk. Max followed him in and closed the door. When Rachel looked up, she smiled. "Isn't this great? Now we can all listen to Trish's proposal."

He sat next to Trish and waited. She took a deep breath and said, "Remember when we worked on the stairs?" Rachel nodded. "You mentioned you'd always wanted to have a bed-and-breakfast and you thought my grandmother's house would be perfect for that." Rachel nodded again, leaning closer.

"You wanted to do that?" Craig asked, sitting up straight. "How come you never mentioned it?"

"What was the point?" Rachel asked. "We never had money. I just thought…when I saw how perfect Trish's house was… Well, I just let it slip out. I can dream, can't I?"

Max came over to stand by her. "Dream on." He turned to Trish. "What are you proposing?"

Before she said anything, Trish watched Craig. Was she looking for his approval? "I've decided not to sell the house, but I'm not going to live in it. I'd like to rent. If you're interested, you can live there with Noah and make it into a B and B."

"You didn't tell her?" Max asked.

Craig shook his head.

"Tell me what?"

"Rachel has agreed to be my wife. So there'd be three of us living there instead of two."

Trish made a slight yelp that she turned into a cough. "Well, that sure is interesting news."

"Here's something else." Craig stood and walked over to stand behind Trish's chair. "I just saw Aunt Jenny and Uncle Arnold before coming here. Since you're getting married, they thought you might be interested in buying their house. They want to move to Florida."

Trish stood. "You have a lot of choices to consider. No rush. You can get back to me once you make up your mind." She walked over to Rachel. "I wish you both the best. And you know, if you decide on a Christmas wedding, Gram's house would make a perfect setting."

Trish headed for the door.

"Lunch?" Craig called out.

"Sure. I have a few errands to do, and I'll meet you at my place."

He walked over and opened the door for her. "You don't have any furniture. Why don't you come to mine?"

THAT HADN'T GONE so well. Why did Craig have to throw in that sledgehammer and tell them about Aunt Jenny's house?

Trish still had a few days before she had to return to work. Maybe she should find a Realtor just to learn the value of the house and ask for a serious offer from Dave Henry.

In the meantime, she'd get rid of the sewing basket. Trish knew from experience that Gram had enough thread, needles and scissors to accommodate a sewing industry. She headed for the thrift store run by Reverend Meyer's church with the hope someone would benefit from her grandmother's hobby.

When she walked into the store, a matronly woman greeted her. "Hi. I'd like to donate this."

"What a lovely sewing kit. Would you like a receipt for tax purposes?"

Trish shook her head. "Thanks, but that won't be necessary." She started for the door and hesitated. So often she'd sit with her grandmother while they both sewed. Those relaxing, peaceful times. She'd miss those most of all. Trish glanced back at the basket and saw several women already going through it. Good. Gram's love of sewing would continue in another's hands. Trish pressed her lips together and walked out the door.

When she reached her car door, someone

called to her. "Wait. Wait." Trish turned to see the woman from the store waving an envelope. "This was inside the basket. Are you Trish?"

She nodded and headed back to the woman. Trish looked at the envelope and gasped at the handwritten message: HOLD FOR TRISH— ITEMS FOUND IN THE SECRETARY.

CRAIG WAITED IMPATIENTLY while his mother and Max talked about making Trish's home into a B and B versus moving into Jenny's house. He wanted to get back to Trish and tell her how much he loved her and wanted to marry her. If he carried potential heart problems in his genes and couldn't have kids, they could always adopt. Providing Trish would settle for someone with the sword of Damocles hanging over his head.

"Could I interrupt, please?"

Max and Rachel turned to him. "Of course. What is it?"

"I need some answers." Craig took a seat opposite her. "Was Noah born with any heart problems?"

Rachel covered her mouth, and her eyes bulged. "What happened? Is he okay?"

"He's fine. I need to know… Did Noah inherit the same heart problems I have?"

Rachel gripped the desk. "What are you talking about?"

Craig walked around the desk and placed an arm over his mother's shoulders. "I need to know if this heart business is passed on from generation to generation."

She fluttered her hands in a shooing motion. "Oh, will you go sit down." Once he moved away, she said, "No, it's not genetic. I had that concern when Noah was born. The doctor told me Noah is fine. Of course we didn't learn you had the problem until you were a teenager, but the doctor said it's not passed from one generation to another. You know that."

"I just needed to be sure."

"Why is this suddenly so important?"

Max came over and began massaging her shoulders. "Because Trish is back."

Rachel glanced his way before turning back to Craig. She patted Max's hand, then folded hers on her desk. "Life is taking chances, Craig. Some chances are worth the risk."

Max rested his chin on her head. "I second that."

Craig shot from his chair as relief flowed

through him. "Thanks." After heading out the door, he went straight to his van. He was nearly out of the parking lot when he heard Max shout, "Aren't you dropping off the knuckleboom?"

Craig stepped on his brakes. "Yeah," he called out the window. "I'll turn around." With Max's help, they detached the knuckleboom.

"You might want to slow it down a little. I'm sure Trish would prefer to have you in one piece."

I'm asking her to marry me! Craig repeated over and over as he drove back to his apartment. He could father children with her…if she'd have him? Trish had to marry him. She had to.

Trish gripped the envelope. Did this contain what Craig had left in the secretary? Inside she found a folded piece of paper. Her fingers trembled as she opened it. A large brown spot next to the writing looked like something had been pressed there.

Dear Trish,
Someday when I'm older and you finally take me seriously, I want to marry

you for real. I will do everything possible to make you happy and love you forever.

Butchy Craig Cadman Jr.

She put it back in the envelope. Did he still feel that way?

Trish drove to his apartment and parked by the entrance. She waited impatiently for him to show up, unable to concentrate on anything but him.

Craig wasn't the only one with the threat of mortality. She realized death could come anytime. Today she'd actually come close. Life was so precious, and no one could predict when it would end. She needed to grab on to it, grab on to Craig. What little time they both might have, she wanted it to be with him.

Children no longer mattered the way they had before. Craig mattered. Maybe he might even consider adoption. She had no problem with that. He'd be a wonderful father.

When she saw Craig's van, she waited for him to park and come around to the front door. He walked toward her as though he didn't have a single care. Well, she intended to upset his contented world. She opened the car door and stepped out into the cold air.

"I have a few things to tell you, Craig Cadman."

"And I have something to tell you, as well." He grinned and raised an eyebrow. "Gentleman that I am, I'll let the lady go first."

She handed him the envelope from her grandmother. When he glanced at it, his jaw dropped. "You found it!"

Trish nodded. "Open it. Is this the note you wrote?"

Craig gave her a skeptical glance. "You know, let's wait on this." Without opening the envelope, he stuck it inside his jacket. "Let's go inside, where it's warm." He wrapped an arm around her shoulders and directed her to the door.

"I found your phone, by the way." She held it out to him. "How come my picture's on it?"

He just smiled, took his phone and placed it in his pocket. "Come on. I'll explain everything in front of the fireplace, where we can stretch out and relax."

When they reached Craig's apartment, Trish went directly to the fireplace and turned it on.

He helped her out of her jacket. "Decided not to fix this?" He pointed to the rip.

"I told you, I'm buying a new one." She grinned. "I gave Gram's sewing basket to Reverend Meyer's thrift store. Never even looked in it, but the woman there found the envelope inside and gave it to me."

When they settled on the couch in front of the blazing fireplace, Craig breathed deeply and focused on the envelope. "Have you read it?"

"Of course."

"You have to remember, Trish, I was thirteen." He placed his arm around her shoulders and drew her close. "You were leaving and I was very upset."

"I know. Now read."

He read it out loud. When he finished, he grinned and tapped an index finger on the brown spot. "You see that? I sealed it with blood to prove my sincerity."

"I have one question for you," Trish said. "Is there a time limit on your proposal?"

His brow furrowed. "A time limit? What do you mean?"

She took the paper from his hand. "Is this as valid today as it was ten years ago?"

His lips slowly curved into a smile. "Yes."

Craig took the paper back. "Maybe even more so."

Trish cuddled closer. "Then, Butchy Craig Cadman Jr., I love you and I accept."

Craig pushed her away and tossed the paper. "That's not good enough, Trish. Do you promise to marry me, love me forever and have my children?"

"Have your… What do you mean?"

"I mean, you can write on my forehead that I want to have children with you. Only you." He bent over and whispered, "Noah doesn't have a heart problem, and it's not anything I can pass on to our children." She watched his blue eyes. "Are you willing to take the chance?"

Trish returned to the warmth of his embrace. "Yes. Just let me know when we can start."

"Right now has wonderful possibilities."

She started to chuckle. "Sorry, Craig. You'll need to have patience."

"What do you mean? I'm the poster child for patience. I've been waiting for you to agree to marry me for the past fourteen years. And remember, I may not have that much time."

Trish sat up. "Craig Cadman. This stops

right now. Don't you ever talk like that again. Promise me."

He pulled her back against him. "Okay. I promise." He kissed her forehead. "Then let's make it quick. I liked what you told my mother about a Christmas wedding. Does that appeal to you?" His phone rang. Craig pulled it from his pocket and scowled. "My mother. Do you think she has some special radar?"

His scowl morphed into a grin, and he kissed her forehead again before clicking the phone on speaker. "You picked a very inopportune time to call, Mom. Trish just agreed to marry me, and we plan to celebrate."

"That's wonderful! Did you hear that, Max? Craig and Trish are getting married." A little disturbance followed.

"Hold off on the celebration for a while," Max said. "Your mother and I want a tour of Trish's house. We might be interested in making it into a B and B."

Trish sat up. "That's great. We'll be…"

"We'll meet you for lunch at The Country Barn to discuss it." Craig clicked off the phone.

When she tried to get up, Craig pulled her onto his lap. "They can wait." He caressed her face. "I need to smell you, taste you and know with every one of my senses that you're mine forever."

Trish curled against him and kissed his neck. "Two can play that game, Mr. Cadman."

"Call me Butchy."

EPILOGUE

THANKS TO CRAIG and Max, the Riverbend Bed and Breakfast had white icicle lights dangling from the gingerbread trim. A balsam fir stood near the curved staircase, decked out with all of Gram's decorations. A large sign in front of the staircase announced that the marriages of Trish Lowery to Craig Cadman and Rachel Cadman to Maxwell Moody would take place at 7:00 p.m. on Christmas Eve. The Reverend Meyer would officiate.

Trish made a final check of the chairs set up in the living room for their guests. She'd finished putting place cards on the dining room tables when Craig came up behind her and kissed her neck. "You only have two more hours to change your mind."

Trish turned and put her arms around his shoulders. "Why? Are you getting cold feet?"

"Never. What about you?"

"I intend to place my refrigerator feet on your back tonight to warm them."

Craig picked her up and twirled her around. "Can't wait."

When he placed her back on the floor, she kissed him with the promise of more. "Come on. I want to show you your Christmas present." She dragged him to the living room.

"You want to exchange gifts now?"

"Yes."

"Well, you'll have to wait for yours. I planned to give it to you tonight."

They stopped in front of the secretary, now sporting a large red bow. "This is yours. And if it reminds you of elephants, all the better."

"I love it. But we'll have to keep it here until we find an apartment in New York." He maneuvered her closer to the mistletoe. "Thank you. I've always wanted this, elephants and all."

"So, how long do I have to wait for mine?"

Craig checked his watch. "The service is at seven. We eat following that. Then we dance." He twirled her around before pulling her back into his arms. "After everyone has gone, I take you up the stairs... I don't have to carry you, do I? It could put a strain on my heart."

"Craig?" That scowl again. He had to remember to mention his heart only in romantic references.

"After we walk up the stairs to the honeymoon suite, I'll carry you over the threshold and throw you on the bed."

"I don't consider what normally comes after a wedding a proper Christmas gift."

He held her face in his hands and drew her closer. "I promise you, my darling, I'm full of surprises."

TRISH, DRESSED IN white satin, and Rachel, in cream-colored lace, descended the staircase to greet the men who would walk them down the aisle. Trish placed her arm on her father's, and Rachel took Noah's hand. When Mendelssohn's "Wedding March" began, they entered the living room and married their respective spouses.

After everyone had left, the Moodys went to Max's apartment and her parents to Aunt Jenny's, because none of the other rooms in the B and B were furnished yet. Alone at last, Trish and Craig walked up the curved staircase. "Too bad your grandmother couldn't be here."

"Oh, but she was. I felt her spirit surrounding us with all her love."

Craig picked Trish up and opened the door to the bedroom. Her gram's furniture remained the same, but what had been a closet now served as a bathroom with a shower.

"Oh, my," Trish gasped, her hand covering her mouth. "How did you…?" Red rose petals littered the floor leading up to a bed covered in red heart balloons. Was this her gift? And how did Craig get the rose petals and balloons in? None of it had been in the bedroom when Trish and Rachel used it as their dressing room before the wedding.

"Follow the trail. It's on the bed," Craig whispered by her ear. She looked for her gift and felt a little disappointed when she couldn't see anything.

Trish began brushing the balloons off the new king-size bed. "What am I looking for?"

"You'll know it when you see it." Craig lifted her onto the bed, set pillows against the brass headrest and joined her.

When her hand hit a hard surface, she scraped through additional rose petals and came up with his iPad. She handed it to him, feeling an additional letdown. Pictures? Her present was pictures?

After a few quick finger movements, he handed the iPad back to her. A three-dimensional house rotated on its surface. "This can go on the empty lot next to my aunt's place."

"Our place. Your aunt and uncle agreed to sell it to us when they move."

"I designed this especially so it should blend in with the other architecture." She gaped at the image as it opened and showed various views of the interior rooms.

"You designed this?"

"If you don't like it, I can—"

Trish put her fingers against his lips, turned off the iPad and placed it on the nightstand. "Craig Cadman, I love it."

"I'll need Victor, my architect friend, to approve it, and I can work on it during weekends when I don't have classes."

She leaned over and kissed him. "You, my dear, sweet husband, are going to slow down. You have way too many projects. And I intend to make sure we put time into other pursuits."

"Such as?"

"A little relaxing before your classes start

and I go back to work." She tapped his nose with her finger. "I plan to show you how my small apartment can suit our needs to perfection with only one improvement."

"What's that?"

"We add your fireplace." She smiled. "It will provide some excellent possibilities for unwinding."

* * * * *